# Cherry Blossom Girls

## ~Book Four~

By Harmon Cooper

# Chapter One: Nothing to Sneeze At

*Mother died today. Or maybe yesterday; I can't be sure.*

Nope, the line from Albert Camus' *The Stranger* didn't begin to describe my situation, but the title of Camus' work *did* describe the guy I knew as Father, who had seemingly rescued my creative nonfiction gamer sci-fi writing ass from dying in a Nevada desert.

"So we're still in Nevada then," I said, thoughts whirling around my head as Father and I helped Stella into the trailer.

While it looked pretty rundown on the outside, the inside of his space was quite clean, cramped, and a bit campy, but there was ample space on the couch for a hot superpowered with a Dutch braid and a penchant for giving me skeptical looks.

"I already told you that," he said as he started boiling water on the stove.

"And you're Father."

"I already told you that too, and you're Gideon Caldwell. Ken told me all about you. As I said before, glad you could make it." He laughed, his eyes flaring again as he did so. I didn't know if he had a power or not (one did not assume in my line of work), but a man with eyes that flared yellow at times definitely had something supery going for him.

"Dr. Kim?" I gulped.

"Yes. I believe he sent you the same information that he sent me. Although I already knew some of it. There may be more information he has for you as well, but that remains to be seen."

"This is all so... confusing," I finally said. Tears came to my eyes and I tried to suck them back. I'm not one to weep in front of a complete stranger, and while I may be somewhat of a soy boy, a beta male with a bleeding heart, I was well aware of the unspoken guy code about crying in front of another male.

But I couldn't help myself, there was true fear in those dollops of lacrimal jizz-straction too, fear that I'd never see Grace again.

Or Veronique.

Or Dorian.

Or hell, Michelle, even though she was the newest member of our little ragtag band of supers.

"Do you need a minute?" Father asked.

"No," I told him, trying not to sob. "This is just a lot to take in. And it's so random. How the hell did you know we'd be out here?"

"Call it a lucky guess," said Father as he continued to stir a pot on the stove. Whatever he was cooking was odorless, which led me to believe he was boiling water. "And it's too bad what happened to Dr. Kim. Good guy, really."

As he continued to boil the water, and as I looked over to Stella to check that she was indeed resting peacefully, I thought of Ken Kim and how he'd come into my increasingly odd narrative: from an email, to a phone call, to the codes that unlocked new powers for the CBGs, to his final will and testament, the trove of info and the app that had proved especially useful.

He really was a good guy.

Father brought me a soup cup of boiling liquid. "Drink this."

I took a sip from the cup and was surprised at what I tasted. Every craving I'd ever had and every bout of hunger I'd ever sat through were instantly cured by the liquid.

"What is this stuff?" I asked, instantly feeling rejuvenated.

"Special recipe," he said, as he sat down across from me.

Father was grizzled, that was for sure. While there was an edge to him, from his scraggly beard not unlike mine to the lines on his forehead, there was a softness to his eyes that I recognized. He was a little pudgy at the middle, but not by much, and I could tell that there had been a point in his life that he was pretty fit.

Stella stirred, the trailer vibrated, and she was suddenly standing, her fists at her sides as she took in the man.

"Gideon!"

My body whipped away from the table. Stella grabbed my wrist and blew the door off the trailer, her vector power lifting us out of the trailer.

Even as we landed out in the Nevada nothingness, and Stella started to drag me forward, Father's only reaction was to stand from his chair and follow us out.

"Relax, Stella," he called out. As soon as he stepped foot on the soil, the door pieced itself back together, its hinges locking into place.

"You're... one of us?" she asked, surprise painting across her face.

"One of you?" Father considered this for a moment. "That's a good way to put it, actually. Now, stop blowing shit up and let's talk about what's happening, and more importantly, your next step."

"Our next step?" I asked.

"What? You thought I called you out here just for my own amusement?" He sighed audibly. "No, hell no. You're out here for a reason. And the others will be here shortly, so we'd better get started."

"You're a powerful one, aren't you?" Father asked, after Stella used a wave of vector energy to *knock his trailer over*.

She continued to hold my wrist with one hand, clearly protecting us with a shield.

She was squeezing tight too, so tight that I was afraid she'd snap my wrist. Thing was, Stella was scared. Really scared, especially since she'd struck Father with a wall of sharp rocks, which he'd somehow managed to avoid. Not even a nick.

He hadn't been swept off his feet, and he hadn't met the same fate as his trailer, which was toppled over, the windows shattered, any item not pinned down tossed out the window.

"Now, I bet you're wondering who the hell I am, or how I came to be out here," he began to say, "and I'm guessing that Aida has scrubbed everything there is to know about me from the Agency of Enhancement and Future Logistics, from AEFL. Hell, Ken wouldn't even have found out if I hadn't contacted him."

"You contacted Dr. Kim?"

A yellow glint flashed across his eyes. "You could call me his handler, but you could call me a lot of things."

"You're a super, I see that, but what is your actual ability?" I asked.

Stella had relaxed her guard some, still unsure of how she should be handling herself. I could tell by the look on her face that she was overheating, likely from stress this time though, as I'd done all I could to adjust her abilities.

"We're not here to talk about my powers, *we're here to talk about yours.*"

"I don't have any powers," I told him.

"Yet you tried a little telekinetic trick not too long ago. You have some of Sabine's power right now, do you not?"

*How does he know all this?* But rather than ask the question that continued to boil to the surface of my mind, I just went with it. "That's right."

"And you were briefly part of the experiments at the Rose-Lyle facility."

"That's… right."

*Is he a psychic?* He had a power, clearly, but was that what he was using? I focused on him for a moment and decided to give it a test.

11

*Father. Can you hear me?*

I stared at him for a moment, and once it was clear I wasn't going to get a read on the mysterious man, I exchanged glances with Stella.

"You've got lots of questions, and rather than ask them in my stuffy trailer, let's gather some of that brush over there and start a fire. It's going to be a cold night."

He glanced toward a stack of wood, which seemed a bit out of place seeing as how we were in the desert. But hell, it was the 2030s, and freaking EBAYmazon could probably get someone a bundle of wood in a three-hour timeframe just about anywhere in the contiguous United States.

"Grab the brush over there, just some tumbleweeds and other dried grasses I picked up today."

I did as instructed.

For her part, Stella simply took a seat on a large rock that faced the firepit. She was weak, and I was just about to ask Father to make her some of that wicked rejuvenating juice he'd made me back in his trailer when he...

*Read my mind?*

"Get the fire started, and I'll bring you something to drink, Stella."

"What am I supposed to do with this brush?" I asked him.

"I already told you, start a fire. Don't people from Connecticut know how to start fires?"

"Born in Rhode Island, but raised in Connecticut, and to answer your question, yes, I'm certain New Englanders know how to start fires. And I once researched building a fire for a scene I was planning for a book called *Breakpoint Online*." I gulped. "But, um, I don't know how to build one. Just put this shit on bottom and put some logs on top, right?"

"You'll figure it out. Have Stella help you." He turned back to his toppled trailer, and as he did, it righted itself.

*Using vector manipulations?* I thought as I stacked wood on top of the fire starter. Friction could cause a fire, and friction was a form of kinetic energy, so sure, why the hell not?

"Stella, can you light this on fire?"

She gave me a curious look.

The moon was partially visible overhead, adding just enough illumination for me to make out her features. Half Grace, half Veronique, Stella had replaced our metal vampire as the most unmanageable in the group.

I cleared my throat. "So, can you? We need a fire."

Two rocks floated above the firepit, Stella controlling them by lightly stroking the fingers of her left hand together. As she picked up her speed, the rocks began sliding against one another.

They slid even faster, to the point that were somewhat blurred, which created a series of sparks that fell onto the dry brush beneath the fire, fizzling out before they could start the flame.

"Closer," I told her.

The rocks continued to rub rapidly against one another as they lowered over the firepit. Soon we had a flame, which I tried to stoke by getting on my hands and knees and blowing at it.

The fire was raging by the time Father returned with a soup cup of liquid for Stella, which she stared at skeptically as he handed it to her.

"It's fine," I told her. "I drank it, and look, my ass is still here. Wherever here is. Where are we anyway?"

"In Nevada. I've already told you this."

"I know that, but where in Nevada?"

Father considered this question as he sat down. The act of him sitting instantly cooled the flames to a manageable, much chiller level. I'd been worried for a moment there; any higher and the flames would have singed the tips of my beard. Even with the relaxed flames, I could still feel the sunburn-like heat against my skin.

"In Nevada," he finally said. "So let's get down to business. There are a few things to discuss, and I'm getting tired. Let's start with you asking me three questions for tonight, then I'll have a question for you."

Stella took a sip from the liquid Father had given her, cocked her head towards me, and with a satisfied grin on her face, she quickly downed the cup.

"What superpower do you have?" I asked. "Let's start with that one."

"My superpower?" Father ran his hand along his chin as he considered this. He now wore a bucket hat, which obscured his beady eyes. "I have the ability to manipulate reality. That pretty much sums it up."

"Manipulate reality? That sums absolutely nothing up…"

"My power is how I knew you'd come, how I'm able to modify the environment around me, and how I generally have a clear understanding of the future. This isn't always the case, I should say, as my ability is very subjective. Other people, their desires and actions do factor into the outcomes I create."

"Can you show me an example?" I asked as Stella set her soup cup down. "Also, I don't want this to count as a question, so if it does, we can move on."

"I've already shown you examples. How do you think I know so much about you? Or the fact that Dorian banished you to the desert, or that you'd eventually get here?"

"And the trailer."

"The trailer," he agreed, referring to Stella's failed attack. "And the liquid."

"What was that stuff anyway? Again, please don't count this as a question."

"I should count it as one," he grumbled. "It was water that I infused with various nutrients necessary to maintain homeostasis. Sugars, fibers, vitamins, protein, that sort of thing. I did this using my abilities."

"You're like a god."

"No, I'm like a man. I am a man, a normal, just like you."

I had to laugh at this. "A 'normal' like me? You just told me you can manipulate reality; there's nothing normal about that."

"Normals manipulate reality too, it just takes them longer. Next question."

"What is your relation to Mother?"

"Aida," he said fondly.

"If she's Mother, and you're Father, I mean, you've got to assume I've put one and two together here."

"And got what?"

"And got Stella."

"Gideon," Stella said.

"What? She's Mother, he's Father, where I'm from that pretty much sums up the birds and the bees, even if you are lab grown. And shit, don't take being called 'lab grown' as an offense. I can't wait for the day in which 'normals' like myself grow their offspring in labs. Call it the sci-fi writer in me, but the possibility for calamity coupled with the cool factor has me foaming at the mouth."

"Is he always this talkative?" Father asked Stella.

She nodded, and it felt like I'd been punched in the gut. Look, I didn't have a filter – still don't! – but that didn't invalidate my points.

"Anyway," he finally said, "Aida and I never had something going, but we do have something in common."

"What's that?"

"We're brother and sister."

"I'm throwing in the towel," I said, as I buried my head in my hand. "So they aren't your test tube babies?"

"Some are mine, some are hers, but never are they ours together because they'd be inbred if that were the case."

"That didn't stop Angel."

"Ah, Angel, are you referring to his relationship with Aida?"

"Yes, I'm referring to their weird-ass relationship. She's prego with his baby."

"Angel is my son. So it's still wrong."

"Wait, why didn't he tell me this?" I recalled the time I called Angel a 'motherfucker.' The shoe still fit, but now it was more like an aunt-fucker, which said aloud conjures an image of the muscle-bound greasy-haired super getting nice and cozy with a Jurassic-sized fire ant.

*God, am I glad no one around me can read my mind.*

"He didn't tell you this because..." Father shrugged. "Why would he?"

"Good point. Okay, so some of the test tube supers are yours, others are hers. Which is why you go by Mother and Father. Got it. Surely you want me to call you something else."

"Jim. You can call me Jim."

I exchanged glances with Stella; seeing the light of the flames create shadows on her face took me away from this strange moment. For that single instance, we were camping, telling stories around a campfire, not in the middle of Nowhere, Nevada getting truth bombs dropped on us.

"And to continue answering your question, not only are Aida and I brother and sister, we are twins. She is my twin."

"And she's the evil twin and you're the good twin."

"I'm not good. It was only a few years ago that I realized the error in what we are doing and moved out here, away from it all, protected by my own superpowers."

"So you had a falling out? Also, I'm trying to include this under the 'what is your relation to Mother?' umbrella, so please don't count it as question number three, and if you are, let me know."

"We did have a falling out. And I won't count it, so don't worry. Aida and I haven't spoken since the incident. She may know where I am, but she knows better than to come and try to find me."

"So we are safe?"

"Is that your third question?"

"No, I'll save that one then. Um…" I offered Stella a quick grin. Her response was indecipherable. If she was warming up to me, her body language and facial expressions didn't show it.

"So, you can manipulate reality, which means that you can bring Dorian, Veronique and Grace here," I said, the light of the flames flickering across Father's face.

"Ah, your third question."

"That wasn't technically a question," I reminded him. "I'm just saying, *you could,* if you were so inclined."

"As I said, my abilities don't quite work like that, and I've already told you they are en route. Final question, Gideon; it's getting late."

"Where did your powers originally come from?"

A smile stretched across his face. "That's a good question, and one that you should know more about. The simplified version is as follows: all humans have the propensity for superpowers, or should I say, enhanced control over their body at the molecular level which *seems* like a superpower when used in front of another person. The problem is, humans don't have the ability to tap into these powers, so they lie dormant."

"And you unlocked them."

"Aida and I unlocked them over twenty-five years ago. You are aware that the American military is usually a decade ahead of the technology they show the general public, right?"

"I've heard the claim."

"The same can be said of the biomedical field, but not necessarily in America due to Christian morals and directives put into place by the FCG to placate the public. Now, in other countries, especially in the EU, the ability to experiment is much laxer than it is here. That's where our story begins."

"In Europe?"

"At a lab in Switzerland, where both Aida and I worked as lead researchers. Through gene therapy, we were able to increase our own powers using a bio-neural operating system that I developed, which enhances certain chemicals in the body. Suspend your disbelief for a moment as I tell you that the animal kingdom is already populated with superpowered beings, creatures that can do things, lift things, move through things by changing their colors, forms, spin webs a thousand times the lengths of their bodies, change their forms when certain conditions are present, operate on land and in water and in the air in ways that we can't. Until now."

He cleared his throat, letting me process this. "What we learned was that some people, like you, and like us, have the predisposition for these abilities, usually a certain ability or two that is triggered when our neural changes are put in place in a person's body. What we later discovered was that creating beings with a predisposition for said abilities allowed them to be much stronger than we ever thought possible. So that's what we did, and what they continue to do. For people like us, it's an upgrade. For people like you, Stella, you're born with it."

"Then why was I tested?"

"Because we would still like to be able to backdate, as it were, people and give them powers. That's what the Federal Corporate Government originally wanted through the AEFL program, but this has of course changed. We were close, too, but what we really got good at was creating these beings. Since both Aida and I both have a predisposition for these powers and their advancement, we created them from our seeds and eggs, never mixing, of course, using lab selected

23

donors to complete the equation. Since I've left, Aida has taken over the operation fully, but any of the ones you have associated with could be mine or hers, as well as the other part from a random donor. Does that answer your question?"

"I ..." I shook my head. It was hard to process, and I'd have more questions, but for now it made sense. "Yes, that answers my question."

"Good, now onto the other part of this conversation: tomorrow, we will convert you fully to a superpowered being."

I felt the blood drain from my face. "We'll do what?"

"You will never be like Stella, or any of the others you've associated with," he said as he stood. "But you will be like Aida and me, which is nothing to sneeze at."

# Chapter Two: Gideon
# Version 2.0

Father returned to his trailer, leaving both of us to our thoughts.

*Become a superpowered person? Is that even something I want?*

*Fuck yes,* Bad Boy Gideon said at the back of my skull.

And he wasn't wrong; there would be another encounter with Mother and her team of second-rate antagonists. Hell, the odds of Angel being there increased every day given the aunt-fucker's ability to grow a new body...

With a superpower, I would no longer be the weakest link. I'd actually be useful for once.

"What kind of power do you think you'll get?" Stella asked, interrupting my silence. Next to her was a tent and a pair of sleeping bags. Before officially retiring to his trailer, Father had brought them both to us and told us to 'figure it out.'

Since I was as good at nature-y things as I was sports, this likely meant I'd be sleeping in the sleeping bag next to the un-erected tent.

"Beats me," I told her. "Also, notice that he didn't say how he was going to give me this power, which leads to me to believe that it may be painful."

"Only time will tell," she said, which was the most philosophical thing I'd ever heard Stella say. Our relationship had been rocky, and it generally revolved around disputes between Veronique and her, Yours Truly trying to calm the flames.

A child of the twenty-first century, I felt for my phone in my pocket and looked at the cracked screen. *Yep, still broken,* but habit caused me to check anyway.

"What kind of powers do you want?"

I looked at Stella and shrugged. She was still in her black mil-spec stuff, but she'd pulled the zipper on the turtleneck collar down, revealing a sliver of skin. Her braid was a mess, a bit of dirt smudged on her cheeks.

"No preference," I finally told her. "I honestly just want to make sure the others are okay."

"Ingrid and Fiona," she said, the look on her face souring.

"Look, that wasn't our fault," I told her. "It really wasn't. We can't believe what Mother said, that they are dead. I believe..." I gulped, trying to put some weight behind my statement. "I believe that Fiona and Ingrid are alive, and that we will save them. We'll save everyone."

"You really think that?" she asked, not at all what I was expecting her to say.

"I really do, Stella."

She just nodded for a moment, staring into the crackling fire. "Do you know how to set up a tent?"

"Does a dog know how to create a GoogleFace account without the help of its owner? I have no earthly idea. You would think that if Father's power is to manipulate reality, he'd have manipulated this tent into erected existence, but whatever, I'm down for sleeping under the stars. We'll figure the tent out tomorrow."

"Then you do that. I'm going to sleep in the trailer." She stood, a thin smile on her face. "Unless you build the tent. Then I'll sleep in there with you."

"Challenge accepted."

Inspired by the prospect of sleeping next to a warm body, I got to work trying to figure out the tent, using the light from the fire to read the directions on its mesh packaging. It was getting cooler out; Stella had unrolled one of the sleeping bags and was using it to cover her legs as she watched me struggle with the tent.

It took me a little time, but I got that shit set up and was proud of my outdoorsiness when I finished. I stood before it, both hands on my hips as I stared at my creation. Cliché as it was, a Henry David Thoreau quote came to me: 'Time is but the stream I go a-fishing in. I drink at it; but while I drink I see the sandy bottom and detect how shallow it is. Its thin current slides away, but eternity remains.'

Stella walked over to the tent and looked inside, judging the space. "It looks a little tight in there."

"It's says it's a two-person tent."

Stella looked from the trailer to the tent and back again.

"Fine, I'll sleep out here, but if you so much as touch me…"

"Whoa," I lifted both palms in defense, "that was definitely not part of the plan."

"I just want to be clear that I'm not part of your odd relationship with Dorian, Grace, and Veronique," she said, taking a step closer to me. "We are not all the same."

"Never said that."

She placed a hand on the back of my neck and adrenaline surged through me. I was aware of what Stella could do at close range.

"Are you afraid of me?" she asked, her head tilting ever-so-slightly.

My immediate reaction was to say 'yes,' but the word that came out of my mouth surprised even me. "No," I told her firmly. "My fear of supers has become increasingly manageable."

"Good, you are, after all, our fearless leader," she said as she slipped into the tent. "Are you coming?" she asked, poking her head out.

"Did you just call me your 'fearless leader'? Because that is definitely, *definitely*, something I haven't been called before. Thanks!"

I tossed the sleeping bags in, and crawled in next to her.

The space wasn't as tight as I had originally anticipated. Still, there wasn't a lot of wriggle room, which forced Stella's thigh into my side as she lay on her back, staring at the roof of the tent.

I kicked my shoes off at the entrance – no sense in getting sand in my new sleeping space.

"I should take off my boots too."

"Yep." I unclipped my bulletproof vest and fashioned it into a hard-ass pillow. I'd been wearing it since we arrived, mostly for its warmth. My ballistic helmet was around too, likely in the trailer. I'd been so surprised when we first came up that I didn't remember taking it off.

And that's how Stella and I ended up sleeping in a tent in the Nevada desert.

No funny business, and both of us fell asleep in a matter of minutes, Stella thinking about God knows what, and me like a kid on Christmas Eve, wondering what Daddy and Mommy – or in this case, Daddy – were going to give me the next day.

The morning came, the sun stretching into the cramped space of the tent.

My lips were dry, my back hurt from sleeping on the hardened soil, and the bulletproof pillow left a crick in my neck. These small issues were soon cured by some of Father's magic brew, which seemed to both rejuvenate me, and make my aches and pains go away.

"We need to get started," he said, as I finished the holy water.

Stella was across from me, sitting on one of the rocks surrounding the firepit and braiding her hair. She had one leg crossed over the other, sexy in the way only a female can make that look, and as she braided her hair, she glanced over her shoulder at me.

She smiled, and I swear my little writer thumped against the inside of my jeans.

I almost scolded it for being so goddamn horny. And really, I didn't know when I'd become such a damn horndog. I was never this way back in New Haven, and aside from the daily Pornhub perusal, that part of my life usually kept to itself.

"I've already set up the trailer," Father said, interrupting my inner monologue. "It's going to be a full-day procedure, and there may be a few growing pains. Then again, maybe not. I really don't know. Follow me."

"It isn't going to hurt, is it?" I asked, as he led me to his trailer.

"I don't have any painkillers, so yes, it is going to hurt, but not much."

I stopped dead in my tracks.

"No pain meds?"

"Nope. Don't need them." He looked over his shoulder at me. "Relax, Gideon, I'll handle everything. That's the last thing you should be worrying about."

"And what's the first thing?"

"If you're ready or not." He pointed at his couch, which was now covered with a white tablecloth. There was also a small table near it with surgical equipment on it.

"It's not going to look as perfect as the others," he said, "but I will do my best with the equipment I have."

Stella entered, and he nodded her over to a table near the kitchen. She sat, and looked at me curiously as I tried to get comfortable.

"You're putting a port in my neck, right?"

"I'm putting in a modifier," he said from the kitchen.

"And why didn't they try this when I was a kid?"

"We weren't putting modifiers in people's necks then. AEFL was testing for propensity, and as you know by now, you have this propensity. The FCG changed leadership around that time, hell, that was before it was the FCG, and so the public program ended."

"And you don't know what powers you're going to unlock?"

"No idea. Usually, with the labgrowns like Stella, we start to see their abilities around the age of four, sometimes younger, like Veronique. We then have to classify them, and as I'm guessing you've seen, especially since you know Dorian, some abilities become apparent later."

"So you really know every super there is?"

"I have the same files that Ken gave you. These, I'm afraid, don't account for every super, but I believe they cover most." He walked over to me and handed me another cup of liquid. "Drink up."

"Okay." The liquid was flavorless, but it made me feel like I'd smoked a gram of some Vermont bud and finished up by rubbing some CBD oil on my chest. I relaxed even further into the couch, if that was possible, and my mind came back around when Father snapped plastic gloves on his hands.

"So, just to be clear, I'm going to install one of these modifiers in the side of your neck, behind your ear." He showed me the small device; the input side was flesh colored. "This isn't an easy surgery, and it will take me a few hours to get it in place and tested, but the good news is that I'll be able to heal you up after, so no need to worry about recovery."

"Wait, why mini-USB for the ports?" I asked, a question that had been at the back of my mind for some time now. "Been wondering about that."

"Lots of reasons. For one, it was pretty universal at the time when we made our first modifier. This, by the way, is the modifier, not a port," he told me, showing me a small, dime-sized electronic grid coated in what I assumed was silicone. "This will go in your neck."

"Got it," I said as drowsiness set in.

"Anyway, there was the opportunity to upgrade to USB C, but I was against it at the time. Maybe I should have done that, but what can I say? The mini USB worked for me. And they never changed it after I left, even though they should have. Hell, they should have digitized it, you know, no physical modifier needed. Bluetooth would have sufficed. But that's the thing with technology, sometimes; if it isn't broke we don't fix it, and not focusing on the data relay and adjustment method allowed us to focus on tweaking the modifier's ability to tap into a person's innate power."

"Interesting ..." I mumbled, the word seeping out of the corners of my mouth. It sounded garbled, like someone else had said it.

Father's medicine was working.

He kept talking about how the modifier worked as I drifted further and further away from reality. The first wave of emotion to hit me was guilt: I'd done a hell of a lot, to a hell of a lot of people. And what of those people's lives? What about the mother whose minivan we stole? Or the countless denizens we'd ripped off outside of banks? The people who had been exploited, the people who had died.

Aside from the trail of dead, there were others who may have experienced anguish as a result of our actions. I knew that AEFL and whatever quasi-investigative cover-up operations they employed did terrible things as they tracked us across the country. The people whose homes we'd stayed at or who had helped us, like the abuela and her big grandson in Austin, surely had received a visit from those Agent Smiths.

Thoughts zipped through my mind in a series of flashes as the medicine chilled me the hell out. I tried to speak, pretty sure I even managed to open my mouth, but then I saw Father looming over me, his beady little eyes, lantern jaw, no discernable scent about him, not that I could smell anyway.

Stella's face came into the picture as well.

*Is he showing her how this works?*

That was what it looked like at least, as he pointed at me and drew a loop in the air. She nodded, looked back at me, and I tried to smile at her.

No return smile, which meant I probably wasn't actually able to move my face muscles anymore.

No pain either as Father returned to my field of vision, a surgical mask over his face and a scalpel in his hand. Yup, I had officially lost my mind to the point that I was allowing some random-ass dude to do surgery on me in a trailer, in a forgotten corner of Nevada.

Stella's hand came over my eyes, and suddenly, everything was dark.

I awoke with cottonmouth.

It took a lot of effort to peel my eyelids open, and when I did, I noticed everything in the trailer had an odd patina to it, a yellow haze, the setting sun seeping in through any crack it could find.

"Welcome back," Stella said, excitement on her face. She was next to me on her knees, looking down at me. "Shhh..." she said, lightly patting my arm.

I instinctively reached my hand up to touch the side of my neck, only to have my paw lowered by Stella.

37

"You shouldn't touch that right now."

"He awake?" Father asked from the back of the trailer.

"Yes," she called to him.

"Good. Let's take a look at you."

Sounds came to me: water being poured, Father's feet on the tile flooring, Stella's knee cracking as she stood. The urge to vomit came over me and I swallowed it down. The act of swallowing forced a sharp pain to spread from my neck to my chin line.

"Glad to see you're awake," he said as he handed Stella a water bottle. "Your neck will be fine, and is now completely healed. What can I say? I'm good at what I do. The procedure went more or less as planned. I'm no surgeon, but my ability to modify reality could be described as a form of artificial luck, which I used to steady my hands and to make sure your body doesn't reject the modifier, which it hasn't as of yet. It may itch, though, so be prepared for that, and don't scratch it. Let it set."

Stella gave me a bottle of warm water; it only took a second after it reached my lips for me to know that it was

Father's concoction. I instantly felt rejuvenated, and the daze I'd been in moments ago was suddenly lifted.

"I bet you're wondering what abilities you've been granted," he said, as I finished the water. "Well, you and me both."

Father showed me a device that reminded me of a cobbled together smartphone. It was three times the thickness of a normal smartphone, and it had a few buttons on a panel that jutted out from where the receiver should be.

"Yeah," he said as he registered the look of skepticism on my face, "it's old school, but it works. Charged it too," he said as he reached the cable towards my neck. "It's going to be a little tender, but just relax for me."

"Got it," I told him, my voice finally my own again and sounding about right in my head. "What time is it?"

"Five-thirty."

"I've been out all day."

"Not an easy procedure," he said as he pressed the mini-USB cable into my neck. He was right: it was tender enough to make me wince as he adjusted his device, which caused the cable to tremble ever-so-slightly.

"That feels so fucking weird."

"That's one way to describe it," Father said as he powered up his device. "Let's see…" He scrolled through his modified phone for a moment, mumbling as the data populated. "In case you're wondering, I'm checking the bioneural operating system, and it's running a pre-installed update. There are no updates from here on out, but it does update to the latest version I have once it is first installed."

"So you'll never update it again?" I asked.

"No plans at the moment," Father said, as the system continued to load. Stella was next to him now, her arms crossed over her chest and propping her breasts up. Rather than focus on the peculiar strain I felt at the side of my neck, I focused on my breathing, recalling the yoga class I took for my P.E. credit at Southern Connecticut State (go Owls!).

"Hmmm…" Father finally said. "I haven't seen this type before."

"What type?" I asked.

"No talking," he reminded me as he noted something on a legal pad that he'd brought over to my bed. Father played around a moment with his modified, brick-sized smartphone, and once he was finished, he turned the device to me.

The only problem was, I couldn't quite read it. "Glasses," I whispered, finally realizing that my poorish vision was to blame for the blur that coated everything I saw.

Father pointed to my glasses, and Stella brought them over and placed them on my face.

I was still groggy, but not groggy enough that I couldn't understand the transformation that has taken place within me. I swore the smile that crept up my face reached all the way past the tops of my ears, a Joker smile if there ever was one, and the smile never left as it continued to dawn on me just how powerful I was about to become.

"Take a look," he said, waving the device at me.


## Main: Superpower Manipulation and Modification

Power Learning: 7

Storage Capacity: 3

Energy Channeling: 4

Ability Imprinting: 8

Borrowed Power Propensity: 7

"I'm a mimic?"

"I believe so." Father unplugged from my neck, giving me a moment to consider what he'd just shown me. "And from what I can tell here, you are able to store up to three powers at a time."

"Let me get this straight..." I had sat up by this point, not sure of how I should be seated after having neck surgery. My neck didn't hurt that much, but it was just a little sore. "I have the ability to absorb other people's powers, which could explain why Grace was able to give me some of hers. Correct?"

"Correct," said Father. "From the stats that you have, you're only able to have three abilities at a time. Now, similar to the dials that you were able to use to modify the others, you can modify yours, but you can't modify that one. I have already taken the liberty of modifying your abilities to some degree, increasing your Borrowed Power Propensity and your Ability Imprinting. I believe, and I may be wrong here, that you will never become more powerful than the person whose power you have borrowed, but you will be more powerful than you were before. Notice any differences?"

"Should I?"

"Stella, move closer to Gideon and let him touch you."

The vector manipulator shot him a funny look.

"Mimics act by touching the object they absorb, so you'll need to touch someone…"

"And how will whatever powers I absorb appear in my list of abilities?"

"I don't think there would be a way for us to code whatever ability you have currently absorbed. There have been others who had a portion of your powers, as their second ability, but none who had it as their main."

"You've been able to do all this with the modifier," I said, sweeping my hand from my neck to Stella. "It seems to me that you would be able to do something."

Rather than say anything, he picked up his notepad and jotted a few things down.

"Do you still want him to touch me?" Stella asked.

"Please."

I reached my hand out and placed it on Stella's arm. I felt a strange sensation roll over me, akin to the feeling I got right before I peed, that moment in which I could either hold it in (presuming there's not too much) or let it all blast out.

There had to be a better way to describe it, but that was what it felt like. It felt like a bodily urge, and I could either contain it, or release it.

"Has it taken?" Father asked.

"I...think? Yes, I believe it has."

"Good. Don't do anything yet. Let's go outside to test it."

I had no idea how to use my newfound power.

There were no labels, no constructs that told me which one I was using, but it was clear when it was in use, especially after Father told Stella to use her power to toss a handful of rocks at me.

And I'm not talking about a simple toss. Stella hurled them at me, and just before they reached me, I instinctively lifted my hand and *swiped them out of the air.*

"Now, lift the rocks and throw them back," said Father, no astonishment whatsoever on his face.

Rather than focus on the rocks themselves, I instinctively focused on the space around the rocks, noticing something in this space that was almost tangible, even from a distance.

The rocks rose and fell back to the ground.

"Try again," said Father, and once I focused on the space around the rocks again, I was able to keep them suspended long enough for me to be able to throw them back at Stella. It wasn't a hard throw, nothing like the way she'd tossed them at me, but I got the hang of it after a couple more tries.

*This has to be her ability,* I thought, as this feeling of total control washed over me. And I'm talking all the way down to the molecular level; I felt like I could even control a single vein in my toe if I wanted to.

*Does she have this much control over her own body?* I looked over at the woman with her big Dutch braid. There was no way I would ever know that, but this was definitely one ability that I wanted to hold onto for a while.

Still, it begged the question:

"How do you think I relinquish an ability?" I asked the mysterious man. Even though I knew his name was Jim, I still had the notion to call him Father. Weird.

"I don't know," said Father. "We're going to need a few more supers to test that out. But I think they will be arriving soon."

"They're coming here?" I dropped a large rock on to the ground. It rolled once, and stopped on its side.

Even with the excitement of my newfound abilities, my heart skipped a beat. And it skipped another in the time it took Father to casually answer my question.

"Grace and Veronique should be here shortly, but I think I already hinted at this. This I'm sure of. And that's the good news. The bad news is, I believe that Aida will be sending her people as well. There's also Chloe, who is still out in the desert somewhere."

I remembered Chloe, the super who could use sound as a weapon. Dorian had banished her almost immediately at the start of our last fight. "And Dorian?" I asked, thinking of how it had ended with her.

"Dorian banished everyone for a reason. She knew that Mother had taken over her psyche, and if you haven't figured it out already, Dorian was actually trying to help all of you. She banished you all to save you from Mother's forces."

"But she's not okay?"

Father's eyes darkened. "Her reality is not one that I'm able to touch at the moment. Now this doesn't mean she is gone for good, but you're likely going to have to get her back. You should be happy that she had the wherewithal to get all of you out of there. It could have ended even more poorly than it already did."

"Were you insinuating that a fight is coming our way?" Stella asked, obviously not at all concerned about Dorian's well-being. It was too bad too, because Dorian liked Stella better than the others seemed to.

"Just be prepared," Father told her. "Now, back to your powers, Gideon. We will need to practice relinquishing control, but that'll have to wait until the others arrive."

47

"You have powers…" I suggested.

"We're not going to play around with my powers for the time being." He cleared his throat. "Too dangerous. Anyway, you challenged me to figure out a way to display this skill of yours on your modifier. I've got the next few hours to do that, and you've got the next few hours to play around with Stella, maybe even train a little bit, and wait for the others to get here."

"Play?" I gulped, a smile taking shape on Stella's face.

"Let me know when you're hungry," Father said as he turned back to the trailer.

# Chapter Three: Come at me, Stella

Damn, did it feel badass saying those four words to the vector manipulator. So badass in fact, that I had to say them again: "Come at me, Stella."

She had already blasted me with a wave of force that I had mostly blocked. It did sweep me off my feet though, and it was a good thing that I was wearing a ballistic helmet because I cracked the back of my head against the ground on the recovery.

And no, I wasn't quite seeing stars à la an old Warner Brothers cartoon, but I was definitely a little dizzy when I got to my feet. The sun was setting now, the temperature had started to drop, the horizon a shade of pink that made me understand the appeal of living out here.

"Are you okay?"

"I'm fine," I said as I shook it off. Like any superpowered, I thrust my hand in the air before me and curled my fingers, twisting my wrist as I aimed my palm at Stella.

Stella started twitching, her eyes blinking rapidly. She regained control of her body, and sent a kinetic scythe of energy at me that seriously left me winded.

"So that's how we're doing this," I mumbled, as an idea came to me.

A rock came flying in my direction, and I shattered it with a wave of my hand, following up with a powerful blast that pinned Stella to the ground.

It was only a second before she was up, but then I hit her with her own ability, increasing the pressure on top of her by manipulating the molecules in the air.

And after keeping Stella pinned for a good thirty seconds, I let her up.

Sweat was scattered across my brow, and I was breathing heavily.

It was miraculous what I had just done, and the fact that Stella didn't walk over to me and slug me in the face showed just how impressed she was.

"That was cool," Stella said, as I offered her a hand.

As soon as our fingers touched, she blasted me away, a good thirty feet up, and I could have died right then and there if I hadn't stopped myself from hitting the ground.

*I can levitate?* I thought as I righted myself in the air.

I recalled the first time that we encountered Stella. She was in her room at the New Mexico facility, floating horizontally, *levitating.*

"Pretty sweet, isn't it?" Stella called over to me.

"That was a surprise attack."

She smirked. "What did you expect from someone like me?"

"Someone like you?" I asked, still tingling from the fact that I was floating. If it hadn't been such a serious situation, I would have done a flip in the air like I was Peter Pan.

But I kept my maturity to that of someone five years away from thirty, and slowly lowered myself to the ground.

*How do I activate it?* I thought, as I tested the buoyancy of my knees. I jumped into the air, and there I was, floating again. It just sort of happened, a natural extension of my being.

"Holy shit, this is so cool!"

Headlights on the horizon put an end to my fun and games.

From what I could tell, there were two Jeeps approaching, evident in their circular lights and the dust they were kicking up behind them, and it only took a moment for Stella and me to get into positions to attack the Jeeps.

Stella took her place to my left, floating in the air. To match her, I did the same, and she offered me a curt little smile as she floated just a little bit higher.

Not about to get in a dick measuring contest with a powerful super female who could squash me in an instant, I let her stay just a foot higher than me as the vehicles approached.

They were still far enough away that I wasn't able to see if there was a mounted weapon, or anything of the sort. That said, I was ready to blow the first one off its tires, and would have if I hadn't sensed a voice whispering in the back of my head.

*Relax, Writer Gideon, it's me.*

My heart shattered. Father had been right.

# Chapter Four: Pitching a Tent in a Tent

The door of the first Jeep opened, and about thirty seconds later, I felt a person leap into my arms.

*You're still invisible,* I thought to Grace as she kissed me.

*We can fix that.*

*How? My phone is broken.*

*The man inside the trailer…*

*Ah! Good idea.*

Father had stepped out, a thin smile on his face.

"It might look weird right now," I told him as I continued to hold invisible Grace, "but I have someone in my arms. Got a USB cable?"

Father returned a moment later with his brick phone and a mini USB cable, which he handed to me.

"Sabine?" he asked.

"Yes," said Grace as she guided my hand to the port, I mean *modifier,* on her neck. I ignored the rest of her stats and turned her Opacity dial up to ten, so her second ability was maxed out again.

Main Second: Shifter

Speed of Change: 10

Texture Consistency: 10

Opacity: 10

Voice Match: 10

Grace's form was back to normal in an instant, and as soon as she was herself again, I removed the mini USB cable and handed it and the heavy phone back to Father.

Stella chuckled as she took in the psychic shifter's appearance. "Is that your desert wear?"

"Survival gear," Grace told her with a wink.

The theme she'd gone for was a female Indiana Jones cosplay: a short-sleeved khaki shirt unbuttoned at the front and tied just beneath her bust line, her midriff revealed, her khaki shorts sat low on her hips, barely held to her body by a thick leather belt. Completing her getup was a pair of leather combat boots, the laces loosened.

Veronique stepped out of the second Jeep, still wearing the gear she'd worn back in the battle against Mother. Her ballistic helmet under her arm, the sexy metal vampire shot me a toothy grin, which didn't fit so well on her sharp face.

"I see you have leveled up a bit," Grace said, her eyes flashing white. She came to my right side, and looped her arm around my waist.

I felt a strange change, as if two invisible paths had opened up before me.

I chose the path on the left, it washed over me, and somehow, I knew it was Grace's psychic power. This became even more evident when I heard faint whisperings, the surface thoughts of those gathered around me.

"That's how it works?" I asked, watching Veronique approach. She reached her hand out to shake mine, and as we shook hands, she drained just a small amount of my life force.

I also felt that sensation of an energy coming over me, this one a more aggressive feeling, a thirst.

"What was that?" she asked as she let go.

"Long story incredibly short: I have superpowers now. Got a port too," I said, showing her the modifier on my neck.

"You?" Veronique asked, a wolfish grin now on her face.

"Want to test me?"

One of the Jeeps started backing away, interrupting our little moment. The other stayed put.

I would have asked Grace who she had found to drive them here, but I already knew the answer. And it wasn't even whispered in the back of my head or anything like that, it was just there, clear as day, as if I had been there on the trip with them.

Grace and Veronique had been teleported to the same area.

Able to levitate, Grace had lifted into the air, looked around for a moment, and found signs of civilization. But civilization was a lot further away than they hoped, and they ended up walking almost an entire night until they saw a small gathering of trailers, people who mostly lived off the grid and still thought the federal government actually gave a shit about their lives.

Once Grace and Veronique were in range, Grace had been able to send out a mental message to have the two picked up. They came here after she noticed the signal, something that I assumed Father had sent out.

Perhaps it was part of his reality manipulation ability, but as soon as Grace got the signal, they had come.

"You actually stole some of my ability?" Veronique now asked me. "Prove it." She pointed at the Jeep that hadn't backed away yet.

"Are you asking me to strip the Jeep of some of its metal or drain the driver?" I felt evil just possessing a sliver of Veronique's power, and maybe this was the closet Puritan in me, or maybe it truly was a fucked-up power to have, but it felt wrong to attack a person who had helped them in the first place.

"Both."

"It's evil, but it's a good idea to see what you can do," said Grace. "I'll have him get out of the vehicle."

Stella, who stood off to the left now, didn't say anything. Father was quiet as well, seeing where this was going.

"Um, okay, but not so much. Just to test."

A guy stepped out, short and stout. He had a sick mustache beard thing going on, something that would have made a guy in Mark Twain's day proud. The man was in a vest, under which he had an American flag shirt, the flag cast in black, white, and blue to honor the police. He also wore a pair of cargo pants and DisNike sandals.

I raised my palm in his direction, a cold feeling coming over me. I visualized a vortex at the center of my palm, sucking energy in my direction. My fingers glowed red, and as the man's life force came into me, I felt rejuvenated, as if I had just eaten a satiating meal. I let go almost immediately, the man's shoulders slumping forward.

"That is…" I gulped, not sure of how to describe the feeling of consuming someone else's energy.

"Try the other part," Veronique said in a coy voice.

Not wanting to destroy the man's only means of getting the hell away from here, I simply stripped one of the railings off the top of the Jeep. The metal tore off the top of the vehicle, spun into the air, and twisted into a cone. My hand still charged red, I drove the railing into the ground, erecting it as if it were a totem pole.

Still looking at the man, I went ahead and took over his mind, telling him to get back in the Jeep and drive as far away from here as he could, to forget all this.

"Grace, back me up."

The guy did as he was told in an instant, gone just about as quickly as he came.

"Anyway, Sabine and Veronique, I am glad you could join us," said Father. If he had any feelings on what had just transpired, he didn't share them. "And Michelle, is she en route?"

Grace shrugged. "I've done all I could to send out as many people as I came across to look for Michelle. I believe they will find her, and when they do, she'll be brought here."

"Okay, great, then tomorrow. She'll come tomorrow, and our attackers will come tomorrow night or the following morning," he said, grimly.

"Our attackers?" Veronique asked, her face tensing.

"How can you be so sure?" I asked Father.

"As I have suggested before, my ability doesn't allow me to see the future as much as it allows me to modify it, and I've already modified it to the best of my ability to prevent them from coming today. The thing is, we're sitting ducks out here. I don't personally want to be involved in any of this, having long ago gotten off the grid to avoid this type of situation. But I have no choice in the matter."

"But didn't you modify reality enough for Dorian to teleport us in your general vicinity?" I asked, realizing just how strange that question sounded.

"I did, and I'm afraid that's all the help I'll be able to provide. I promised Dr. Kim I'd lend a hand, and this is it. That said, after tomorrow, you are on your own again, and I suggest you continue the mission that you've already started."

"What about Dorian?" Veronique asked, surprising me with her concern.

"Unfortunately, Dorian won't be joining us, as I've already told Gideon here. My guess is she is in Sacramento, at the holding facility."

I remember the three facilities we had left: one was in Sacramento, one on Santa Cruz Island, and the final one was in Washington, in a place called Humptulips which sounded made up.

"At least it was the holding facility back in my day," Father continued. He bit his lip, the last sliver of sun lightly touching his face. "When I left, the facility was mostly used for holding supers that were going to be retired."

"You mean…"

He gulped. "Yep, retired."

I exchanged glances with Veronique. Before she had joined us, there was a good chance she was going to be retired in this way as well. It was one thing that fueled my desire to see an end to these places.

"Do you think Fiona and Ingrid will be there as well?" I asked. I still had hope that Mother was lying, that she hadn't killed them as she'd relayed to us. I couldn't imagine a world in which they simply killed two powerful assets like that.

Then again...

I glanced at Stella, and saw a muscle in her throat tighten at the mention of their names.

"That remains to be seen," Father finally said. "I'm going to be making food soon, and as per your request, Gideon, I'm still working on a way for you to better observe the abilities you have taken. I believe I will have something for you tomorrow, but I may have to work all night to get it right."

"Am I sleeping in the tent again?"

Father laughed as he turned back to his trailer, leaving me with the three superpowered women.

After drinking a little of Father's invigorating 'Super Juice,' which sounds dirtier than it is, the CBGs and I chilled out around the fire. Grace was next to me, still in her Indiana

Jones cosplay, Veronique was to my left, and Stella to my right. While we kicked it, Father caught Grace and Veronique up on his role in this affair, and the fact that he was likely related to them.

"A DNA test would tell us for sure, but I don't have any of the equipment for that out here."

"I kind of don't want to know," said Veronique, the reflection of the fire dancing across her dark eyes. "I am happy with just being me."

I appreciated that response.

Sometimes Veronique's bluntness made her seem cold; other times, it was the best way to respond to the situations we found ourselves in.

It was also strange how readily Grace and Veronique accepted Father's explanation.

This led me to believe that Grace knew more about the operation than she was letting on, which was likely as she seemed to *always* know more than she was letting on.

As Father continued on, telling them about early experiments and their first facility overseas, I leaned back, taking a good look at the stars and wishing I had an app or something that told me what constellation I was looking at.

It was downright chilly in the desert, but nothing as bad as New England. The temperature reminded me of a trip I'd taken to Brattleboro, Vermont with my ex in the spring of 2029. It was just the right temperature of cold, and had we gotten along better, it would have been a pretty good trip.

Thinking back, it was hard to imagine that the heavily wooded, retired hippy haven that was buried in three feet of snow for four months out of the year was somehow related to the dry Nevada desert. If anything, this adventure had given me perspective on America, its size, diversity, and the uniqueness of its regions.

There was plenty of time to wax poetic and reminisce after Father retired to his trailer, but my mind kept coming back to the sleeping arrangement. I was definitely going to crawl up into that tent, and I had no idea who would crawl in there with me, but whoever it was...look out!

I kid, I kid, but it was nice to think about something other than all the stresses of my life at the moment, all centering around the fact that we'd lost three members, especially

Dorian, the punk rock teleporter who was one of my favorite people.

Rather than turn down the path to melancholy, I focused on the center of the fire, and lifted my hand in its direction.

Without really paying attention to what I was doing, I used Stella's power to mold the flame into the outline of a voluptuous woman.

"Really?" asked Veronique.

"Sorry," I said as I cast the flaming woman away.

"You really are a perv," Stella said, a hint of humor in her voice.

"I think he's sleepy," Grace said, "and maybe he should go to bed."

"Yeah, yeah, you're right." I stood and stretched my arms over my head. "I'm banishing myself to the tent."

I unzipped the tight sleeping space and crawled inside, kicking my boots off at the entrance. With a deep sigh, I slipped into the sleeping bag, determined to get to sleep and forget about who might try to get into the tent with me.

I wasn't there for more than a minute when I was disturbed by...

*Dorian?*

The woman that crawled in next to me was the spitting image of the punk rock teleporter, from the red bandana she occasionally wore, to the leather jacket, to the fishnet stockings.

She faced me now, her black bangs in her face.

"Just be yourself," I told her, and in an instant, she was the Grace that first appeared on my doorstep, nude as the day she was created in a lab.

"I thought that seeing Dorian would cheer you up," she said.

"We may have to add Dorian to the list of people that you shouldn't turn into…"

"So many rules," she said lightly, as she moved in to kiss me. My hand was on her waist, and I shifted it up to her breast, cupping it, touching her nipple with my thumb.

"Give me some of your sleeping bag," she said.

"Will do," I told her as I unzipped it to cover both of us.

"Make room for me," Veronique said. Without waiting for me to do as she instructed, Veronique pushed her way into the tent onto my right side.

It was quite cozy now; Veronique also didn't have a sleeping bag due to the fact Stella had been using it to cover her shoulders, and had likely taken it into the trailer to sleep.

It took all the power I had, and I mean all of it, to suppress the idea of suggesting a *ménage à trois*.

I seriously had to use Grace's power to put my brain in an empty state, and even with my brain in that state, I couldn't prevent my mini writer from leveling up.

"Something's poking into me," Grace whispered.

"Don't worry about that," I said as I shifted to my back.

"This is like your fantasy come true, isn't it?" Veronique whispered in my other ear.

"Just go to sleep," I told her.

*I'm pitching a tent… in a tent.*

The thought escaped, and Grace couldn't help but laugh.

"Shut up," I told her, and any future thoughts that threatened to squeak out.

"It's cold," Veronique said, her hand now on my chest, and her head nuzzled in my armpit. Ever so slightly, her fingers began to move down my chest until they stopped just at my belly button. She pressed her finger into the fabric over my belly button, pushing it in as deeply as she could.

I tried not to squirm, but it wasn't easy.

I didn't want to let Grace know that Veronique was finger-fucking my belly button, but there was really no way around it considering our proximity.

The tension increased when Veronique dropped her hand beneath my belly button, so it was in the space just above my raging hard-on.

My mouth was dry now, and I even entertained the idea of zapping her hand away using some of my power – or Stella's power to be exact.

*Need some help down there?* Grace thought to me.

*You know, as much as I like the attention, and as much as I have watched animes and blasted the main characters for not making moves when they should have, this is neither the time nor the place to get that going. We're in a goddamn tent in the middle of Nowhere, Nevada.*

*We're a couple miles away from Lincoln Highway, near Fallon, Nevada. So not nowhere.*

*You know, I was thinking of something just now. Remember when you possessed me, and used my body to fuck Veronique? By the way, I'm pretty sure that's some type of rape that has never been classified, but regardless, remember that time?*

*It was fun, wasn't it?* Grace thought back to me, as Veronique continued to finger-bang my navel.

*Well what about this: what if you possessed me and then fucked you? That would be crazy, right? Then you could give it to yourself the exact way that you want to have it given to you.*

*That would be interesting, it would also be interesting to take part in one of the sessions you've had with Dorian and Veronique.*

*I never thought you'd be into that...*

*You never asked.*

Veronique's hand fell to my member. She squeezed it once, sapped just a small amount of energy from me, and took her hand away.

"You wish," she said as she turned her back to me.

*Anyway,* I thought back to Grace, finally able to breathe again. *Veronique has given up, which I'm fine with, because like I said, we are in a tent and I'd rather not get a situation like that started. Let's get some rest. Take over my mind and put me to sleep, please. Tomorrow should be an interesting day.*

*If that's what you'd like…*

I suddenly found myself getting sleepier, just barely able to keep the conversation going in my brain with Grace.

*Regardless of what happens to Dorian and the girls, we have to see this mission through. That is one thing I am certain of, Writer Gideon.*

*I agree, and after Michelle comes, we'll get out of the desert and see what we can do next. Also, Father hinted that Chloe may be somewhere in this desert. Have you sensed her?*

*No, I haven't. But I'll keep trying. My ability to sense someone, as you know, isn't that strong. I need to be able to see the person to really do damage. There are other telepaths that can work at a longer distance, and I believe Mother is one. But not me.*

*Yeah, I remember that. It's pretty strange having a conversation with you like this while you're lying next to me.*

*Would you rather us talk out loud?*

*No, because Veronique has passed the hell out.*

*That quick, huh?*

*Can't you hear her snoring lightly?*

Grace was quiet for a moment.

*Ah, I hear it!*

*I don't know how much more tent life I can take...* I thought to her as I grew drowsier.

# Chapter Five: A Mirage in the Dark

A bubbling blast of light struck our tent. The blast would have burned our three-way cuddling asses to a crisp had it not been for the fact that my borrowed abilities kicked in immediately, instinctively protecting us with a vector shield until Grace could respond with telekinetic protection of her own.

As the tent melted away, an earthquake started beneath us, making it impossible for us to get our footing.

*Chloe,* I thought as I got my bearings.

"Where is she?" Grace asked, struggling to get to her feet, her eyes blinding white. The psychic shifter was no longer nude; she was now in her tight black get-up, the one she wore from time to time that meant business.

Veronique moved into a defensive position in front of me, even though the ground continued to rumble beneath us.

Her eyes were trained on the horizon, her hands flaring red.

By this point, Stella had already run out of Father's home, instinctively casting a protective barrier over the trailer.

The four of us waited, our nerves firing as we stared into the darkness of the Nevada desert, the cold, starry night, waiting for something to give, for Chloe to show herself.

A blast hit the ground before us, followed by a high-pitched screech. The shield Grace had erected protected us from the debris; I didn't know how much longer I could keep my own shield up. It was exhausting keeping it powered, like I was running full speed on a treadmill, my heart racing, the sense that my legs would slip out from under me ever present.

Veronique used her power to lift small pebbles from the soil, anything with a trace amount of metal in it.

"I'll find her," Veronique hissed.

With a flick of her wrist, she sent a wave of pebbles and rocks spiraling around the area. Had I been able to see this from an aerial view, I likely would have seen that

Veronique's control over metal was even greater than I had originally anticipated. Like a game of Snake, she sent the wall of rocks circling around the campsite, spreading out just a little bit further with each pass until...

*She struck Chloe.*

"Eleven o'clock!" Veronique shouted to Stella.

A light cut across the darkness as Chloe fired another blast at us, followed by an ear-piercing sound meant to throw us off guard.

The sound manipulator knew she was outnumbered, and as the moments continued to stack up, Chloe switched tactics.

It began as a soft whisper in the distance.

It was Dorian's voice calling me forward, and regardless of the fact that I knew it couldn't be real, I took a step in her direction.

There was nothing else before me now, just a straight path towards Dorian, who stood in the darkness, a shadow enveloping her form, a bittersweet mirage in the darkness. As Dorian sweetly whispered my name, I felt a warm sensation moving through me.

It started at the top of my head, the tingling sensation growing hotter.

But I didn't mind, I was close to her, she was just a few feet away now...

"Gideon!"

This sound came from over my shoulder, a man's voice that felt like it was screaming from miles and miles away.

I came to a stop.

A man was approaching from my left, slow, calculated, unaffected by Dorian's sweet whispers.

The man cleared his throat, his eyes flaring yellow.

A blast of kinetic energy swept Dorian off her feet. Suddenly, Dorian was no longer her punk rock self, she was Chloe.

And she was being dragged over to us by an unseen force.

Chloe was a shapely brunette with an oblong face. Her skin was a shade darker than the others, and I saw immediately the similarities between her and Father, who still stood at my side, his arms crossed over his chest.

We were all in front of the fire now, which Stella had stoked to provide a little more light.

"Thanks," I finally told Father.

Had it not been for his reality manipulation ability, Chloe would have definitely gotten her shot off. No one said it, but I knew I'd been dangerously close to being cut in half by her power.

Aside from Father, Grace was the only other one who hadn't been enchanted by Chloe's Sonic Stimulation ability. The warmness I had felt could have been my demise.

I knew that, and just looking at Chloe, I felt a wave of anger come over me.

And it was unlike me to have this wave of anger – well, unless I was having an argument with Angel – and my first response was just about as 'Veronique' as I could be.

I lifted my hand over Chloe's body and began draining her life force.

A grin spread across Veronique's face as she did the same. I felt my energy swell, and it was only when Father told us to stop that I quit sapping her energy. Chloe was on the verge of purple now, her skin dry and shriveled. I lowered my hand, glancing from Stella to Grace.

"We should hold her for now," Father said firmly. "She'll be more useful to us that way."

"Do you have any extra metal?" asked Veronique.

"I have some clothes hangers in my closet."

"That will work."

Father turned back to his trailer, leaving me with the CBGs and Chloe's unconscious body.

"What should we do with her?" Stella asked.

"Let's keep her prisoner for now," I said, my anger at her waning. "Hopefully, we can turn her. Maybe, once she's awake again, Grace and I can do some psychic rearrangements."

"She's dangerous," Veronique said.

"And so were you, well, you still are dangerous."

Veronique turned to me. "Is that how you see me?"

"No, I see you as, um, a sometimes misguided superpowered female who is incredibly cool and, um, hella powerful. Pretty too."

Stella laughed.

"What?"

"Sometimes I think you're a genius, but most times I think you're an idiot."

"Well, first off, thank you for calling me a genius," I told Stella, "and *second off,* if that's even a thing someone can say, I'm not really an idiot as much as I am an amateur. A lot of this stuff, scratch that, *all* of this stuff is new to me. Even though we've been going at it now for a couple weeks, it's still pretty crazy, and it still takes me time to process it and figure out what to do next. And look, I'll be the first to admit it, I know I've made mistakes."

This last sentence created a spell of silence between the three of us. We all knew what Stella was thinking, and it was no surprise that a part of her still blamed us for the loss of the two super teens, Fiona and Ingrid, even though I knew in my heart they were still alive.

"As I was saying, this is still new to me, so keep that in mind. And we should give Chloe a chance, just as we gave you a chance," I said to Veronique. "And Dorian. Maybe Chloe will be the same."

"That remains to be seen," was her only reply.

"Here are the hangers," Father said to Veronique. "And Gideon is right, she deserves a chance. Let's just make sure Chloe can't attack us. I've already tried modifying her reality, but as I believe you'll come to see, she's stubborn, and it's hard to gauge how well my influence will work."

"Another hard-headed super?" I smiled at Stella. "Well, I've dealt with them before, and I'll deal with them again."

"I'm not hard-headed."

"Yes, you are," said Veronique. "But it's fine. We all have our issues."

"Do we now?"

"Yes. Gideon's issue is he doesn't trust his own powers and judgment and gets too carried away in his thoughts.

Grace's issue is that she's too nice and never pushes her power to its natural limit. My issue is that I'm not so personable, due to the fact my ability has changed me into someone that can be a bit cold-hearted."

All of us turned to Veronique, shock registering on our faces.

"But these are just my observations," she said with a shrug. "Our tent is destroyed. We need a new place to sleep."

"How about the bed of my pick-up truck? It should hold the three of you," Father offered. He glanced up at the sky, nodding towards the distance. "The sun will be up in an hour or so. I'll make some breakfast once some real food is delivered."

"A delivery?" I asked.

"It's easier to manipulate the reality of normals. I have a guy who delivers groceries to me once a week. And I usually have him come pretty early, about 5:30 to 6 AM. So at least we'll have a nice breakfast."

He turned to me.

"Regarding an ability to gauge your powers: I'll get into that after breakfast. We'll also need to experiment with switching out your powers, and now that we have Chloe

here, we have someone we can experiment with."

# Chapter Six: Getting My Ass Kicked

The truck bed was cold, but at least I had two toasty bodies on either side of me to keep my wacky ass warm. And we only slept an hour anyway, and hell, I could hardly call it sleep, as my toxic thoughts had me on edge.

We just needed Michelle to come. Once she was here, we could continue forward and try not to look back too much.

Father's grocery delivery service woke me; the guy wasn't there for very long before his old truck started up again and he drove off.

Grace had said that we were somewhere off Lincoln Highway, not too far away from Fallon, Nevada.

Later, I would pinpoint our location on a map to see that we were between Harmon Reservoir and the highway. And what a strange name for a reservoir anyway, Harmon. It seems like it would be a good pen name for an author, but that's about it. Hell, I wouldn't even name a cactus Harmon.

"I'm awake," Veronique announced to both of us.

"And let me guess, you want some coffee?"

"Yes, but only if it's strong."

"You've been drinking coffee for what, a week and a half? Two weeks? And now you have a preference for its style?"

"Just be glad I haven't tried McStarbucks."

I gasped. "How do you even know about McStarbucks?"

"Commercials. They seem to really target people who watch the home improvement channel."

*So advertising does work,* I thought as I sat up. Grace wasn't so interested in waking up, and instead, she stretched out like a starfish as soon as both of us were out of the bed of the truck.

"She sure looks comfortable back there," I told Veronique as we stopped to look at her for a moment.

"She always looks peaceful; it's one of the ways that she deceives people."

"I can't argue with that."

We found Father already cooking inside his trailer, and Stella was awake too, sitting on the couch with one leg crossed over the other.

It had been awhile since I had taken a shower. I knew I didn't smell like fresh musk apples, or whatever Old Spice Right Guard deodorant flavor they had for men nowadays, but for some reason, the CBGs looked relatively clean.

And they shouldn't have looked clean, but even sitting on the couch in the dusty trailer in the same clothes that she had worn for two days now, Stella still looked way cleaner than me.

Maybe this was a female thing.

Maybe men always smelled no matter how hard we tried to cover up this fact.

Yesterday, I had tried to wash off in Father's shower, but the water was freezing cold, and it smelled funny too. The sulfuric stink made me feel like I was bathing in farts.

We needed a hotel badly. Privacy would have been nice too, but a hot shower…

What I wouldn't give for a hot shower.

I now sat at the trailer's dining room table next to Veronique, who had just poured herself a cup of coffee. She sipped it with both hands, a strand of her blond hair falling into her face.

Her dark eyes fell on me as I watched Father cook.

The chair next to me scooted against the linoleum flooring; Stella had used her power to prepare her seat, and as she sat, I felt her thigh brush against me.

"So I've got good news, and I've got bad news," Father said, as he fried some bacon. "The good news is that I figured out a way for you to see the abilities you currently possess. That is, until you are able to recognize their feelings more precisely."

I nodded; I had a sinking suspicion that a point would come when I would be able to sense which abilities I currently held.

"And the bad news?" I asked.

"There's no way, at least through bio-digital means, for you to switch these abilities out or increase or decrease their powers," he said over the sizzle of the bacon. "You switch them out by absorbing another ability. And now that we have Chloe out there, we can really do some experimenting with that."

"But if I plug in now, I'll be able to see which abilities I am currently holding, correct?" I asked, going for a cup of coffee.

I added some French vanilla powdered creamer and half a packet of sugar; it wasn't the best stuff I had ever drunk, and definitely not as good as the fancy schmancy shit we had in Colorado, but it was good enough.

"That's right, you'll be able to see which abilities you currently have." Father set a plate of bacon on the table. There were things that were more gorgeous than a plate of bacon, including all the CBGs, but that being said, a plate of bacon was, and still is, a sight to behold.

I dug in almost immediately, disregarding any sense of table manners my parents had instilled in me.

"I'm glad you're enjoying yourself," Father said as he returned from the kitchen with a pan of scrambled eggs. "I have some Tabasco sauce if you need it."

"Green or red?"

"Red."

"I'm fine," I told him. "Anyway, back to what we were talking about. Let's test it out as soon as we finish here. And once Michelle comes, and damn I hope that's today, we'll be out of your hair. We have things we need to do."

"That's true, you do have things you need to do."

While we ate, Father told us a little bit more about living out here. He was actually starting to open up to us, something that he hadn't done when it had just been me and Stella.

The gist? The man known as Jim Mathis in some circles, the Father of all supers in others, had been out here for a couple years. He liked the isolation that came with being off the grid, and he especially liked the desert during the winter.

Grace came in just about the time we were all finishing breakfast, looking fresh as ever, as if she'd just stepped out of the shower and took an hour pampering herself. She took the scrambled eggs and scooped her bacon onto my plate, which I gladly ingested.

Outside we went, where we found Chloe lying sideways on a blanket, her wrists and legs cuffed behind her by Veronique's hanger arrangement.

She was breathing lightly, still passed out.

"We need to move her to the shade after this," said Father. "She'll get burnt if we keep her out here any longer."

"We could move her onto your couch," I suggested.

"Yeah, that would probably be more humane. But before we do that, take her power and see which ability it replaces."

The CBGs were behind him, Grace still eating from her plate.

"I'm supposed to just feel it?"

Father retrieved his modified smartphone and a mini USB cable from his front pocket. "Yes, but to be sure, we're going to check using your modifier. Your abilities will be listed in the order that you have taken them, so that means you will have Grace's telekinetic ability, Veronique's power, and Stella's, based on the changes you recently made. Let me double-check that before you absorb Chloe's power."

I sat to make it easier for Father to plug into my neck. I noticed when he plugged in that I wasn't feeling any pain associated with having a pretty major surgery less than twenty-four hours ago. I hadn't looked at myself in the mirror yet, but if I had, I would have seen that the skin around my port had already healed up completely.

Father showed me the readout on his smartphone. "That is what your abilities currently look like, the powers you are currently mimicking."


<u>(1) Psychic</u>

* Second Sight

* Psychometry

* Telepathy

* Psychokinesis

* Hypnosis

* Nightmare Sight

## (2) Metal Absorption and Modification

* Wielding Capacity

* Adaption Speed

* Alloy Integrity

* Blood Metal Conversion


## (3) Vector Manipulation

* Kinetic Energy Manipulation

* Vibration Emission

* Inertia Negation

* Telekinetic Regeneration

* Velocity Manipulation

* Aversion Field Creation

* Overcharge

I saw how they were listed, and was impressed by how detailed they were, especially considering they were borrowed powers. No, there weren't any numbers associated with the powers, but at least I got a sense of what I could do. I also had no earthly idea of how he'd come up with a way to list it, but I never let those types of questions get in the way.

I was impressed, both with his skill at bio-hacking and what it truly meant to be a mimic. It explained why I could still hear surface thoughts of those around, mostly Veronique thinking about feeding, and how I had Stella's sense of the web that connected all of us.

"Go ahead and absorb Chloe's abilities," said Father, his hand coming up to his scraggly beard. "We'll see what happens."

With Father still plugged into my neck, I reached my hand out and placed it on Chloe's cheek.

I felt the strange sensation that I had felt before, as if something was coming into me in almost a spiritual way.

At the same time, I also felt something go out.

Suddenly my surroundings weren't as crisp as they were just moments ago. Looking over the CBGs, I noticed that I could no longer sense the space between us, at least that was the way my mind was able to describe it.

Before, with Stella's power, I was keenly aware at the molecular level of the energies surrounding us. Now that feeling was gone, and everything was back to normal.

Or so it seemed. My awareness of sound had increased, and where I'd felt Stella's understanding of the nature of time and space, I could now feel *sound* as if it were a tangible thing. It wasn't super strong, but the feeling was definitely there.

"Interesting," Father said as he checked the readout on his phone. "Your abilities cycle through, and once you have three, the next one will replace the last one in the list. That said, I have this feeling that once you get good enough, you'll be able to pick which abilities you want to replace." His eyes suddenly went golden and dark again. "But that's a discussion for another time. Look."

Father turned the face of his smartphone to me:

(1) Acoustokinesis

* Sound Sculpting

* Acoustic Acceleration

\* Sonoluminescence

\* Rhythm Manipulation

\* Sonokinetic Combat

From what I could recall, I was missing a few of Chloe's abilities, like Extreme Sound Detection. So it seemed as if I didn't get the full power, only portions of it.

Figuring I'd switch back to having Stella's power, I cycled through by literally playing a weird, hardly sexualized game of Duck, Duck, Goose until my powers were, in order: Veronique's metal ability, Stella's vector badassery, and Chloe's sound power.

"Who's up for a little fight?" I asked the CBGs, jokingly cracking my knuckles.

I liked Veronique, really, I did, but boy did it feel good to give her a taste of her own medicine.

The first person I went for in our little melee was the stone-cold metal vampire, draining her before she could drain me.

I had first told them all to come at me at once, which had been an incredibly stupid idea because they beat me in about twenty seconds.

This time around, at Father's suggestion, we decided to separate it out.

And Veronique had been the first to volunteer to kick my ass.

As she returned fire, this time with another gravel attack – something she'd been experimenting with – I activated Chloe's power. I still didn't know the correct verb to use for how I activated and/or switched the powers; it was more of an afterthought than it was a predetermined attack.

My natural instinct took over when it came to selecting the superpower to use, and I had a knack for it, likely because of a youth spent consuming superhero comics, gaming, and being a fantasy writer.

I wasn't OP, far from the term, but I felt confident, adjusted, like I truly could take them on. It was a feeling that I would grow more accustomed to as the days passed, that I was born for this.

But in the desert of Nevada, it was still an incredibly new sensation. I opened my mouth and a sound emitted from my body, but not from my pie hole as I'd thought it would.

The sound originated at my throat, and as it rushed forward it turned into light energy that landed at Veronique's feet and tossed her to the side, ripping her vest off her body. I hit her again, this time a total perv attack that blasted her shirt off.

Funny part was: I had no idea how I was doing this! I was simply going for it, not holding back, and I was quickly brought back to earth when a rock struck me in the back, sending me stumbling forward, where I was caught by Veronique's powerful vampiric grip.

As my energy left my body, and as her hand grew red, a smile twisting across her face, I threw in the towel, gasping for mercy until she finally let up.

"Sorry about your clothes," I said, as I sucked in deep breaths.

"Why do I feel like you did this on purpose?" she said as she walked toward Father's trailer.

"Ha! Can you imagine stripping someone's clothes off as a superpower? Wait a minute, I think that might be one of the main powers in *High School DxD*. Back to the drawing board..."

"Careful next time, Gideon," Veronique mumbled as she retrieved her shirt and vest.

I rubbed my hands together. "Who's next? I'm ready when you are. Stella? Grace?"

Grace stepped before me, and as she did, she took on the form of Michelle, the speedy super teen with a pink streak in the side of her black hair.

"Please don't attack me, Gideon," she said in Michelle's cute voice.

"Grace, why is it that you always have to do the most fucked up thing possible?" I laughed.

"I'm not Grace, I'm Michelle. Please don't hurt me."

"You know that's not going to work on me," I told her, and even saying it, I noticed that I was starting to believe the phony Michelle in front of me.

I had seen Grace do this to other people before, take a form and augment her ability by using her telepathic powers, but I couldn't recall being on the receiving end of it, aside from the first night in my garden apartment back in New Haven.

And I knew it wasn't Michelle, I could tell, I mean...
*Right? It can't be her.*

Michelle placed her hands behind her back and squirmed, balancing on the balls of her feet. A sudden wind lashed at her hair, and she looked to the wind, just as Michelle would have done if she had experienced something like that.

"Huh, it's windy today!"

And that's when a wave of force threw me backwards at least fifty feet.

I hit the ground, tumbled a few times, ate gravel, and managed to finally stop myself by boosting forward. Having control of vectors allowed me to do some pretty crazy things, but they did nothing against someone manipulating my mind, or putting thoughts into my head, visions, like the one I was now seeing of Grace lying on the ground, nude, a pool of blood forming around her head.

*Grace!* My mind screamed out.

*Help me, Gideon!*

I knew in my heart of hearts that it was not real, but that did not stop me from averting my attack at the last moment, which caused a crater to form where Stella had just been standing.

"Watch it!" Stella called to me.

"Sorry!"

The headache started at the back of my skull and moved forward, swimming through my cranium. It bloomed into something entirely terrible, an image that I hoped to never see.

Dorian was dead. She lay on the ground, a large slab of steel sticking out of her chest. Veronique was next to her, her neck in an awkward position, clearly broken. Staggering now was Grace, whose arm was broken, dangling at an awkward angle, her knees buckling as she reached her free hand up to me.

*Please, Gideon...*

I saw the panic in her eyes, the splattering of blood dripping from her nostrils and streaked across her hair, over her lips, dribbling down her chin.

I panicked.

Racing down to the ground, I reached my arms out to scoop her up. I was flying, using a power that I still wasn't a hundred percent comfortable with using.

And I wasn't able to put the brakes on in time.

I cracked into the ground, feeling my shoulder rip towards my spine, my chest scrape as I slid for a moment.

"Gideon!" Everything was back to normal, and Grace was standing next to me now, trying to help me to my feet.

"Let him be, let him be! Don't move him," Father said as he approached.

Everything around me was a blur, and I noticed that I was now whimpering. It was a sound that was coming from my chest, as if I had...

It was getting hard to breathe. Each breath in felt like I was inhaling daggers.

Father was next to me now, an annoyed but concerned look on his face. I could barely hear him now, everything was slipping away, but his voice eventually made it to my ear, where it was translated to a sound that I could understand.

"Damn it, this is not how I wanted to do this, but it's now or never. Gideon, if you can hear me, I want you to take my power. But not my reality manipulation power. I want you to focus, and only take my ability to heal. Sure, you have some healing capacity with Stella's power, but nothing like what I can give you."

"You can heal?" Veronique asked.

Her hand was charging red, that she was ready to take Father down. I would have also seen Stella, her hair flaring up as a shield formed around her ready for the attack that was to come, and Grace, her eyes flaring blistering pearl, ready to spring into action as well.

But for the time being, they were blurs on the periphery, and I was more focused on trying to catch my breath.

"I've never been one to show all my cards in the beginning. To answer your question, yes, I also have the ability to heal, but that's not what is important right now. What is important is that you take this ability and use it to heal yourself, Gideon. I was going to show you this ability later, but you need it now. Heal yourself, Gideon, *take my power…*"

"I … I… try…"

Father placed my hand on his arm. I felt that sensation that was growing more familiar to me, the ability to take someone's power or leave them be.

Even as I was losing oxygen, and as my brain and body were registering the fact that I was in critical condition, I tried to focus on only taking Father's ability to heal. My eyes were closed now and I got this strange vision of two channels. While they weren't labeled, I sensed that the left lane was Father's healing ability.

I moved into that lane, and as soon as his power came into my body, replacing Chloe's, I immediately began to feel a healing energy spread through me.

The first part of this feeling reminded me of what it was like to take your first sip of a carbonated beverage; it almost hurt in this very good way, but this was quickly replaced by an entire full body experience in which I felt myself growing stronger, my limbs looser, my muscles hardening as my bones moved back into shape.

I sat up, looked to Grace, who had just about the most ashamed look on her face I think she could muster, and smiled.

"That was... badass."

"I'm sorry, Gideon," she said, swallowing hard.

"If that's what it's like to be on the receiving end of your nightmare abilities, jeez, we have got to use that one more. I almost flew into the ground."

"You did fly into the ground, and you almost died," Veronique said, lowering her charged red hand.

"I'll have to be a little more careful next time."

I got to my feet, feeling as healthy as I had been before Grace's hallucination had caused me to dive head-first into the hard Nevada soil.

"So you were holding out on us," I told Father.

"No, I just wasn't telling you the full truth."

"Why didn't you just heal me?" I asked.

"Because I was going to give you this ability anyway, after you got used to cycling through powers. I figured now was as good of a time as any." Father looked at me curiously for a moment.

"What?"

"I wonder if your power would work with saliva?"

"With saliva?"

"Or urine, or even better, blood. Yes, blood may work. Who is ready to be part of a science experiment?" Father asked the CBGs.

I was the only one to raise my hand.

I currently had Father, Chloe and Veronique's powers, in that order. This left Grace or Stella to donate a small amount of blood to see if I could activate their abilities in this manner. Stella was skeptical, as was I, but if Grace had any thoughts about the experiment, she wasn't showing it on her face.

She was feeling guilty, evident in the way she held her shoulders when she saw me.

*I'm not mad at you, Grace, I wanted you to do something like that,* I thought aloud.

*If it weren't for Father, I might have killed you,* came her response.

*Stella has somewhat of a healing ability, not as good as his, but that would have helped. I think.*

*Maybe. I'm sorry, Writer Gideon, please forgive me.*

*I've already forgiven you.*

*Then let me make it up to you.*

*You make it up to me by just being you.*

*Well, then let me make it up to you anyway. Next time we're alone.*

*That's how you want to make it up to me?*

*Are you opposed to this?*

*Nope, sounds good to me!*

I offered Father a toothy grin, rather than Grace.

"Why are you smiling like that?" Father asked.

"No reason. Let's get this party started."

Father now had a plastic glove on and a syringe. He pressed the needle into Grace's arm, took a small amount of blood, and squeezed the blood out onto a petri dish.

We were back in his trailer, Veronique and Stella on the couch while Father, Grace and I were huddled around the petri dish in the kitchen.

"So there it is, just touch it with your finger."

Father already had his phone out, ready to plug into my neck and confirm if I had taken her ability or not.

I did as instructed, pressing my finger into the small pool of blood in the petri dish. I kept it there for a moment, and... I felt that familiar sensation again, the one that was asking me if I wanted to take someone's ability.

And just like Father, I was presented with two paths, and I instinctively knew that the path on the right was her psychic ability, not her shape-shifting power. So I took it, and as I took it, I felt another energy leave me, which if I was not mistaken was Veronique's ability.

Father plugged into my neck and turned the smartphone screen towards me.

<u>(1) Psychic</u>

* Second Sight

* Psychometry

* Telepathy

* Psychokinesis

* Hypnosis

*Nightmare Sight


<u>(2) Cell Regeneration</u>

* Regenerative Healing Factor

* Regrowth

* Cellular Activation

* Flawless Restoration

<u>(3) Acoustokinesis</u>

* Sound Sculpting

* Acoustic Acceleration

* Sonoluminescence

* Rhythm Manipulation

* Sonokinetic Combat

"That confirms it, you can take someone's ability by simply touching their blood." He nodded, offering me a firm smile. "In that case, I have some shatterproof test tubes that I've been saving, mostly because I thought they were interesting."

"You thought test tubes are interesting?" I asked.

"Once a scientist, always a scientist, and yes, I like the way that they were designed." He shrugged, turning to his backroom. "Anyway, I will get them ready for you. I have this sense that Michelle will be here soon, and you'll likely want to get on your way at that point. You should just be able to dab your finger with my blood to take my healing ability."

"Got it."

Father stopped before he could reach his bedroom. "But remember, you shouldn't take my reality manipulation ability. And I know that saying that is akin to telling a kid not to eat from the bowl of candy on the table, but you have to trust me: this ability is not something you want to play with. Are we clear here?"

I could tell by the look in his eyes that Father was being serious with me. The way he said this was the way a sniper would tell you that guns kill people: the man had seen it firsthand, was very familiar with the power he possessed, and wished no one else to possess it.

"All clear," I finally told him.

# Chapter Seven: Desert Brawl

Cue the training montage music, and choose whichever tune you'd like. Try to be a little more original than *Eye of the Tiger*, but who am I to judge? If the shoe fits...

*Action, action, action,* as Luke used to tell me.

Which is why I'm offering you the equivalent of a literary montage: picture hot supers coming at me, sweat wicking off their sexy bodies; a few instances where I manage to piss them off; a few instances where they manage to almost kill my sci-fi-happy ass; some touching moments where we go easy on each other; several two-on-one matches in which I am accosted by two hella babes at the same time, a threesome of the utmost extreme.

Hot stuff, really.

And while I continually had my ass handed to me, Father gathered a vial of his blood so that I could now become a healer whenever I needed, as it only took a very small amount of his blood, or anyone's blood for that matter, for me to take their power.

Which was nice, because after a couple of vector powerslams by Stella, and the time Veronique beat the crap out of me with an old metal bumper she'd unearthed, it was nice to heal right the fuck up.

I had also figured out a way to take someone's power mid-fight, and use it against them, which seemed as if it would be handy.

My current skill set, in order: Father, Veronique, and Stella.

For once in my life, I could kick ass, drain ass, and heal ass.

"You sure are looking smug," Stella said as she dropped down next to me.

"Just enjoying the view," I told her, referring to the horizon, but also possibly in reference to the fact that Veronique and Grace were approaching me, Veronique now in one of Father's shirts which she had unbuttoned and tied beneath her chest, Grace in a tight black outfit.

"Ready to get back to civilization?" asked Stella.

"I've never been readier," I told her. "We just have to wait for Michelle to get here."

It didn't happen the moment after I said that last line – nothing really works like that in real life, or at least not usually – but it wasn't too long after that I saw a black truck appear in the distance.

Two more black trucks appeared behind it, and my excitement morphed to surprise when I saw something fly off the first vehicle.

From the distance, it looked like a kid was floating above the last truck now, small blinking lights surrounding the kid's body. Only when it got closer did I realize that this kid had the head of an adult, a head covered by long, greasy black hair, and defined by its scowl.

"It's Angel," I said, and I was just about to fire off a shot at his truck when Grace stopped me.

*Let us do it; keep your skills secret,* she thought to me. *For now.*

*Good idea.*

Stella had already made a shield as Father stepped out of the trailer, looking nonchalant as ever in his off-the-grid attire.

"Grace already go over the plan with you?" he asked.

"I think?"

"Good, act weak, act like normal."

*Like normal?* I shot him a dirty look.

"I'll try to talk them out of what they're planning to do."

The three trucks came to a stop, the first one turning to the side so we could see the contents of the bed of the vehicle. I gasped as I saw a large metal cage, a female inside with black hair and a pink streak at the side.

It was Michelle, and worse, they had bound and gagged her, stuffed her in a big cage.

"Fuckers!" I shouted, feeling vector energy moving through me in response. Grace shut me down in an instant, her voice suddenly all around me.

*Relax, Writer Gideon. Remember, your power is a secret.*

In the back of the first truck was Victoria, already in her metal form with a ginormous blade coming out of her back, scorpion-like.

Augustin, Mr. Fire and Ice himself, hopped out of the second truck bed, a supervillain scowl on his face if I'd ever seen one. He struck a pose and his right fist ignited.

But that's not what got my attention.

What held my attention now was the man, or should I say, *men* getting out of the driver's seats of all the trucks. The men wore black MercSecure gear and all of them were identical in every way, shape and form.

*They have a replicator,* I thought to Grace.

*Remy,* she thought back to me. *But I can't tell which one the real version is. They all share the same thoughts.*

"Got it," I said as the biggest auntfucker this side of the Pacific descended to the earth.

Angel looked... better.

Actually, it looked like someone had taken his normal-sized head and plopped it on the body of a muscular twelve-year-old. Sort of a bobblehead thing going on, but at least he was a muscular kid, and making fun of him was going to come easy, if I got the chance to speak.

Father, his eyes flaring yellow, frowned as he looked from Angel to the replicating super known as Remy. "I believe we have someone you may be interested in, and you have someone we may be interested in."

"We aren't interested in Michelle," Angel growled. "We captured her, and figured we'd come and deal with you four next, well, and you, Jim."

Father took a long, hard look at Angel, who despite his size still had his gruff, tough guy voice. "I was hoping we would be able to do this the easy way. But seeing as how you have shown up here uninvited and kidnapped a young girl, treating her like she was no better than a barnyard animal, I guess things aren't going to be so easy this time, son."

"I guess not," Angel said, flexing his muscles, "Dad."

I couldn't help myself, I had to get a jab in.

"Hey," I said, stepping up. "What's it like to have sex with your aunt in the body of a kid? Okay, let me rephrase that because that sounded even worse out loud than it did in my head. Fuck you, Angel," I said, hurriedly, realizing my little shit talking session was petering out. "I don't have any good one-liners right now, but fuck you."

Angel snorted. "I am going to enjoy killing you, Gideon. I'm going to take pleasure in your death, in breaking every one of your bones. It's going to be like a fine wine to me, I'm going to savor it, hell, I may save a little of it for the next day if you get my drift. I'm going to even share a little bit of it with my friends here. Point is, you're mine, and I can't wait to crush you, slowly, so that you feel as much pain and humiliation as you have caused me."

"You know, Angel, I never took you for an eye for an eye type of guy. I mean, I knew you were a douche-biscuit, but didn't know that you would look like a flying bobblehead the next time we met."

Rather than reply, the aunt-banging fuckboy rose into the air, allowing Augustin to send an arc of ice and fire in our direction.

Stella protected us from frying and/or freezing to death, and as she did, Remy quadrupled the number of forms he had on the battlefield. They ran toward us now, Veronique trying to take them down with rocks and any metal that she could find aside from Father's truck and trailer.

114

Remy's clones didn't fight us, *they exploded*, vamoosing into fiery bits once they met the shield that Stella had created around us.

"They're suicide bomber clones?" I cried out.

"Never mind that," said Stella, seething. "Once they finish I'm going for Michelle!"

"Grace!" As soon as her name left my lips, she knew exactly what I wanted her to do. A telekinetic shield formed around us, the glimmering energy reminding me of plastic wrap. It stretched back until it also protected Father's trailer.

Remy's clones kept slamming into the shield, allowing Stella to focus on rescuing Michelle.

"Veronique, go for Michelle as well! The truck too!" I shouted, and without looking at me Veronique turned her attention to one of the black trucks.

It was pulled into the air, smashing into Victoria's steel body.

Why they kept sending a woman made of metal after us was beyond me, and this time, Veronique didn't play nice.

In fact, it was one of the more gruesome things I'd seen her do.

The truck still on top of Victoria, Veronique ripped all the metal pieces off and began stabbing them repeatedly into the steel woman, each shard of metal zipping through the truck's frame to reach its buried target.

Only thing was, the metal didn't just hit Victoria's body, it melted into it, creating something that looked kind of like a voodoo doll with a bunch of pins sticking out of it once Veronique kicked the truck away.

Veronique's eyes were red, and not glowing red like Grace or Father; no, her pupils were red, a predatory grin on her face as she began closing her fists, pulling them away from one another as far as she could.

Veronique tore Victoria's body apart, pulling until all that was left was just a stub of body, a single leg, and a shrieking super seconds from death, her neck bending backwards as Veronique drove a portion of the ripped truck into her exposed throat.

And that was when Victoria disappeared.

I recognized the person who took her, too. It was only a flash, and if I had blinked I wouldn't have seen it, but it was clearly...

*Not Dorian.*

I exhaled audibly, at once saddened and also relieved, a part of me sickened, as I glanced from the now empty space in the battle to Victoria's body parts, which were still scattered around, portions of them covered in metal and the others covered in red tendrils of flesh.

"It wasn't Dorian." I had to verbalize it.

And I was relieved that it wasn't her, but also, part of me just wanted to see her, to know that she was okay. That she was with us.

My strange, mixed emotions were interrupted when Augustin lifted pillars of fire from the ground. One came up right in front of Father, and as it did, it simply skipped to his right. As casually as one would walk along the beach in the moonlight, Father made his way over to Augustin.

Even Remy's clones, which were doing their damndest to explode their bodies against him, missed every time.

Father paused, looked up at Angel, *his fucking son,* and slowly clasped his hands behind his back as Remy's clones descended upon him.

I couldn't see the look on his face, and his pose seemed very low-key, but I could tell he was taunting Angel, letting the flying bastard know just how powerful he was.

Stella, having battled her way through a series of explosive clones, reached the truck and used her power to hurl caged Michelle in our direction, where she was intercepted by Veronique who brought her safely behind Grace's shield.

Michelle rescued, Stella turned her attention to Augustin, who was trying to blast her with a great ball of fire. The fire reached Stella and dissipated, like someone blowing out a candle.

Stella encompassed Mr. Fire and Ice in a blurry cocoon of power. I realized when his hands came to his neck that she had taken all the air out of the cocoon.

And she would have killed him right then and there if Danielle the teleporter hadn't appeared, grabbed Augustin, and zipped away.

"That fucking teleporter," I said, the urge to roll up my sleeves and make my way onto the battlefield surging within me.

But I kept back; after all, it was part of the plan. As Stella engaged Angel, I used Veronique's power to snap the lock off the metal container, freeing Michelle.

"Michelle," I said, focus entirely on the young super.

There were bruises and scratches all over her body, and a particular bruise around the upper part of her arm in the form of a handprint showed me where Victoria had latched on to her.

"Gideon?" Michelle asked as I helped her out of the cage.

Turning my back to Grace's telekinetic shield, I stepped into Father's trailer and placed the young super on the couch.

I grabbed the blanket, and covered her, noticing a translucent light spreading around my hand. *Father's healing power.*

I placed my hand on Michelle's forehead and her bruises began to fade.

"Just relax," I told her, explosions and chaos ringing outside the trailer.

The black and blue splotches on her face disappeared, and color returned to her skin. She opened her eyes, blinked, and stared at me curiously for a moment.

Finally, Michelle giggled. "Since when did you become a super?"

I whipped my hand away, thought better of it, and returned it to her forehead, feeling a powerful, caring energy move through me.

"That tickles a little," she said, not at all bothered by me pressing so hard onto her head.

I lessened the pressure some, right before I heard a loud, concussive explosion outside that I could feel in my chest.

"Stay here," I told her, as I ran to the door.

What I found outside was more or less the best scenario possible: one of the trucks was on fire, another one was upside down and stripped to its frame after Veronique had used its pieces to skewer Victoria to death, and the final truck was still intact.

The CBGs stood tall, Stella and Veronique closer to each other, and Grace surveying the area as she reduced the size of her telekinetic shield.

Father had his arms crossed over his chest, shaking his head at the entire scene. "Well," the bearded man finally said, "at least you have a truck now."

# Chapter Eight: What Happens in Reno, Stays in Reno

Father's home was surprisingly close to Highway 50, and by 'surprisingly' I mean it was a good twenty minutes to the highway.

We got on the road pretty much right after the fight ended, not wanting to stick around for any longer than we had to. It had been one hell of a battle, a battle in which Veronique had proven just how lethal she could be. Not that I didn't know she was capable of that type of destruction, but knowing and seeing were two different things.

And it wasn't that we didn't want to hang with Father; rather, Father sort of pushed us out, telling us it was time to start our journey, ushering us away before more calamity could come.

Landmarks in the area were also discussed, in case we were able to rescue Dorian. Fuck, I hoped we would be able to rescue Dorian. About the only other thing that Father gave me was the vial of his blood, just in case I needed to activate his healing powers. I had to admit, this was definitely a turn of events that I hadn't seen coming, but then again, becoming a superpowered seemed like the best logical next step for me.

There wasn't enough room for all of us in the truck, but it did manage to fit Grace and Stella up front, Michelle in the small seat behind mine wearing an oversized t-shirt of Father's from a video game expo hosted by the Proxima company. Veronique was in the back with Chloe, keeping low by lying down next to the sound manipulator, her hand wrapped around Chloe's wrist just in case she stirred.

It would have made for an odd visual, that was for sure, a shaved headed dude with glasses and a facial scar driving a truck filled with hot women, this coupled with the teenager, and if they were really looking, two bodies in the back, one awake and one clearly passed out.

And besides, our current ride, a Ford F-150 was lifted, meaning it was a good several feet higher than any vehicle should be.

It was cool too, off-roading. It wasn't something I'd ever done before, and there were a few times that I hit a bump that had all of them laughing, aside from Veronique. Well, she could have been laughing, but I couldn't actually see her face.

*So this is what off-roading is like,* I thought as we ran down a small cactus, Michelle cheering me on. I kicked up speed once we hit the highway, and set the truck to auto drive as we blazed toward Fallon, Nevada.

Everyone was hungry, which was something Michelle reminded me of every five minutes or so.

"But we need clothes, first," I reminded her. Everyone aside from Grace was looking pretty gnarly, and we certainly couldn't go to a restaurant wearing body armor…

*Or could we?* It was the southwest, after all, and Nevada had just flipped from blue to red in their last governor race.

"I like the clothes I have," Michelle said.

"I definitely need new clothes," Stella said as she turned up the A/C.

"Grace?"

The psychic shifter, who sat next to me with a clever look on her face, raised her hand into the air and snapped her fingers, her features splitting down the middle. She had gone for a redheaded woman, freckles across her cheeks, big green eyes, large breasts barely contained by an American flag tank top.

"We're going to WalMacy's," I said firmly, to Grace's pouting.

We pulled into the WalMacy's in Fallon and kept just about as low of a profile as we possibly could by parking at the back of the store, near the auto bay that had closed an hour ago.

The CBGs knew that we could get fancier shit later; for now, they just needed some basics, as did I, and naturally, it was Grace and Yours Truly who undertook the mission of shopping for the others while they stayed in the truck, Veronique still lying in the back with Chloe.

It was better this way.

In the off chance we were attacked, Grace could alert them, and I had some powers as well.

"It's shopping time!" I told Grace the redhead as we were greeted by an older man with a glass eye.

"Do you like shopping here?"

"Not really. You?"

"It's great for decorating," she said as she hooked her arm through mine. "When we get our own place, I really want to be in charge of decorating. The others can be in charge of other things."

I smiled at her as we made a beeline for the clothing section. "You really think we'll have a place one day? A headquarters?"

"*Cherry Blossom Girls: Superheroes for Hire*. That could be the name of our show."

"Are we being hired out now?"

She thought about this for a moment. "I guess not. Although, I could play a good matchmaker."

"Using your power to force someone to like someone else is *not* matchmaking."

"It worked for you and me," she said, moving past me, my focus dropping to her hips and her tattered short shorts, which should have been illegal, yet were longer than the short shorts I'd seen other women wear back in New Haven during the humid summer months.

Go figure.

WalMacy's was like every WalMacy's I had been to in America: cavernous, bland, somehow frightening, yet also comforting, familiar.

I got some men's clothing, a pair of Wranglers (not the cowboy cut, though), two shirts, undershirts, undies and socks, while Grace went for the women's clothing, filling up our basket with anything they could want.

I met her after I'd stocked up, and helped her pick clothing for Veronique and Stella, wishing that WalMacy's had a better lingerie section.

That left basic clothing for Michelle, and I tried to choose the coolest stuff I could find at WalMacy's. A few DisNike princess shirts, some exercise clothing, and triples of everything we put in the basket. Michelle went through clothing rapidly, and we'd need to carry extra with us just in case she hit the gas pedal.

We also got backpacks, toiletries, and bolts and nuts to fill Veronique's backpack, so she could use them as projectile weapons.

Our final stop was near the automotive department, where we got a tarp to cover Chloe's body. Grace worked her magic at the front register, and we were out of there in under thirty minutes, which must have been some sort of record.

"Find something to put on," I told Michelle and Stella as we got back in the truck. Even though the space was small, they managed to change relatively quickly while I tried on one of the shirts I'd picked out. It was a cotton number, a deep maroon, almost a sari cut. Not bad.

Veronique changed too, slipping into one of the tank tops Grace had picked out.

After we were all dressed for a night out, we followed the highway west until we reached a restaurant known as the Depot Diner. The reviews were good enough, the food was Guy Fieri, and our waitress was like something out of a movie about a diner in, well, Nevada.

"What'll it be, sweetheart?" she asked, smacking her gum. The woman had a smokey voice, her teeth stained by nicotine and her skin leathered from the years upon years of chain-smoking. She had a nice smile though, which she flashed at me as she readily awaited my drink order.

"A beer, and a glass of water," I told her.

"All right."

"I'll have iced tea," Grace said.

"Two sodas please," said Michelle excitedly. "Large, no, extra-large if you have them!"

"All right, sugar."

"Orange juice," said Stella.

"A beer too," came Veronique's response.

I cleared my throat, not too keen on dealing with a drunken metal vampire. She waved my concern away, her eyes jumping from my face to just over my shoulder. The place had been empty, allowing us to park directly outside our booth. This gave Veronique the vantage point she needed to keep an eye on Chloe.

"And a coffee," Veronique said before the waitress could leave with our drink orders.

"A coffee and a beer, huh?"

"That's right," I told her.

"A coffee, two beers, two sodas, orange juice, iced tea, and some waters. Got it. I'll be back shortly to take your food order."

I glanced at the sticky menu. An angus beef burger sounded nice, cheese sounded even better, and a cheeseburger sounded like something I could throw my full support behind. I chose the salad as my side, just to be healthy, and closed my menu before I started salivating at the other pictures.

"Grilled cheese sandwich with home fries, a side of bacon, sliders, and mozzarella sticks, fried pickles. What about you, Stella?" Michelle was in a pink shirt that said I Love NV, a shirt Grace had picked out because she thought it would be cute.

Stella closed her menu, and scowled at it, willing the sticky listing of food items to death. "There's no pizza here."

"I noticed that. That's why I ordered the mozzarella sticks. Sounds pizza-ish."

"There are other foods besides pizza," I told them both.

"But are they as good?" Stella asked. "I'm kidding. Don't take me so seriously, and I'll have the chicken and waffles."

"A mighty fine choice," I said, as the waitress made her way over with our tray of beverages.

Once our bevs were down and distributed, we placed our orders, Grace ordering the cheddar-topped barbeque meatloaf, which I had to say looked freaking delicious when it came out about fifteen minutes later.

"It's nice to eat with all of you again," I said after the first bite of my hamburger, half the beer now sitting in my gut.

God bless America, and god bless hamburgers.

Secretly wishing I'd ordered fries was an understatement, especially because the dinner salad was basically white hunks of romaine lettuce with a sliced tomato on it and a single baby carrot, but the meaty goodness of the hamburger more than made up for the healthy-ish not-so-goodness of the salad.

"What's the plan for after?" Veronique asked as she took another sip from her beer. She was taking it slowly, which was a good thing, as I didn't feel comfortable with the way her dark eyes had settled on me.

"The plan?" I asked her, washing down my salad with a bite of hamburger.

"The plan."

"The plan is as follows." I cleared my throat and clasped my fingers together on the table. "Tonight we get to Reno. We'll switch out vehicles along the way, and send the other vehicle heading in a different direction. We'll stay at a nice hotel, get cleaned up, get some rest, and go to Sacramento tomorrow so we can plan our assault on the next facility. With any luck, Dorian, and hopefully Fiona and Ingrid, will be at the next facility. We'll save them, they'll join us, and we'll work to take out the next facility, on Santa Cruz Island. All we can do now is hope."

"And eat," Michelle said, her mouth stuffed with food.

"And that."

"Did you say it was on an island?" Stella asked.

"That's right, but let's just focus on getting to Sacramento for the time being."

My only knowledge of Reno came from a show I watched when I was a kid, *Reno 911!*, and what I found instead was a decently sized city with a ton of casinos, which meant beautiful hotels.

We had exchanged cars outside the diner, trading our F150 for a newish Chevy Tahoe, which was most definitely large enough for the CBGs, one super teen, one crazy-ass writer, and one passed out villain.

To keep things simple, and also because of the fact I didn't yet have a smartphone, we kept to the highway, cruising along Dwight D. Eisenhower Highway at a comfortable speed, Michelle with her window down in the back and her hand out the window, flicking the air with her fingers.

It was a nice drive, and the desert air was cool, the sound of passing cars music to my ears. A moment of calm at the end of a pretty killer day.

I didn't know why we were sitting in silence, and at some point, when we were halfway to Reno, I asked Grace to play some music.

"Anything but country music, unless you can find some classic country, some Johnny Cash era stuff," I told her on the tail end of a yawn.

"It's *This American Life*, I'm Ira Glass. Each week we drop in with famous sci-fi writer Gideon Caldwell. Hello, Gideon."

"Famous?" I asked, raising an eyebrow at her.

I checked the rearview mirror to see that, once again, Veronique was staring at me with her dark eyes. Stella, who sat next to her, was looking out the window, and Michelle, who sat on the other side, was still playing with the air whipping by the vehicle.

"Well, Gideon?" Grace asked in Ira Glass's voice. "Is there anything that you would like to say to our millions and millions and millions of listeners?"

"I kind of doubt that NPR has millions and millions of listeners, but fine, if that's what you think, then let's go with it. To answer your question, Ira, I'm fine. How about you?"

"Of course I'm well, I'm Ira Glass. I have lots of money and beautiful, superpowered women throwing themselves at me. Plus my voice is very sexy. Do you like my voice?"

"Yes, I like your voice."

"It is very sexy, isn't it?"

"Barf!" Michelle called out from the back.

"You kids keep quiet back there!" I said in a cranky old man's voice.

Michelle laughed, and even Stella turned her attention from the passing cars to me.

"I can't wait to get to the hotel," Veronique said, her sharp voice cutting through our small moment. "There are so many shows that we have to catch up on."

"I agree," Grace said in Ira Glass's voice, "we will have a wonderful time binge watching some quality programming."

It didn't take us long after we reached Reno to find a badass looking hotel. No, it wasn't the Marriott, but it was twenty stories tall, and there was a casino on the bottom floor. The place was called the Silver Circus Legacy, and whatever the hell that meant, it lived up to its name.

I knew getting into this hotel would be a little trickier, as there would be more people in the lobby. So I parked the Tahoe and the rest stayed in the vehicle, while Grace and I slipped inside, as casual as ever.

I didn't know quite what rich gamblers looked like, but I tried to play the role of a high roller in WalMacy's clothing, which was just about as hard as I figured it would be.

Luckily, I had Grace, a woman who could charm just about anyone who laid eyes on her, male, female or genderqueer. I didn't know where she had pulled her next avatar out of, but it was a good one: tall and thin, small waist, medium-sized chest, cute black skirt that matched her jacket, glasses, and perfectly combed bangs.

Grace had a suite for the CBGs in no time, a suite already paid for by CBG Incorporated.

"Also," I told the clerk, "I need two burner smartphones, three mini USB to mini USB cables, and a laptop delivered to our room. Just bill it to our room."

The clerk nodded, and we turned away.

We met the others, and were then tasked with figuring out how to get Chloe up. This part wasn't going to be easy, especially with the fact that the lobby had a good number of people in it, some of them going to their rooms, others moving in and out of the casino, some drinking casually.

"We could float her all the way up to the top," I suggested, only realizing a moment after this suggestion left my lips how stupid it was.

So how do you bring a passed out person to the 19th floor of a busy hotel?

Damn I wished I had a smartphone at that moment to contact Luke, who always had an idea. I was sure he would have figured something out, but for now, I was on my own, and I didn't think wrapping Chloe in a tarp and bringing her up would do the trick.

"Just carry her," said Veronique. "I heard in a movie that what happens in Vegas stays in Vegas, so I don't think anyone will care."

"But we're in Reno."

"What happens in Reno, stays in Reno?" Michelle suggested.

So we did just that. And without Grace having to mind-wipe anyone, we made it to our floor, room 1969, Chloe in my arms and Veronique not too far away, just in case she needed to act.

Our room was hella swank, easily the size of my parents' home in Rhode Island. (Speaking of which, fuck, I needed to call them, but I kept getting distracted.)

There was a huge window that looked out onto Reno, the lights of the city reflecting off the Truckee River below, and since there were three separate bedrooms in the suite, each of us had a place to crash.

Veronique gravitated toward the Keurig machine, and brewed herself a cup of something that had a cinnamon tint to it, maybe a chai. Meanwhile, I set Chloe down on the sofa chair in the living room area, and reminded the others to keep an eye on her.

"She won't be waking up anytime soon," Grace said as she stepped over to Stella, her body morphing to her base form, wearing the clothes I'd given her back in my basement apartment. Still didn't know how that worked, and I don't think I ever will.

As everyone settled, I found the bedroom with the desk and put my flag in the ground. "As soon as the laptop gets here, I'm going to crank out some papers. And Michelle, I'll need your help."

"You got it, Gideon!" the young super called out to me, her voice already drowned out by the noise of the television.

# Chapter Nine: The Pace of Our World

"You want to touch me?" Michelle asked, suddenly suspicious.

"Not like that, dammit!"

"Not like what?"

I took a deep breath and explained to Michelle how my superpower worked.

"So you want to run really fast?" she asked, the look on her face softening.

"Not exactly; just trust me on this one."

"Okay!"

Michelle stuck her arm out, and I placed two fingers on her arm, immediately feeling her power move to me. I knew that Father's healing power had been on top, followed by

Veronique and Stella, which meant Stella was on the way out. As soon as the smartphone arrived, I could confirm this, but for now I just had to keep tabs the old-fashioned way.

"Did it work?" Michelle asked.

I glanced down to see my hand twitching, my feet ready to shuffle. I felt more alive than I had just a few moments ago, the urge to move swelling within me, my heart going crazy inside my chest.

*Move.*

I nearly took off, and had to physically stop myself.

"How do you control this?" I asked, feeling panic rise in my chest.

"You're as fast as me now?" she asked.

"No, well, I don't know. I just need the speed."

I noticed too that my thoughts had sped up, a blistering array of concepts smashing into my psyche that was working overtime to deal with the onslaught of ideas. A deep breath calmed this a little, but not much.

"How do you do this?" I asked, taking my first step forward. *Was it faster?*

I took another step, and felt a buoyancy I'd never felt before.

"Let's give it a try." Michelle motioned me towards the main living area, where Veronique was watching a home improvement show, Grace on one side of her and Stella on the other. Chloe was there as well, passed out, her wrists bound in hanger cuffs.

Even odder, Grace had taken the form of one of the property guys, which made the fact that he was currently speaking on the television even stranger. *Psychic shifter is definitely, without a doubt, one of the cooler combo powers a super can have,* I thought as Michelle walked me to the end of the hallway.

The layout of the suite was relatively simple.

The front door opened to an open living room space with windows. The hallway attached the living room area to the three bedrooms, each of which had their own bathrooms. I didn't know what kind of family would stay in this place, but damn, talk about some sweet Reno digs.

"Go to that end, near the bar," she told me.

I did as I was told, and Michelle appeared in front of me faster than I could blink.

"Now you try," she said before vanishing to the opposite end of the hallway.

"I'd better get a safety net in place. Stella?"

"Fine." Stella stood from the couch and made her way over to me without taking her eyes off the television. Once she reached me, it took all the power she had to pry her peepers away from the property bro. "What do you need?"

"Go to the end of the hallway and put up a shield, *a soft shield,* for me to run into. I've taken some of Michelle's power."

"Why?"

"Why put up the shield or why take her power?"

Stella smirked. "Why take her power?"

"Ever heard the author phrase 'show don't tell'?" I asked her.

She shrugged.

"Well, that's why," I said, more excited energy spreading through me. "Just do it. I don't want to smash into the wall and create a Gideon-shaped hole into the room next to us."

"This should be fun," Stella said, getting into position, which for her was the entryway to the other bedroom.

"Yes it should." I did a jogger's stretch, just to be playful about it. In actuality, my pulse was hammering in my chest; I was nervous as hell about testing Michelle's powers.

*Here goes nothing...*

I plowed into Stella's invisible shield two seconds later, not even realizing I'd left my former spot.

The impact definitely cracked a bone in my arm, but before I could cry out, I naturally started healing it with my other hand.

Michelle was still laughing by the time I could put all the pieces together and finish healing myself. "You have to be more careful than that!"

"I'll... I'll try again," I told her as I got back into position. This time, I tried to visualize a stopping point, which resulted in me tripping and slamming into Stella's shield.

I can't emphasize enough how quickly I went from standing on one side of the room to cracking my chin on Stella's shield and nearly knocking myself out. One second? The blink of an eye?

Something like that.

I healed my face this time – I suddenly had a bloody nose – and noticed that the fabric between my legs felt rather odd, like it had been rubbed to threads.

An idea came to me.

I quickly – very quickly! – found a few plastic cups in the kitchenette area. I filled one halfway with water and grinned at Michelle.

"That's a creepy grin!" she said, a smile still on her face that nearly matched mine.

"Let's see what my reflexes are like," I said as I tossed the water from the left cup in the air. Everything was suddenly cast in slow motion, Stella nearly frozen as she started up another shield, the television flickering, Grace and Veronique practically manikins.

The only thing moving, *slowly moving,* was the water, which shimmered as it fell from the air.

Oh, and Michelle, she was moving too, bobbing from foot to foot as she watched me catch the water in the other cup, every last drop.

"So cool," I said, as time returned to its normal speed, or rather, as I slowed down to the speed of our reality. This was something else I noticed: the reason Michelle was so twitchy even after I'd brought down her Overcharge, was because of the fact that she was having to constantly monitor herself to stay in tempo with our time, the pace of our world.

I could sense it now. Even a small movement like lifting my hand, part of me wanted to do it faster and the other part of me had to actually control my speed to slow me down.

"I definitely can't do this forever…"

"Neither can I!" came Michelle's response. "You want to race?" she asked, cocking her head to the right and squinting.

"No, *hell no*, but I'll need to practice running in a more open environment. For now, I'll use your power with my original intention in mind."

"You still didn't tell us why you need her power in the first place," Stella said, an annoyed look on her face.

The doorbell rang, and I smiled. "Well, that came faster than I expected."

# Chapter Ten: Luke, I Have Superpowers Now!

I moved over to the door and checked the peephole to see a room service guy holding an EBAYmazon package.

There are a ton of things writers, especially indie writers, do to game the system. The richer ones hire the poorer ones to ghostwrite books for them. This isn't to say they didn't have a part in it; hell, the richer writer may have plotted every single detail in the book, but it's something that happens and something that people have issues with.

More technologically inclined writers do things that involve attempts to trigger EBAYmazon's natural algorithm to better showcase their books. After all, who doesn't want free advertising on the world's biggest online bookstore? The debate rages on as to if this is gaming the system or *knowing* the system, and figuring out the best way to make one's book visible for the longest amount of time possible.

After all, the longer a book is visible, or 'sticky' as it is known in some circles, the better chance the author has to sell their wares. There have been issues with this in the past, but as with everything, cunning writers continue to figure out new ways to exploit and work around the algos. After all, there's a lot of money at stake.

A lot.

Others track their word count in public groups; pay for outside editors to plot their books; drink a crapton of Bull Bean energy drinks; hit fat rails of coke à la S. King before his wife found his stash in the trash can; and do all sorts of weird stuff to get in the zone and write more.

More, more, more – write!

Of course, I didn't tell the CBGs all this as I moved from the common area to one of the bedrooms, careful not to walk too quickly. It only took me a couple minutes to get the laptop set up – the phones could wait because I *needed* to try this.

Once it was set up, I logged onto the hotel's Wi-Fi and pulled up *Mutants in the Making 3.*

"You have to finish this tonight," I told myself as I started frantically looking through the manuscript, scrolling as I speed-read the shit out of it.

I had to be careful not to put too much pressure on the equipment, but I was definitely able to move a hell of a lot faster than normal.

And once I started typing, it was all over.

*I need to get a handle on this power,* I thought as I busted out words, mostly spelled correctly, my sweet, sweet fingers a direct channel for all the shit in my brain.

Father? You bet his ass I put him in there, and a cliffhanger too!

Angel? I mean, come one, the aunt-banging bobblehead man is practically my arch nemesis by this point. All the other details too, everything, I swear I was able to pack a ton in, my fingers firing away as the words flowed freely onto the blank white page.

It felt good.

It felt damn good.

And I kept at it, my speed steadying as I focused even harder. No noise; my ears were simply filled with a buzzing sound.

*The end.*

I finally got to the last chapter and wrote those final sweet, sweet words that exist in the dreams and nightmares of all authors.

Finally.

*Finally.*

And after I got a cover together, I could edit the rest and get it up. I'd already read through some of the beginning stuff, so I knew what was going on there. I'd still re-edit it though, tomorrow.

"Good job," Grace said, suddenly at my side.

"How… how long has it been?" I asked.

"Three hours, no, three and a half."

"Has it been that long?" I asked, just now noticing I was quite sweaty. "I need to drop Michelle's power for a bit."

I noticed that I was covered in sweat, that my feet were thumping against the ground, that I was breathing in short little breaths.

"Let's take that power away for now," Grace said, placing a hand on my head.

Two channels appeared, or rather, I *sensed them*, and I took Grace's psychic power again. By my calculations, my order of powers now was Grace, Michelle, and Father, which meant I needed to touch two more supers to get Michelle out of my system.

"Be right back," I said, almost colliding with the door. "Besides, I should probably edit sober. Ha! Sorry, writer joke."

Grace giggled, obviously placating me.

I raced into the living room, touched Stella to replace Father's power, and as I walked by the couch, I placed a hand on Veronique's head.

"I'm not your pet," she said, craning her neck to look around me at the TV.

Grace, who had come out of the bedroom, laughed again. "She'd make a cute cat."

"I would be a panther, not a cat."

"I always pictured you as…"

"What?" she asked, her dark eyes narrowing at me in a playful way.

"Never mind, Michelle is officially out of my system!" I said, mentally noting that my powers, in order, belonged to Veronique, Stella, and Grace. "Everyone, keep watching TV. I need to get the phone set up and make some calls."

"Move, Gideon," Stella said.

"Oh, sorry, blocking the TV, my bad."

"Gideon," Luke said, excitement spreading across his bearded mug. He had his headset on, appeared to be gaming, and looked both relieved and happy to see me.

"Sorry, I know it's been a minute," I told him, "but the last few days have been pretty crazy. Or last day. I don't know when we spoke last. Anyway, I was in a fight in the

Nevada desert, and then I was transported to another random part of the desert, where I met this old guy who turned out to be a super, and then eventually I made it back to civilization, but not without getting attacked and, um, there's one more thing."

"Go on."

"I will, but I keep meaning to do something, so hold up a moment."

I set the phone against the wall so that it could balance on its own.

"I need to sign this EBAYmazon contract," I said as the laptop screen powered on.

"You asked for more stuff, right?"

"What do you mean more stuff?"

"I mean, things like audiobook rights, the possibilities of publishing audiobooks of your works, that sort of thing. It doesn't hurt to ask, and you've kept them on the hook for a few days now, which may be to your advantage."

I considered what Luke had said for a moment. "Are you telling me I should refuse to sign anything until I get the promise to republish *How Heavy This Axe?,* because if you are…"

"Why not? Don't sign anything; instead, write a message to them letting them know your demands. Play hardball."

"Actually…" I scrolled through my email inbox and found the latest from Jake Archibald, my eyes widening. "Speak of the devil. You're not going to believe this, but my rep, this guy named Jake, believes I am trying to hold out and has already offered me a new contract that includes publishing *How Heavy This Axe?,* and putting the audiobook to work even sooner to build buzz for *Mutants in the Making.*"

"And you had *How Heavy* edited, right?"

"Yep, cost me a thousand dollars too, and not Canadian dollars, mind you."

"Our currency caught up to yours mid-2020s."

"Even better, I just finished the third *Mutants* book, so I'll publish that after an AI edit, and then EBAYmazon will later publish the trilogy of novellas as a single book, and they'll have that re-edited. Sorry, my beautiful reality is coming to me all at once."

Luke laughed. "Apparently."

"Point is: I'm signing this new one," I said as I skimmed through the contract. "Says they'll start the *How Heavy This Axe?* in audio format as soon as I sign it. Great! And the book is in present tense, so that should keep people on their toes."

Luke squinted as he tried to get something out of his teeth with his tongue. "That's right, it's in present tense. Man, some people really hate present tense."

"Oh, I know, I've seen the reviews. They blast books that are in present tense and say that they read like a script, which really, is that a problem? Haven't we grown up on movies? The funny part about the argument against present tense is that all dialogue is written in present tense, and we like dialogue in books. I mean, a lot of times, it's the dialogue and the way it's mixed into the action that makes a book feel like it's fast-paced or a thriller or whatever. Dialogue isn't usually written in past tense, unless someone is explaining something that already happened."

Luke's head bobbed back and forth. "Huh, I never thought of that."

"Well, think about it now, best-selling author of Star Defacer," I told him with a smirk. "Almost all the dialogue in your book is in present tense, so when a reader reads your series, they are reading a collage of present and past tense, which is funny considering how much heat present tense books get. But that is beside the point: EBAYmazon is really throwing everything but the kitchen sink at me to publish with them, and I'm going for it!"

"Yeah, they are."

"I'm going to keep the cover for *How Heavy*, however, because I like it."

"You totally should."

I closed the laptop and returned my focus to Luke. "Okay, author talk is over unless you got anything to share."

"Just waiting on some artwork for the Patreon. I swear it takes my artists forever, but you already know that."

It was true, I'd heard Luke lament about waiting for artists for some time now. "Okay, let's get back to the crazy shit that has happened to me over the last two days."

"Yes, let's do, because I was getting pretty worried there, and was about to leak all the information that you gave me access to."

I'd given Luke all the information handed off to me by Dr. Kim, just in case something unthinkable happened.

"Hold off on doing that for at least a week whenever I disappear," I told him. "And anyway, there's another interesting thing that happened to me."

"What's that?"

"I have superpowers now."

# Chapter Eleven: Obligatory Sex Scene

I was surprised to see Stella enter my office, AKA my bedroom for the night. I had just finished my call with Luke, and while he mostly believed me, it was only when I showed him that I could make things levitate that he finally realized I wasn't lying about my superpowers.

And I didn't blame him. I mean, wouldn't you be skeptical if your friend told you over a video call that he or she was now a superpowered individual?

Probably.

"Are you finished yet?" Stella said as she approached me.

Even though we had new clothes for Stella, she was still in her black, MercSecure outfit.

Stella placed a hand on my shoulder, and turned the chair around so that I faced her.

"You know, it was cool being with you in the desert."

"It was?" I asked her.

"I feel like I got to know you a little better, and it was kind of cool having you all to myself."

"Yeah, same to you. It's always good to get closer to a teammate."

"And that's why I'm here now. Unzip your pants."

"Wait, what?" I pushed back from the desk.

"You heard me," she said, narrowing her eyes at me. Stella got to her knees, and positioned herself between my legs.

She reminded me again to unzip my pants. Eventually, Stella reached up and helped me, my little writer growing to epic proportions (ha!) and practically springing out of the opening on my boxer briefs.

And sure, the zipper teeth weren't far away from the bottom of my shaft, but that was not what I was focused on; I was focused on the fact that Stella had placed her mouth around my member and was *a lot* better at this than Veronique.

I started to moan, the chair creaking as I leaned back.

"Quiet," she said after she pulled her head back and wiped her mouth, a strand of hair falling from her braid. She started using the slickness from her saliva as a lubricant to jack me off, staring at me intently, in a way that made me nearly come just by looking at her.

My breaths were shortening as she went for it again, her head moving up and down. Eventually, my hand found a place on the back of her braid, flowing with her as she continued sucking me off.

I felt 100% like John Updike as his phrase "she's really going to town on my prick" came to me, seemingly out of nowhere, my brain commenting on what was happening.

*You okay in there, Writer Gideon?*

*Yes!* I thought back to Grace, trying to shut my mind down from that point forward.

"This can't be happening," I whispered. I didn't think that Grace would ruin the surprise blowjob, but I didn't want to find out if this was a possibility either.

Stella switched hands, and brought her neck back, looking up at me as she continued jerking me off.

"Are you going to come for me?" she asked, a melody to her voice I hadn't heard before. She spat on the head of my throbbing Johnson to add more lubricant.

I was literally seconds away, when a doubt came to me.

"What?" Stella asked, licking her lips. Rather than wait for an answer, she moved forward and placed her warm mouth around my cock again.

*I know it's you,* I thought to her as her head moved up and down.

*It took you this long to figure it out?* Grace thought back to me.

With that, and while still latched onto my proof of writerhood, Stella's form morphed to Grace, who was in a black bodysuit, similar to the bathing suit she'd worn the other day.

"I have an idea," Grace said as she grabbed my arm and moved me to the bed.

I instinctively got out of my pants, and leaped out of my boxers. She stood before me, one finger in her mouth as she looked at me innocently.

"I think you have done enough tonight," I told her as we shared a mischievous grin.

"You didn't like that?"

"Maybe…"

"I could turn into a man, if you'd like to try that."

I laughed awkwardly. Even though we were having a conversation, she was still looking hot as hell in front of me and my member was responding accordingly, a little wet from our previous encounter, and ready to go.

I wasn't about to have another dialogue with him, as I hated talking to my dick, but I got the feeling he was telling me to go ahead and wrap the conversation up.

"No, not too interested in a guy," I finally told her.

"What about a hot ladyboy?"

"Where are you getting these ideas?"

"I don't know," Grace said as her eyes flashed white.

"There's nothing I can do about some of the strange places I have found myself while perusing porn! Seriously, that's a private matter, something I really have no control over once curiosity takes over. I told you before to stay out of that part of my mind, and I would appreciate it if you listened."

Grace smirked. "But going to that part of your mind is why I'm better at this than the others, at least Veronique."

I recalled Dorian and her explosive pussy. I had no idea how "good" she actually was at sex, but I had this strange feeling that it would be pretty great with her.

*Damn, did I miss Dorian.*

"Would you like me to change to her?" Grace asked, reading my thoughts.

"No..."

"Then let's try this."

I felt a sensation starting from the back of my head spreading forward. I was familiar with what I was experiencing: Grace had done this to me before, and it indicated to me that she had taken over my psyche.

*I'm going to fuck me as you,* Grace said, her voice coming from every direction inside my skull cavity.

"You're going to what?" I asked, my voice suddenly far away.

With complete control of my body, Grace laid me onto the bed and put a pillow under my head.

She straddled her thighs around my head, and lowered onto my face, grinding up and down, her pussy growing wet almost instantly. My hands lifted and cupped her ass as she did this, and I could hear her moaning, but her moan was long-distance, at the opposite end of a canyon.

She grabbed my head with her hand, and adjusted the position, smothering me with her lady parts.

Once she was good and wet, she moved down and started kissing me as I slipped inside her. We did it much slower then we'd ever done it before. In fact, had I been in control of my body, I don't think I could have done it this slowly.

I was still fairly certain that sex with Gideon Caldwell wasn't great. I didn't have that much experience, even if I'd gained a lot since meeting the CBGs, and I pretty much just did what I had seen done in, well, porn.

To put a woman in control, completely in control, gave me a lesson in love-making that money couldn't buy.

Grace moved up and down at a snail's pace, finding a rhythm that was half the tempo of our normal speed as her skin began to change, Grace morphing into her true base form.

"There you are," I heard myself whisper.

And there she was, the real Grace, thinner, shorter, with perky nipples and brown hair that framed her face. Gaunt cheeks, thin lips, more like...

*Mother?*

Her form reverted back to what I'd grown accustomed to, a platinum blonde bombshell.

I wanted to tell her to be herself, to stay in whatever form she felt most relaxed in, but I couldn't speak, all I could do was fuck.

# Chapter Twelve: Reno
# GTFO

So that was weird.

Grace and I had finished thirty minutes ago. She was now asleep at my side, in a frilly, one-piece thing that I was sure she'd stripped from my spank bank. I had just been schooled in sex, and it made me question my whole conception of carnal acts – or carnal art? Both worked.

"Shit!" I shouted as a blast in the living room tore me awake. This was followed be an ear-piercing screech.

Chloe was awake.

Not a second later, Remy duplicates burst into our room, their forms exploding as they reached the shield Grace had erected around us.

We both stood on the bed, and rather than cower like Gideon of the past, I sprang into action with Chloe's power.

The first Remy duplicate to meet my vector attack was tossed backward, where he slapped into two other clones, triggering another of their explosions.

The bedroom space was too confined to have a clear-cut battle, a problem remedied when the rest of the wall came down, and the ceiling started to bulge inward.

"We've got to get out!" I shouted to Grace, just as all the windows shattered and we scrambled into the main living area.

Her eyes white, Grace kept her shield up as she monitored the action in the living room.

Veronique had subdued Chloe; now she was fighting off Remy clones with Stella, while Michelle...

"Michelle!"

"Gideon!" Michelle said, appearing next to me on the bed and hugging my side. She was in a robe, the fabric warm, as she'd been running back and forth in the room at the start of the mayhem.

"Are you okay?" I asked.

With a flick of my wrist, I cut through another explosive clone beating against Grace's telekinetic shield. One of the creepier things about Remy's clones was that they all had this twisted, Joker-esque smile on their faces, almost like the titans in *Attack on Titan*.

"I need my pants and possibly my laptop. Can you get those? And how did you get through Grace's shield?"

"Grace has a shield up?" Michelle called to me over the chaos.

"Never mind; get my pants and my laptop!"

I needed my pants, the pockets stuffed with Father's blood, my phone, the thumb drive that contained all of Ken's information, even though I also backed up on the cloud, and the USB key that disabled GPS. If anything, having my pants was imperative.

"Forget the laptop," I started to tell Michelle, but she was already back, the laptop and its cable under her arm as well as my pants.

The laptop had been fried by one of the explosions, so I focused on getting into my pants, my hands patting my pockets to confirm that all my stuff was still inside.

*Whew.*

"This place is going to come down!" I told Michelle and Grace, Veronique and Stella continuing to fight off Remy's clones. "We're either going down with it, or we're going out that window."

"Do you think you can float us down to the ground?" Grace asked, all her focus on protecting us from Remy's explosive clones.

I gulped, not knowing if an uber-super-rookie like me could carry three people.

*You have to try,* Grace said inside my head. *I can take over from there.*

"Wait, what are we doing?" Michelle asked, panic in her eyes.

"We're getting out of here! Grace, did you alert the others?"

"They know!"

I watched more explosive clones slam into Grace's shield, my thoughts firing as I made a quick calculation of our trajectory. "Okay, jump out the window with me, I'll levitate us, Grace can take over once we're out."

"You can do it!" Grace said, her white eyes still focused on protecting us from the explosions.

Michelle, likely from her training (and evidence of my lack of training), had her hand on the small of Grace's back, so that the psychic shifter could maintain the shield while she got to her knees, scooted off the bed, and joined us by the window.

I cleared what was left of the glass of the floor-to-ceiling window away, closed my eyes, grabbed Michelle and Grace's hands, and together, we jumped out of the 18th floor window of a resort hotel in Reno, Nevada.

The wind whipped past my face, everything coming at me fast, and my adrenaline was so through the roof that I could barely form an actionable thought.

My vector manipulation ability completely took over, suspending us for just a moment before Grace could get her shield up. We were at about the sixth-floor level, defying all laws of physics. And sure enough, floating down to us were Stella, Veronique, and Chloe, who was flung over Veronique's shoulder.

Remy clones began spilling out of the window above, falling on top of Stella's shield and exploding upon impact.

She held strong all the way to the ground, but more clones fell from the sky as she did, creating craters in the ground, mutilating the building's structure, exploding into some of the rooms and sending debris into the air.

The street also had several cars in it, and a few of the clones landed on top of the moving cars, creating movie-like explosions all around us as we landed.

It caught my eye at the time, and I didn't put all the pieces together until later, but to our left, a parked truck exploded of its own accord, liquid flames moving from the truck to the side of the hotel as people fled and were struck by debris.

We joined Stella and Veronique as soon as we touched down.

"Are you okay?" Veronique asked me. With a charged hand, she lifted one of the smaller parked vehicles and tore it apart, sending metal everywhere.

As I opened my mouth to tell her that we were fine, just a little shaken up, all the Remy clones suddenly disappeared.

A single man staggered away from us, *the real Remy,* a hunk of metal sticking out of his shoulder.

"Kill him!" I shouted, surprised to hear those two words come out of my mouth. But he was gone in a flash, thanks to Mother's teleporter.

"Everyone do a body check!" Stella said, holding back the panic in her eyes. The sounds of panic reached us, from the minor explosions, to sirens, to people screaming. One glance up and I saw a body fall from one of the rooms of the hotel and smash into the pavement just fifteen feet away.

"Eeek!" Michelle cried out.

"Check, body check!" Stella reminded us all. "Everything intact? Are we good to move?"

"Good," I said, still breathless, still filled with terror, shirtless, barefoot, my brow covered in sweat.

"Good," said Veronique, her hands flaring red. "Grace?"

"Good."

"Good!" said Michelle, whose young eyes were as wide as I'd ever seen them.

And that was when a ring of fire ten feet tall formed around us.

# Chapter Thirteen: Away from the Pandemonium

"I'll take Chloe!" I told Veronique, as Augustin lowered over the wall of flame. The bald-headed Fire and Ice guy stood on a blackened cloud, a wicked look on his face.

Another explosion outside the ring of fire sent the roof of a smaller vehicle into our vicinity. As Veronique handed Chloe to me, and as I tossed the partially shriveled woman over my shoulder, Stella whipped this debris away.

Ice armor formed over Augustin's body, an instant sheen to it due to the proximity of heat, sharp pieces framing the chiseled muscles caused by the ice.

"We don't need to fight this one," I said, suddenly. "We need to get out of here."

You bet your ass there were sirens blaring in the distance, and once law enforcement showed up, there'd be helicopters, more guns, more innocent bystanders.

I had no idea how many casualties this fight had already caused, but there were definitely people driving the cars that the clones exploded into, and people in the hotel had certainly died.

"Let me finish this." Veronique pushed out of our protective shield and raised her hand at Augustin, who vanished into thin air.

Suddenly, a hunk of ice cracked Veronique in the back of the head, sending her to the ground. Stella's shield moved to compensate for the fact that Augustin was now behind us, but by this point, he was gone again.

"Veronique!"

"I've got her, Gideon," Grace said, Veronique's body lifting into the air. She floated vertically now, her head slumped forward.

"How is he so fast?" Michelle asked, watching as Augustin appeared again and blasted our shield with a huge burst of flame, hot enough to make us feel the heat.

"I think I know how he's doing it." I looked to Michelle. The young super with the pink-streaked black hair was bobbing left and right on her heels. "Can you start running inside our circle as quickly as you can? Once you see Augustin reappear, focus on him and see what happens in slow motion. Does that make sense? Tell me if it doesn't make sense!"

"It makes sense, don't yell!"

A blast of ice hit our protective barrier, a mist of coolness reaching my skin. I still held Chloe over my shoulder, my hand naturally settling just beneath her ass cheeks. "Stella, I'll add my vector shield to yours to double our strength. We really need to start moving toward a car. Fuck, I wish Dorian were here…"

I felt a breeze blow past me as Michelle slowed down. "It's a woman bringing him here and there," she said. "The woman appears, touches him, and they reappear."

"Okay, then it's Danielle. That confirms it; he's using a teleporter to attack us. Anyway, we've got to go."

Even as Augustin continued to blast us, we made our way out of the fire, heading north, where we encountered a three-car pile-up.

With Veronique passed out and floating near me, there wasn't anyone who could get the vehicles out of the way.

And I could already see sirens, which mean the police and first response teams had closed in on us.

*How do we get out of this situation?* I thought, looking around for some exit, some way to save the CBGs, to live and fight another day.

*The hotel parking garage,* I thought, as I saw a valet parking guy running for cover.

I was just about to tell Grace to do her thing, but by that point, she'd already taken over the guy's mind, sending the kid into the garage, his eyes completely white. Another explosion inside the hotel showered the street with debris. People scrambled over the rubble, thick black smoke filling the air.

We turned into the garage, Stella's shield still protecting us from Augustin's attacks. My shitty-ass shield barely doing anything as my full focus was on instructing the team.

It was cooler in the parking garage, and even though we could still hear all the chaos happening outside, I felt slightly removed from it, away from the pandemonium.

*If only.*

Veronique floated like she was a ghost, shoulders slumped forward, her head hanging, her hair in her face.

So maybe a drunk ghost.

Stella focused on maintaining the shield, Grace was next to me, and Michelle was on my other side. With Chloe slung over my shoulder, we backed deeper into the parking garage in search of a ride.

And that ride came to us moments later as the valet parking guy skidded to a halt at the end of the driveway. He drove a white Suburban, relatively new, and if we truly hoped to get out of here using that thing, we'd need to act fast.

The valet got out of the vehicle, tossed me the keys, only to be lit aflame by a concentrated fireball from Augustin. The poor guy took off in the opposite direction, his arms flailing over his head, his entire body now raging with fire.

"Stella, blast Augustin with everything you have! Grace, give me Veronique, and hit him with a Nightmare Attack!"

"You can carry two women?" Michelle asked.

"I'm not as weak as I look, dammit!"

Chloe on one shoulder now and Veronique on the other, I *definitely* felt the pressure of carrying two women; still, I pressed on, my desire to be an alpha beating my beta-nature.

Stella moved in to engage Augustin, pushing him away from us, the air filled with the stench of burning flesh.

"I'll get the car ready," said Michelle as she quickly covered the distance between the Suburban and us.

The back of the vehicle popped open, waiting for me to carry Chloe and Veronique over. I laid them in the back, feeling bad that Veronique had to lie next to the enemy.

As I did this, Stella hurled energy waves at Augustin, more than I'd ever seen her lob before.

I knew that one hit when I saw one of his flames slap into the concrete ceiling of the parking garage, giving Grace her opening to hit him with her Nightmare Sight ability.

Augustin cried in terror as I scooched into the driver's seat, Michelle already in the back.

"Get him!" I shouted, starting the vehicle. Grace hopped into the front passenger seat, and Stella grabbed onto the back door as we took off, using her power to propel herself forward into the seat, the door slamming shut and the seatbelt warning sounding off.

We took off like the bats in *Fear and Loathing*, barreling towards the exit, where we came out onto a side street that shot us away from ground zero.

I looked for signs pointing to the highway, my heart racing in my chest as I tried to process all of what had just happened. The brakes screeched as I hit a hard right, making a beeline for the highway, figuring that we could turn towards California if we ended up in the wrong direction.

As I put the pedal to the metal, Grace buckled her seatbelt to stop the incessant beeping. "Give me your phone and I'll help navigate!"

I reached into my pocket, found one of the USB cables there, as well as a few other things, including the indestructible vial of Father's blood. "Let's get an hour or two away from the city, get to a hotel… No, let's use someone's home tonight, somewhere nice and big, and get our bearings straight. I don't know how they are targeting us, but we may have to stay on the run. I'm ready for that; I just want everyone to be prepared."

Michelle started to sniff as if she wanted to cry and Stella comforted her.

"It's going to be okay," I told Michelle.

"I just wanted some peace and quiet," she finally said, sucking back tears.

"Yeah, me too. Me too."

# Chapter Fourteen: Gideon, You're Famous!

*Exit 89 towards Tahoe City.*

I'd been driving for a while now in complete silence, and part of me wanted to keep going, to reach Sacramento because it was only another hour or so from here. Then again, saying that things have been hectic as of late would be the understatement of the year, and everyone, including supers and yours truly, could use a small break.

Besides, the homes were probably better in Lake Tahoe. Definitely better, and I wanted the CBGs to really enjoy the next day as I tried to figure out our game plan.

I really needed to dig into the information Dr. Kim had provided me. Now that I had a smartphone, I could access the app he'd created. It wouldn't be hard to get another laptop, or just use the computer in whatever home we borrowed.

"Look, everyone, I know things have been fucked over the last two days, or three, shit, the last week or longer, whatever. Point is, we are going to Tahoe, Lake Tahoe, and we're going to enjoy the next two days and recharge before we make our attack."

"Two days is too long," said Stella.

"I mean that we will stay there tonight, and tomorrow night, and orchestrate our attack the following day. So one day of rest, basically, and we'll get a nice place too. Somewhere secluded, a place where we can all train a little bit. So what do you say?"

I glanced at Stella in the rearview mirror, and for a second, I saw the part of her that reminded me of Veronique. "That's fine," she finally said.

"And another thing, we need a new vehicle," I said as I pulled into a gas station that was relatively packed. It wasn't hard to switch our vehicles. What was hard was to switch out vehicles with two passed out women in the back.

"Let's just have someone follow us," Grace suggested, reading my mind as always.

"Not a bad idea."

We saw a guy that looked like a golfer: polo shirt, pressed shorts, white as Columbian cocaine (not that I'd know), and a green hat advertising a country club in the vicinity.

He was getting into a Land Rover, which we hadn't driven on our trip yet and I figured would be worth a test drive. Besides, we were going to be staying in Tahoe, and it was good to blend in.

"I've got this," Grace said as she stepped out of the vehicle, her form morphing into an incredibly tan blonde in a low-cut blue blouse, jeggings, and sparkly high heels.

Even though the man was backing out, he saw her and stopped, which was all it took for Grace to take control.

She got in the Land Rover with him and I followed them up the road, where we eventually pulled onto an access road to switch out vehicles. Rather than make me do it this time, the man loaded both Veronique and Chloe into the back of his Rover, which gave me an idea: the smell of fresh foliage all around me, and a beautiful star-filled night above, I uncapped Father's protected test tube of blood, put my thumb over the end, and flicked my wrist once.

As it had been before, there were two paths available to me, and I chose the one on the left, sensing it was his healing ability.

If I wasn't mistaken, and I could plug in later to check, my abilities now in order were: Father, Veronique, Stella.

"All good here, chief," the man whose Land Rover we were jacking said.

"Not yet. Just get in the Suburban and wait for further instructions."

"You got it."

I moved over to the back of the Land Rover and found Veronique, who was still passed out from being struck in the back of the head. I placed one hand behind her head, and as I had done to Michelle, I visualized taking her pain away.

Veronique's eyes flickered open. "Gideon," she said, a tight smile spreading across her face as she sat up.

"You got struck by something, but you're better now."

She got her bearings, immediately pushed away from Chloe's body and got in the back with Stella and Michelle.

*Damn, we really need to do something with Chloe,* I thought as Veronique stood and brushed herself off. *Story of my fucking life. How do I keep ending up with knocked out superpowered women?*

*We'll figure something out,* came Grace's reply.

I turned to the psychic shifter, who was still in her preppy blonde mode, and smiled. Our Moment was interrupted when Veronique said she was hungry.

"I had a feeling you would say that," I told her as I nodded to the Suburban. "Take as much as you can from him without making it impossible for him to drive. If you need to top off any further, you can hit up Chloe again."

Veronique approached the driver of the Suburban, who had one arm out the window, ready to go. She lifted her hand, a red glow cutting through the darkened night.

Once she was done feeding, she returned to the back seat next to Stella and Michelle.

"You good?" I asked the metal vampire.

"I'm fine."

"Good, let's go."

Boy did we find a place.

The home we found in Tahoe City, or thereabouts, had a private drive, beach, a boat, and a ton of other amenities that we didn't pay a cent for. The Federal Corporate Government was many things, but if you were rich, it was your best goddamn friend, and if you were loaded, you could use those tax breaks that severely damaged the economy a few years ago to afford some epic living spaces.

And I'm talking *Extraordinary Homes* epic, some Saudi prince shit.

This particular home belonged to a Hollywood studio exec, and he and his wife and two children were currently lined up at the entrance, waiting for our next order.

We'd found the place by chance: a guy driving a sweet Aston Martin cut me off and, figuring he had a pretty sweet home to match his pretty sweet ride, I followed him to his humble abode.

And by humble, I mean that it was about four thousand square feet, a two story McMansion with a separate garage, fountains, a deck with a jacuzzi, a pool for swimming laps, you name it. I'm pretty sure the only thing they were missing was a helipad, and no worries there, as the neighbor had one.

"So take this Land Rover to Portland, Oregon," I told the husband, Grace next to me, her eyes white as a Nor'easter in the heart of January. "Once you get it there, I want you to give it to a homeless person. Just find someone that needs it. Take the tags off, and tell the guy or gal to hide it in the woods. Or try to get the VIN scraped. No idea how it works to get rid of a car, but that's up to you now. You'll figure it out." I took a look at their home. "You seem resourceful. Also give the homeless person some money, just because it's the right thing to do."

"Got it," he said.

"And if anyone you work with calls, say that you had to visit a cousin in Portland. If a family member or friend calls, say you had to make a business deal in Portland. If a neighbor calls, tell them I'm your nephew and I'm just hanging in the place with some of my hot college friends."

"Sure, no problem."

I tossed the homeowner the car keys. "She's all yours."

The man and his family filed into the Land Rover and they took off. By this point, Michelle and Stella were already inside. Veronique was securing Chloe in one of the bedrooms, and Grace was next to me, as usual.

"We've really gone a long way, haven't we?" I asked her.

"It has been quite the journey, from New Haven to here, where there aren't any cherry blossoms."

"It's too bad you missed all the other blossoming trees."

I remembered how the other flowering trees in Connecticut usually bloomed a couple weeks *after* the cherry blossoms. I had never seen anything like it, trees that were completely pink and white, filling the air with a fragrance that only comes around once a year, and that was only if the timing was perfect.

Grace dropped her hand into mine. She slipped back into her base form, in my clothing, and as I stared at her, her face started to morph into mine, still keeping her smokin' bod.

"That's... don't do that," I laughed as her face morphed back.

We entered to find Michelle sitting on the couch, a tray of food before her. She had found the family's refreshments, and as she flipped through the channels, she stuffed nuts, pretzels, and raisins in her mouth.

Stella was sitting on the floor, her back to the couch. She looked up at me as I entered and smiled. It wasn't a big smile, but it was progress.

I plopped down on one of the sofa chairs, and Grace sat next to me on the arm rest. Michelle was moving through the channels pretty quickly, and had I not been watching, I wouldn't have seen the brief flicker of fire.

"Hey, go back to that..."

She turned a few channels back and I saw that the report was about...

*An attack in Reno?*

Grace and I exchanged glances, her brow furrowing almost instantly.

*"An attack in Reno, Nevada, tonight has left fifty people dead and upwards of thirty people critically injured,"* said the female newscaster. *"These injuries were sustained from a bombing on the 18th floor of the Silver Circus Legacy Hotel*

*and Resort in Reno, Nevada, as well as a coordinated attack in the streets below."*

"Shit," I whispered as Veronique came around. She stood behind me, her eyes glued to the television.

"The police are seeking a Connecticut man named Gideon Caldwell for questioning, and say that he may be traveling towards the West Coast with a few hostages."

"Look, Gideon, you're famous," Michelle said as an old picture of me appeared on the screen.

The sound that emitted from my throat was something that I would never be proud to claim as my own. It was a high-pitched squeak, the sound of a creature that knew they were doomed to fail, that a good many people would be watching their epic fall.

*"Police are saying to be on the lookout for Gideon Caldwell, who may be traveling under an alias. He may also have a younger hostage with him, an underage girl. The FBI and police task forces in California and Nevada are working to apprehend the suspect.*

"We are so incredibly fucked," I finally whispered.

# Chapter Fifteen: Face Off

Grace grabbed my hand and pressed it into her breasts.

"That's not helping," I told her, my eyes still locked on the screen. I guess if AEFL had a trump card, this was it. As they had before, two channels had appeared in my mind's eye, but I was ignoring them, still focused on the breaking news story that was unfolding.

I didn't normally watch stations that viewed news more as entertainment than its original intent, but if this was how the mainstream media was portraying me, I knew that the clown show was only a few clicks away.

"Give me the remote," I told Michelle, and it was in my free hand before I could blink. I found the station I was looking for, the one that always portrayed things in a sensationalist, almost nationalistic way.

*"Breaking news out of Reno, Nevada,"* a woman with bleach blonde hair and a red dress said. *"We have*

*confirmation that a terrorist attack took place this evening, and that law enforcement officials have narrowed down the attacker to a man from Connecticut named Gideon Caldwell. What the mainstream media won't tell you is that Gideon Caldwell is a left-wing activist sci-fi writer, responsible for the self-published book series* Mutants in the Making, *as well as a morally empty standalone novel about…"*

Blondie with the American flag necklace cleared her throat, clearly disgusted.

*"…About a transgender dwarf known as* How Heavy This Axe? *What you're seeing on the screen is a recent picture of Gideon, who, I'm just going to be frank here, is an ugly man. You all know me, I like to go off the rails, and that's why you tune into this show. This guy is clearly a New England liberal beta soy boy who wants to take down America because someone treated him meanly in middle school. Womp womp, Gideon Caldwell, what you did was called terrorism, and there is a special place in hell and Guantanamo Bay for those who dare go against the United States."*

I changed the station and tossed the remote back to Michelle. "That's enough of that," I said as I focused my attention on Grace.

"You'll have to start taking my shifter ability when we go out," she said. "My guess is that you won't be able to use it as well as me, and I don't think that you would be able to modify your voice with it, but maybe."

"We'll try," I said, swallowing hard.

The two channels presented themselves to me again, and I intuited that the right channel was her shifter ability. I took this path, and her powers came to me, so I now had her shifting power, Father's healing power, and Veronique's metal vampire schtick.

"Come with me," Grace said, as she led me to the nearest bathroom.

Veronique followed us, and once we got to the bathroom, Grace flicked on the light and told me to step in front of the mirror.

There was a basket of magazines on the floor, and she instructed Veronique to grab one. Veronique grabbed one of those celebrity gossip magazines, and as Grace flipped through it, she quickly settled on a picture of a baseball player who was now dating a famous TwitchTubeRed model.

"I want you to turn into this man, just your face. You don't really have to try for the rest of the body, because we just need to disguise you when we go out. Do you think you can do this?"

"I… sure?" Holding the magazine now, I looked from the man's lantern jaw to my, um, not-so-lantern jaw. My beard was as wild as ever, my glasses scratched up a little bit and the scar on my cheek pink.

"Should I keep my glasses on?"

Grace considered this for a moment. "Father said that your ability wouldn't be as strong, so I don't think any of the absorbing part of my power has come to you. But I don't know. See what happens. Become this man."

I focused on the energy again and told my face to morph into this guy's face.

I didn't want to watch this happen in the mirror, it would be too weird, so I simply focused on the picture while I felt a change come over me.

"Wow," Veronique whispered, and hearing her voice sent my eyes to the mirror to catch her reflection and…

"It worked," I said, seeing the face of a man that was clearly not my own.

"Can you add abs too?"

Grace laughed as Veronique backhanded me in the gut.

"Hey!" And as I cried out in mock pain, my face morphed back to its original form.

# Chapter Sixteen: Cherry Blossom Boy

The adrenaline had long left my body, and I was getting tired. This had been one of the longest days ever, and I'd lost track of time by this point, overcome by exhaustion. And usually, when I got tired around the CBGs, good things happened. Then again, Grace and I had just hooked up a few hours back, Grace revealing her true form to me ever-so-briefly.

So no sex, just some heavy cuddling, and on a California king no less. There was plenty of room for Grace on one side, and Veronique on the other. And this arrangement didn't bother them.

I didn't know if Grace was trying to tell me something, or if I should initiate anything, but like I said, I was tired as hell, and even if my horniness matched my exhaustion, I would have still passed the hell out.

So that's what I did, and I woke up six hours later with Veronique next to me on my pillow, her eyes open as she stared at me.

"It's morning," Veronique whispered.

"I can tell," I said as I reached my hand up to press a little of her hair out of her face.

I dropped my arm under her shoulder and pulled her in closer, so we could hug. Our bodies fit together, her head under my chin. I held her there for a moment, not ready to face the day.

But my phone was already buzzing in my pocket, and I knew that we needed to press forward, that this entire journey was about pressing forward.

"Coffee?" I whispered into the top of Veronique's head.

"Yeah," she said.

We quietly slipped out of bed and made our way to the kitchen, holding hands along the way. The Tahoe family had a pretty awesome kitchen, an island, a trash compactor, all sorts of cool nooks and crannies and hell, even the refrigerator was cut into the wood grain of the shelves so that it was partially hidden.

I found my coffee, and started the machine up as Veronique dipped into the room where she was holding Chloe, and drained just a little more from the woman.

"Do you think she would change to our side, like Dorian?" I asked Veronique, as she returned to the kitchen.

"I really don't know, but she did try to attack us back at the hotel."

"Are there any other experiences you had with her? Like a training exercise, or an extraction?"

"No, she was more on this side of the country and I was on the other."

"East Coast versus West Coast, a tale as old as time."

"Huh?"

"Never mind." I listened as the coffee dripped into the glass pot, filling the kitchen with an aroma that reminded me why it is good to be human.

We drank in silence, and once we'd both had a cup, I pulled out my mini USB cord and plugged into my own neck.

(1) Shifter

* Speed of Change

* Texture Consistency


(2) Cell Regeneration

* Regenerative Healing Factor

* Regrowth

* Cellular Activation

* Flawless Restoration


(3) Metal Absorption and Modification

* Wielding Capacity

* Adaption Speed

* Alloy Integrity

* Blood Metal Conversion

I hadn't really thought about doing this before, but since we had Chloe with us...

"Come on," I told Veronique, as I turned to the bedroom.

She followed me in, and sat uncomfortably close to Chloe as I plugged into the port on her neck.

No password, no nothing, just straight to the base stats. Chloe's first set of deets appeared on my smartphone:

**Chloe, Subject C**

Build: 17.169

Base height: 185 centimeters

Base weight: 56 kilos

Strength: 4

Intelligence: 7

Constitution: 7

Wisdom: 5

Dexterity: 7

Charisma: 4

I scrolled to the folder that contained her powers and was presented with several dials.

## Main: Acoustokinesis

Sound Sculpting: 5

Acoustic Acceleration: 6

Sonoluminescence: 7

Rhythm Manipulation: 8

Sonokinetic Combat: 5

Sound Detection: 4

Sonic Stimulation: 3

Overcharge: 6

I turned all the dials to one, so it looked like this:

## Main: Acoustokinesis

Sound Sculpting: 1

Acoustic Acceleration: 1

Sonoluminescence: 1

Rhythm Manipulation: 1

Sonokinetic Combat: 1

Sound Detection: 1

Sonic Stimulation: 1

Overcharge: 1

"When she does wake up, she'll wake up close to powerless, which might put her in a position where she'll have to negotiate."

Veronique considered this as she sipped from her coffee, both hands holding the mug. "Maybe."

My phone rang, startling both of us.

I looked over to see that it was Jake Archibald, my author rep. With a heavy sigh, I took the call, knowing all too well that I was about to get dropped.

"Gideon? It's Jake, and boy do we have a lot to talk about."

I sat on the floor, and Veronique sat next to me, leaning her back against my shoulder. I pressed the button that put Jake on speakerphone.

"I'm here."

"First of all, is this stuff true? Is what they're saying in the media true? I know it's early, hell, I never get up this early, but I got a bunch of calls from my supervisors and well, here I am. So is it true or not?"

"Are kidding me right now?"

"No, I'm not fucking kidding you. I wake up and my GoogleFace alerts have your name all over them, accusing you of committing a terrorist attack."

I sighed deeply. "I wasn't part of a terrorist attack, and I wouldn't even know how to commit one if I were part of one. Okay, that makes no sense. Point is: I'm being set up."

"By who?"

"By AEFL, Mother, the people I've written about."

"You're really going with that right now?"

205

"Yes," I told him, my voice rising. "This is something that actually happened to me! I'm not making this up, and... I don't even think I'm creative enough to make this up. It's true, I'm sitting here right now with Veronique who I've written about, and we were attacked last night."

"I see... "

"No, I don't think you see, I don't think you really believe what's happening here, and it's all freaking true! So if you want to drop me, and that's it, I'm fine with that. I don't need this pressure anyway. I'm doing the best I can, dammit, and the odds are stacked against me. I can't stress that enough."

"Okay, relax, Gideon, I know you've got a lot on your shoulders, a lot of pressure. Let's not get too carried away here. I didn't say anything about dropping you. Hell, this will sell even more books!"

"This is real life, man, this isn't some sort of publicity stunt," I said, a bad taste suddenly in my mouth.

Veronique placed a hand on my foot; I felt my stomach twist as she drained just a little bit of power from me, just enough to remind me that I shouldn't be arguing with this guy over the phone, that it was futile.

"Good, real life, I like this angle," said Jake. "Maybe we'll get you on some talk shows later, once all this cools down. Your side of the story. Maybe prime time. That could do something…"

"It's not going to cool down."

"I'm sure you'll be cleared of any charges, I mean, I didn't really think that you had it in you to do something like that. It was probably a terrorist, disguised as you, who knows? Oh, and another thing, I actually got some auditions already for *How Heavy This Axe?*, and I figured you wanted to hear them. Okay if I send them over?"

"No, please do," I said, pretty much at a loss for words.

I was part of the system now, a fugitive, and I could hear the hamster wheel in Jake's head turning as he thought of all the angles we could use to make money off this tragedy.

And I hated it.

I wanted no part of it, but it would push the story even further into the forefront of American thought, which would expose just how bad these experiments were.

"Great, I'll send the audiobook auditions later today. Talk soon, Gideon. And stay indoors for a while. We don't need you getting arrested! We have a group of lawyers ready when you need representation, by the way. This is America, dammit, innocent until proven guilty!"

"We really should do something with her," I said, after I'd hung up the phone.

Chloe's brown hair was in her face, and she looked like she was resting peacefully, which told me Veronique hadn't drained too much.

By my estimates, and those estimates could totally be wrong, she would be awake in the next few hours, maybe sooner.

Grace entered the room wearing a sports bra and boy shorts.

She noticed that I stared at her just a second longer than I should have.

*I wore this for you.*

*Aware,* I thought back to her. *Why are you dressed like that?*

"These are my workout clothes," she said aloud. "I wanted to take a jog, and still plan to, but you're right, we need to deal with Chloe now."

"I never said that."

Grace gave me the 'oh child' look.

I didn't have evidence, but it seemed like her ability to read my mind had improved to the point where she could preemptively know what I was thinking.

"I guess Chloe's morning just got a bit more interesting," I finally said.

"I think I can wake her up." Her hips swayed as she approached Chloe, and once we were directly over the woman, white lightning sparked across Grace's eyes. "Be ready, Veronique."

Veronique's hand glowed red as Chloe came to life. Chloe moved away from us, immediately going for her powers.

"Relax," I told her, as a low, ear-piercing sound met my ears.

Dialing back all her abilities had really worked, but that didn't mean she didn't have some hand-to-hand combat training. Realizing her powers were gone, she tried to lunge for Veronique, even though she didn't have the space to gain momentum.

Chloe struck an invisible wall, Grace's doing, and it was at this point that she finally spoke.

"What the fuck do you want from me?" she asked, seething, her hands tensing at her sides as she hunched over, ready to spring into action again.

"We want you to relax," I said as calmly as possible. "Please, just... just chill for a minute."

"I am your prisoner," she said, baring her teeth. I could tell by the daze behind her eyes that she was confused, that she was operating on pure adrenaline. She'd been out for a while now.

I wondered briefly why she didn't go to the restroom while she was out.

*She did, Gideon,* Grace thought to me.

*In her MercSecure jumpsuit?*

*Yes, but it was only some piss.*

*Well, that sucks to be stuck in a jumpsuit with your own piss!*

*Focus, Writer Gideon.*

*Sorry. You know me.*

"You probably want new clothing, don't you?" I asked Chloe. "How does that sound?"

"What have you done to me?" she asked, her shoulders dropping some.

"Long story short: our teleporter, Dorian, banished you to the desert and then you attacked us, and then we took you captive."

"And there was a hotel?" she asked, her brown eyebrows furrowing as she searched her mind.

"Yes," Veronique said, a red glow still moving around her hand. "And you attacked us there."

"And what's happened to my powers?" she asked, fear tinging the edge of her voice.

211

"We'll get to that," I told her. "For now, we want answers, and you have some decisions to make."

She slammed into Grace's telekinetic shield again.

"That's not going to work," I told her, lifting my hand Veronique-style. It flashed red as well, and Chloe's eyes went from angry to confused.

"You're a super?"

"I am," I said, still feeling a bit bashful actually voicing this affirmative.

"They didn't tell me that," she said as she brought her knees to her chest. She looked pretty shaken up, and part of me felt pity for her, but I knew now wasn't the time to let my guard down.

I smiled grimly. "There's a lot of things they didn't tell you, and I'll be honest here, they haven't done shit in trying to rescue you. They've had two chances to rescue you now, and they've left you with us both times. Hell, they had Danielle teleporting into our hotel to deliver Remy. The least she could have done was grab you," I said with a shrug.

Confidence swelled inside me; it was time to flip Chloe.

"They left me?" she asked, swallowing hard.

"Twice. Once in the desert, when Angel attacked, and then at the hotel. So twice. Maybe your power just isn't worth it to them. Mother has been known to cast people aside that she found useless to advancing her cause."

"They wouldn't... "

"They would," I said, leaning on this angle. "They were about to do the same to Veronique, and Grace wasn't far off when she first encountered me."

"Grace?"

"You may know her as Sabine."

Chloe nodded, barely making eye contact with Grace.

"My point is: if they had wanted to rescue you, they would have come for you by now. They came for Angel."

"I was there," she reminded me bitterly.

"And who keeps setting the fucking bombs? There's a question I have. There always seems to be a damn explosion everywhere we go."

Chloe bit her lip. "Augustin," she finally said. "He likes tinkering with those sorts of things."

"He will be dead next time we meet," Veronique said under her breath.

"Watch it," Chloe told her. "Victoria, Augustin and I all trained together."

"Victoria has already been extinguished," Veronique said with finality. I recalled the gruesome image of her pulling metal from Victoria's body and impaling her with it.

Chloe gasped. "You didn't…"

"We all have our motivations," said Veronique matter-of-factly. "Gideon's is to expose these terrible experiments. Mine is to stop anyone who gets in the way of doing so."

"You're a fucking cold-hearted bitch," Chloe said, baring her teeth again.

Veronique shrugged. "No, I'm a realist."

"Next question," I said, interrupting their stare down. "What really happened to Ingrid and Fiona. Are they dead?"

Chloe considered her answer for a moment.

"Remember, we have a telepath," I said, pointing a thumb at Grace. "So your thoughts aren't your own. Do we really need to dig deep into your mind?" I asked Chloe, my voice softening. "I don't think you'd like that."

"They were taken from Colorado to California. That's all I know."

"Sacramento Facility?"

"Yes. Wait, where are we?"

"Doesn't matter."

"But I don't know if they're dead or not," she said. "Mother told us they were, and I'm inclined to believe her. And…" She hesitated for a moment. "I think they've called in some of the more elite of our batch to wait for you at the facility. Mother did mention that."

"More elite?"

I raised an eyebrow in Grace and Veronique's directions.

"You all don't stand a chance–"

"Yeah, we'll see about that."

"–Without my help," she finished.

"Your help?"

*Is she being honest, Grace?* I thought aloud.

*Don't give Chloe her powers back yet. Her intentions seem clear, but there is also something cloudy there, something distant about her thoughts.*

"We're going to need a little more convincing to offer you membership."

"Membership in what?" she asked me, amusement dancing behind her eyes.

"The Cherry Blossom Girls."

I saw Veronique cringe in my periphery.

"But you're a boy... right?"

"Last I checked, yes."

"So one Cherry Blossom Boy?"

I scratched the back of my head. "I never actually thought of it like that."

"It's just a code name," Grace said, coming to my defense.

"It doesn't sound like a good name for a team of superpowered women, and one man. Maybe you should call yourselves Team Super," Chloe suggested. "Or something cool like that. At the very least, you should be Cherry Blossom People, because 'Girls' makes you sound weak. No offense. I feel like it's sexist too. And what is with the Cherry Blossom part? Aren't those things from Japan?"

*I like her,* I thought to Grace.

*She sort of talks like a female version of you, reasoning everything out loud.*

*Maybe that's why I like her.*

I cleared my throat. "All right, we're going to put you on probation for a bit. You will always be supervised by either Veronique or Stella, but gain our trust and I'll see about giving you your abilities back. That is my ability," I sort of lied to her, "to completely take another's superpower. Kind of like Rogue."

"Who?"

"Never mind, and just for your info, I can take slivers too, which is how I'm using some of Veronique's right now. Point is: only I can give your powers back to you. Not

217

anyone else in our group, nor anyone that Mother may know."

"They can just go through my neck," she started to say, her hand brushing against her modifier.

"Not so. Father disabled your modifier."

"Father?"

"You attacked him in the desert. You know Mother?"

"Yes."

"Father is her twin."

"So they're related?"

"Yes."

"Then why is he Father?"

"I don't know; look, don't dig too deeply into the details or none of this will make any sense. Just know that Father fucked up your modifier so that the only way, and I mean *only* way, for you to get your powers back is from me. Are we clear?"

"I think." She relaxed a little. "Do you have a change of clothes? Also, I want a shower."

"I'll watch her," Veronique said.

"Not Gideon?" Chloe asked. "I figured he'd like that sort of thing."

*She has no filter,* Grace thought to me.

*Interesting.*

*Are you thinking about watching her shower?*

*No!*

*That's not what your mind is telling me.*

*Shit, Grace, please follow the rules!*

*Fine, no spying on your thoughts. But I'll keep spying on hers, and she wants both you and Veronique to watch. Weird. And Veronique wants you there as well, but just because she likes being around you.*

"Fine," I announced to the group, "we'll watch you shower."

# Chapter Seventeen: Shower Scenes Rule!

"I'm not going in there while she does that," Veronique said, a disgusted look on her face.

"Well, someone has to. Besides, it can't be much, she has been passed out for like two days now."

"I'm sorry," Chloe said, her face scrunched up, "But I really have to go…"

"I'll go," said Stella, who had just come out of her room. Benefits of having a psychic: Grace had already spread the word of what was happening through the house.

Relief spread across Chloe's face. "Thank you…"

"And if you try anything, I will make the rest of your life very, very painful."

"I just need to shit," Chloe said, casting her eyes at her feet. "Please, before I do it here."

"Let's go." Stella opened the bathroom door and stepped in, waiting for Chloe to join her. They'd chosen the half bath, which meant there wasn't a lot of room in there, and I could only imagine how uncomfortable it was watching Chloe go number two.

"We'll be here," I said as the door shut. "Where's Michelle?" I asked, just so our conversation would cover any noise that Chloe might create.

"The living room, probably watching TV," said Veronique.

"Figured as much. So, um…"

"What?"

"Nothing."

"Nothing?"

"Nothing."

It didn't take them very long, and after a toilet flush, Chloe came out followed by Stella, who had an indecipherable look on her face.

"She's all yours," Stella said, her face red with either anger or embarrassment.

"The shower is this way," I said as we led Chloe down the hall.

"That was very dehumanizing," she said, her head still tucked forward.

"Well, I don't know what to tell you there."

Veronique gave me a funny look.

"What?"

"It doesn't matter if you felt like that was dehumanizing," Veronique said. "You must understand why we need to act in such a way. Now, regarding the shower, you will bathe with the curtain open. And if you try anything, I will make sure that you seriously regret it."

"Does she always bust your balls like this?" Chloe asked, shooting me a mischievous grin.

"Move it," Veronique said as she pushed her into the next bathroom. "And take your clothes off."

I started to look away, but then stopped, realizing that I'd long since moved away from being prudish.

Chloe peeled out of her MercSecure suit and let it drop to the floor. She did smell a little bad, a hint of urine and sweat radiating off her clothing, and she noticed me looking at her as she unclipped her bra.

Her face turned red, but she kept doing as instructed, even after Veronique elbowed me in the ribs.

"What was that for," I hissed.

"You know what that was for," she said.

Her tits were perky, her hips wider than Veronique or Grace's, her bush full grown but nice and trim.

She stepped into the shower, her back to me, and turned the water on.

Veronique's hand was charged, and she'd pried bits of the metal from the toilet paper holder to use as potential projectiles. These projectiles hovered in the air in a way that reminded me of drones, which made me hungry, as I loved getting breakfast delivered by drone back in New Haven.

I was glad Veronique was also watching Chloe, because my thoughts kept jumping from how much I'd like to go to Hamden, Connecticut, to a diner known as Town House for some Scottish eggs benedict to Chloe's nude body, which was pretty fucking choice. Even though her hips were wider, she still had that gap between her legs, 'Toblerone Tunnels,' as my ex once called them.

My first-year roomie at Southern Connecticut was into that gap, and he said mostly Asian girls had it, probably a racist thing to say, but they were generally thinner, which was his reasoning.

I think he ended up teaching English in China and still lives there, last I checked.

Chloe turned so I could see her front. Her eyes fell on me, and even though water was sluicing over her face, she managed to give me a soft smile. I watched as she ran the loofah over her nipples, as she added more soap and washed her nether region.

Veronique shook her head at me. "You would make a terrible guard at a women's prison."

"That I would," I said, for some reason thinking of *Orange is the New Black*. I watched the show years after the series had finished, still good though.

Chloe turned again so she now faced Veronique. "So does everyone share him or something?"

"Excuse me?"

"He doesn't seem like your alpha type to me, but he's cute."

"What, um, makes you think we all share him?"

"Briefings from Mother," Chloe said as she turned her back to me, running the loofah between her legs. No, it wasn't sanitary, but I was too busy watching the end of the loofah pop out of the back of the gap caused by her legs, reminding me of a colorful bunny tail.

This got me thinking about monster girls, and how I'd had a binge fest of monster girl animes a couple years back. I got sick of the shows after a while, mostly because the MC was always such an idiot, but some of the stuff was hot, and I wasn't certain if I was a fucking freak, or cat girls were actually sexy.

Chloe removed the loofah and looked over her shoulder at me.

"Enough," Veronique said, and without so much as a twitch of her nose, the water stopped, the levers both whipping to the right.

A pouty look on her face, Chloe got a towel and wrapped it around her chest.

"Gideon, get her some clothes."

"Um, yeah, will do."

I headed to the master bedroom and started going through the lady of the house's wardrobe.

She had a bunch of fancy stuff, cute summer dresses too, and I selected several as well as a pair of clean undies – a thong, dammit! – and called Veronique into the room.

She came with Chloe to find all the stuff laid out on the bed.

"Wear what you'd like," I said.

"This stuff is kind of ugly," said Chloe.

"You aren't wrong there. I'll go talk to Grace about picking up some stuff from town. Unless you want me to stay…"

Veronique harrumphed. "I've got it from here, Gideon."

# Chapter Eighteen: Shop 'til Drop

After I made everyone breakfast (nothing fancy, just whatever I could whip into the eggs I'd found in the fridge), Grace, Michelle, and I got ready to go to town for some good old-fashioned retail therapy.

Grace told me to take the face of an older man, not too old, but someone who would look right having a hot body on his arm.

"So that's what we're going for?"

"A trophy wife. I saw it in a movie," she said as she morphed into a woman in her late twenties, brown hair that had been highlighted with blonde streaks, a loose flowing blouse which hid artificially inflated tits, tight white jeggings on her legs, the dark panty line visible, and pricey sandals. "Michelle, you will pretend you are our daughter."

The young super, her black hair in a ponytail with a pink streak in it, looked to the living room area, where Stella and Veronique sat with Chloe watching a home improvement show.

This one took place in the Pacific Northwest, on the outskirts of Seattle where the hosts were hoping to score big by purchasing foreclosed homes and refurbishing them to sell to people that couldn't afford to live in the city.

"And they will just stay here?" Michelle finally asked.

"That's right, and we will bring them clothes. They have to watch our new friend."

"Prisoner," Chloe said, with a hint of irony in her voice.

"Don't spoil the little girl's brain," Veronique said, turning up the volume. "Or Grace will spoil yours."

I cleared my throat. "Well, come on, wife and daughter, let's go to town and do some shopping."

Grace and I locked hands and I noticed the channel open up. Since I already had her shifter ability, I figured a little psychic goodness wouldn't hurt anyone. So I took some. Now I had both of Grace's powers, capped off by Father's ability to heal.

We piled into the Aston Martin outside, and I felt like a total pimp as I backed out, revved the engine once, and pulled down the curved road. The inside of the vehicle was lit up like Christmas, if Christmas cost a couple hundred thousand dollars and its design was sleek, sophisticated, and minimalist.

So maybe it didn't light up like my friend's pimped out Honda Civic in high school, but it drove like a beauty, and for just a moment, I even roleplayed in my head what it would be like to live this kind of life.

I needed a cigar or something, and an account in the Cayman Islands. A good accountant too. Hell, I already had a reduced tax rate considering my income level, might as well figure out a way to reduce it even further.

My backstory was simple: I was part of Skull and Bones at Yale; my father gave me a million to start my first business and I wasted it on coke and booze; I sobered up at twenty-four after spending a month at a Malibu rehab clinic by the beach, and went on to start a thriving business through an app I helped create that traded failing currencies for USD; my wife was my better half, and even though she came from money, she was humble, sexy as hell too; and my kids have psychological disorders that only people with too much money get, but not Michelle, she's my golden girl, who'd had her ADHD cured by a Nepali shaman.

"Every time I peek into your mind, I'm frightened by what I see," Grace said as we sped along a nice lane, its sides cushioned by immaculate estates.

"That's a good thing," I reminded her. "A writer should always be plotting!"

Michelle, who sat behind us now, laughed. "That's right, Gideon!" she shouted, startling me. I glanced in the rearview mirror at her to find that she'd already gone from talking to me to looking out the window.

The speedy youngster had eaten her weight in eggs and cereal this morning. Having once taken on her power – and not too keen to use it again – I knew the kind of calories she needed to take in to maintain homeostasis.

For some reason, this got me thinking about Stella having to guard Chloe while she evacuated her bowels, which made me think that I had some serious mental issues and that therapy in my youth would have changed my life for the better.

"It would have," Grace confirmed aloud. "Now stop thinking of crazy things, and focus on the road."

We were traveling on the main street now, Ruta Estatal de California, I believe, and there were tons of shops on the left and glistening Lake Tahoe on the right.

The place was magical, and once I found parking, it took every ounce of self-control not to get out my smartphone and start sending selfies to Luke of my cleverly disguised ass posing with Grace in front of the lake.

To make things easier, we first hit up a bank and had Grace get us some spending cash. This only took a few minutes, and Michelle and I chilled on a bench overlooking the water while Grace netted a cool five Gs from a rich grandma, which would be backup money just in case we needed some dough.

Cashola in our pockets, we headed to the Boatworks Shopping Mall and found the nearest chain retail store, which just so happened to be a Zara.

The male clothing was not my style, I wasn't trying to look like a dude from the Jersey Shore, but Grace and Michelle found plenty of things for the ladies.

"What about Chloe?" asked Michelle. "Should we get her something too?"

"Sure."

"What are her sizes?"

"Just get smalls and mediums of whatever you guys like. I'm sure they will fit, and regarding any styles, have at it."

This last part made me miss Dorian, who was the most stylish of the CBGs. Her leather jacket, black shorts, tights, red leather boots, tattoos – she truly was one-of-a-kind.

I now sat on the loveseat near the dressing room, the place where husbands and boyfriends were supposed to sit while their wives shopped. I was joined by a young guy with his head glued to his smartphone as his lady dropped item after item into a black mesh bag.

"You too, huh?" I said, and he just shrugged without looking at me.

*That's right, I'm an older looking man now,* I thought as I too turned my attention to my phone, and briefly saw my reflection in its surface.

My voice sounded the same, or at least I thought it did, which reminded me that I needed some headphones to listen to the *How Heavy This Axe?* audiobook files that Jake had forwarded to me about thirty minutes ago.

*I'm going to find the Okay Buy kiosk,* I thought to Grace. *I'll be right back.*

After wandering around a bit, I used a hundo from my stack of recently acquired cashola to purchase the headphones from Okay Buy, nice ones too, the ones Doctor Dre makes that are pretty much the same as the Sony's but three times the price.

"They're definitely the best," the nerdy Okay Buy employee said to me. She was female, in glasses, with an arc of zits across her forehead. I saw myself in her, a Gideon from years ago who wasn't the biggest loser at his high school, but was definitely in the top ten.

"Great," I told her as she unclipped the security tag.

I had chosen low-key Bluetooth earbuds, something that would fit in a case, and likely end up in my pocket along with all the other shit I carried now: a mini USB cable, the vial of blood, a thumb drive of data, and the USB key given to me by Dr. Kim.

No wallet, but there was a roll of cash. Shit, I couldn't remember where I'd lost my wallet.

The urge to explore swelled in my chest yet again, and figuring the ladies needed more time to shop, I took a walk around the mall.

It was strange being an older man.

Younger people ignored me, and I kept having this strange sense that no one gave a shit about me. And true, no one gave a shit about me in my normal Gideon form, but I still felt like I was part of something, some misguided movement or whatever defined the youth of the times.

Now I was carefree, so carefree in fact that I bought an ice cream cone in the food court and walked around licking it, enjoying the hell out of my anonymity.

Once I was finished, and the sugar was surging through my veins, I returned to Zara to find Grace paying for everything, the shoppers and clerks in the vicinity quiet as she overpowered their minds.

"We got so much," Michelle said, as she zipped over to me with a large bag of clothes. Grace had one too, which I naturally took from her.

"I can see that."

"Great sales today," Grace commented.

Everything returned to normal as soon as we stepped out, as if we'd never been there.

I noticed this in two ways: for one, people started moving around again; there was also the mental chatter that picked up immediately as we left. Grace's power even felt comfortable after a while, until it was nonexistent due to the fact she'd wiped everyone's minds.

Then you really get a sense for how odd it was.

Back to the Aston Martin the three of us went, where we loaded up our goodies and took off towards our borrowed abode. Not twenty minutes later, we pulled into the drive and started unloading.

"You got clothing for us?" Chloe asked as soon as we entered.

She still sat on the couch with Stella and Veronique, both of whom were fixated on the television.

"Stuff for everyone!" Michelle bolted to the living room to deposit the clothes. She disappeared and reappeared with another bag, a look of pain on her face.

"Moving that fast burns the inside of my legs," she mumbled.

"It's because of the material you're wearing," I told her. Michelle had found a pair of nylon exercise shorts upstairs in one of the bedrooms. She currently wore the shorts and a random shirt she'd picked out from the master bedroom. "You bought something made of cotton, right? Some jeans or something?"

"Yep!"

"Wear those. Shit. We'll need to get you something one day. Maybe a skirt? That could do it. Thinking out loud here about how to prevent chafing."

"A skirt could work..." she said.

"It sure could. Fine, a skirt it is. Now, before this conversation gets any stranger, everyone change to their swimsuits. Or whatever you have to swim in. I forgot to check, you got swimsuits, right?"

Grace's black swimsuit, the one piece that was ridiculously skimpy, appeared on her body.

Michelle laughed. "I wish I could do that."

"Just get your suits," I told them as Grace and I turned to the back deck. "We're going for a dip."

"What about you?" Michelle called after me.

"I have some audiobook auditions to listen to."

# Chapter Nineteen: Audio Badness

"What are you doing?" I asked Stella, Veronique and Michelle, who had all gathered around me.

We were on the private beach, the sparkling water of Lake Tahoe adding a sense of ease to a situation that had been increasingly tense over the last few days.

"This is going to be so funny," Michelle said excitedly.

She wore a large white t-shirt over a pair of lime green running shorts. Veronique was in a tube top she'd found in our borrowed mansion, Stella wore one of the bathing suits that Grace had picked out, a two piece with the lower half a few inches of fabric away from being a straight up thong, and Grace had changed to a dark green top and matching bikini bottom. Chloe was in a pair of shorts, a bikini top and a sun hat.

"What do you mean?" I asked the bubbly young super.

"We want to bury you in the sand," said Veronique.

"Bury, bury, bury!" Michelle began to chant.

"I need to listen to these tracks," I told her, showing her my smartphone and tapping on my earbuds, which were Bluetooth activated and ready to go. I had four auditions sent to me from Jake, and I wanted to give them all a fair listen. After all, a *How Heavy This Axe?* audiobook was something I'd dreamed about for ages.

"Please, can we bury you?" Stella asked, offering me a smile that could melt metal.

Maybe it was the tight bathing suit that framed her breasts and accented her hips, or maybe it was the fact that I was a twenty-five-year-old horndog of the highest degree, but I found myself readily agreeing to her request.

"Fine, fine," I said as I pressed off the ground. "But only if you leave me alone after that so I can listen to these audio tracks."

I moved to a spot in the sand that already had a larger indention in it. Chloe the sound diva took notice, watching with a raised eyebrow as I got comfortable, Stella and Veronique going to town using their powers to kick up sand.

Michelle also helped, shoveling as much sand as she could around me and patting it into place. Grace stood by as well, a crooked grin on her face as I was smothered in sand.

"Leave my hand free," I reminded them. "I need to be able to listen to some tracks."

"Okay!"

It didn't take long for them to have me completely buried.

The sand was everywhere now, in my ass, between my toes, the grains heavy against the top of my body. I was strangely comfortable though; I felt like I was only a few scoops of sand away from meeting my ancestors in Wakanda.

Err, something like that.

"It's so funny," Michelle said. "He's just a head now. A talking head!"

Veronique offered a rare laugh. "He looks like such an idiot."

"I'm right here, you know."

Stella snorted. "It's like he's a ball and we could just kick his head."

"Please don't do that. Now, your request has been granted. I'm buried in sand, and I'd like twenty minutes to listen to these tracks. That was our deal."

"We'll leave you alone," Veronique said. "Besides, I want to get in the water with Grace."

I looked left to see Grace doing her best Jesus impression as she walked on top of the water, her eyes completely white, her body glistening.

The Scandinavian beauty wiped her bleach blonde hair out of her face and smiled over at me.

*Looks like you're having fun, Writer Gideon.*

*The fun is about to begin,* I told her as I played the first track.

*Here goes nothing,* I thought as I played the first audiobook track for *How Heavy This Axe?* I was still buried under the sand, ready to get this show on the road.

I waited a moment for the audio to start.

*Manchester Rich holds her sword at the ready,* a nasally voice read.

*The cave is dark, smelt of swamp ass, and Manchester's tits are sore. They are always sore. Ever since she took the witch doctor's potion that put the former male dwarf on the journey towards female, the same stuff that shrank her former testicles and grew her mammaries to epic proportions, Manchester's breasts have ached at least twice a week.*

*Maybe more.*

*"I really need to see that witch doctor again," she whispers, her voice somewhere between baritone and dainty. Dwarf males had a lot of testosterone, and even though she was officially a woman her voice still sounded manly.*

*At least to her.*

*It was hard to really hear and interpret her own voice, but she tried, yelling into every hole she encountered in Unigaea, hoping to hear her echo.*

*"Manchester! My name is Manchester! I am a woman!"*

I finished listening to the passage. The nasally voice of the narrator made it hard to really get into the character, and there was a little audio skip in the part where Manchester yelled into the hole.

"Next," I said as I started the second track. This one was read by a woman, and she clearly had a cold.

*But yelling in holes isn't the reason I came to the caves south of Drachma (snort). There are treasures in these mountains, treasures that they (cough) say are guarded by powerful trolls, slobbering beasts with clubs and muscles and a proclivity to inbreed (cough, cough).*

*And the trolls know the secret of the caves. (cough) They built their dwellings in catacombs beneath the main passageways, where (sneeze!) they kept the cave slaves, a group of pink skinned carnie folk said to (cough) possess magical powers.*

I had to stop the female narrator there. Regardless of the recording quality, her illness ruined her audition.

"Why the hell are you sending me these ones, Jake?" I whispered, my finger hovering over the next track. I heard Michelle shriek, and I turned to see Stella or Grace (who the hell really knew?), holding her above the water using their powers. The speedy young super laughed and laughed, her shrill laughter at odds with the hiss of the next recording.

*"... I am... Manchester Rich," I... told the troll. At the troll's... feet were two of the pink skinned... carnies."*

I checked the volume on my phone. *Nope, same as the other tracks.* Apparently, this narrator had recording equipment that wasn't quite up to snuff, nor did they understand how punctuation worked, leaving large pauses in the sentences.

*"That is... uncalled for," I tell the... troll. The troll pulls his knob... out and squirts a creamy... bit of piss out... of its tip, shakes... it twice, farts, and... stuffs it back... in, much to the... carnie's delight.*

"Yep, heard enough," I mumbled as I loaded up the next track. Stella launched out of the air, flipped in slow motion and came back down, creating a splash that got Veronique

244

and Chloe wet, both of whom were laid out on the beach, the metal vampire on guard duty.

I pressed play on the next track and nearly whipped my earbuds out.

*"Hey!" I shout to the troll. "That was uncalled for!"*

*"What brings you to these parts, commoner!?"*

*"I am not a commoner, I am from the dwarven village of Scudo! I have come here to take part in the goblin trials! So that I may win the treasure buried deep within the mountain!"*

*The carnies laugh! They laugh until one of their faces turns blue!*

*"That treasure isn't for you, boy!"*

*"I am not a boy, sir! I am all woman!"*

*"You have a dwarf's beard, a maiden's funbags, and the voice of a pipe smoker!"*

*"I cannot help who I am!"*

This was actually a little funny to listen to. I imagined the male narrator in the studio jumping up and down as he overacted the parts. He was definitely overselling it, but it was better than the dude who read with all the pauses.

My phone buzzed, but I ignore it and continued listening.

*"All woman!?" the troll chortles!*

*The carnies laugh again as the troll flicks his gnarled penis, hoping to squeeze a bit more out!*

*"Put away your chode, troll, or face the wrath of Manchester Rich!"*

I stopped the track and checked to see that it was a second message from Jake, this one apologizing for sending the wrong tracks, that these were some of the auditions they were passing on.

"That explains it…" I looked back over to the CBGs, who were still playing in the water while Veronique kept a watchful eye over Chloe.

I had to blink twice as I saw Augustin suddenly standing before me, a sinister look on his face as icy blue energy charged up his arm.

# Chapter Twenty: Mind Over Teleporter

Augustin disappeared just as a large blast of kinetic energy spawned a crater where he'd just been standing.

I was out of my sand trap in a matter of seconds, using my telekinetic force to instantly free myself. The surprise attack had my heart thrumming in my chest as I glanced around to see where Augustin would reappear.

Grace and Stella ran toward land now, where Veronique stood, already having drained Chloe enough to make the powered woman pass out. Michelle appeared at my side, dusting me off as a look of worry cut across her young face.

"It's fine," I told her with finality, stuffing my earbuds in my pocket. "Take cover."

"This ends now!" Veronique shouted as Augustin appeared over the water, cutting an arc of ice in our direction that careened its way to shore. Stella and Grace bailed left, Veronique right; the ice stopped inches away from Chloe.

"I've got her," I said as I ran towards the KO'd super.

Augustin rose into the air, standing on a column of ice as he shot fireballs at the beach. Each fireball caused the sand to turn to specks of glass, and before one of the CBGs could bring him down, he was gone again, his teleportation being orchestrated by Danielle.

An idea came to me and I figured it was worth a shot. "Everyone come to me!"

And thankfully, they did as I instructed, all on the offensive as they gathered.

"Let's form a square, back to back, get ready to attack any position in front of you. We have to bring him down before he teleports away. Stella, give us a shield!"

I was running on pure adrenaline by this point, focusing on my quadrant.

"What about me?" Michelle asked.

"Stay with Chloe, and move her if they try to attack," Grace said.

"Got it!"

Stella faced towards the water, Grace to my left, Veronique to my right, and I was back-to-back with Stella, looking at our borrowed home.

Tension was thick in the air as we waited for Augustin to reappear.

Grace fired off a blast of telekinetic energy that sent a wall of sand spraying into the air.

"I will show no mercy this time," Veronique seethed. I couldn't see her, but I could tell that both her hands were red, the hairs on my arms pricking as she increased her power.

A boulder of ice struck the invisible shield around us, shattering into pieces.

I kept waiting for the fire and ice guy to appear in front of me, ready at a moment's notice to hit him with whatever telekinetic power I could conjure up.

"Got him!" Veronique said. "Stella!"

I turned to see that Veronique had ensnared Augustin with her power. Danielle was flashing in and out of existence around him, trying to rescue him, but Stella had formed a protective shield around Augustin that blew Danielle back every time she laid hands on him.

The female teleporter panicked, and even stopped moving away for a moment as she watched blood pour out of Augustin's eyes, beads of red blood appearing on his skin as Veronique did something I'd never seen her do before.

Augustin was on his knees now, blood trickling out of his mouth and excreting from every pore, staining the sand beneath him.

Danielle locked eyes with me, and for a moment, a literal split second, they were pleading eyes.

But then something spawned behind those eyes of hers, *an idea.*

The teleporter disappeared, and not a heartbeat later, I disappeared alongside her.

Danielle and I reappeared in a staging area in a location I'd never been to before. My initial reaction was to cry out, and I would have done this if I hadn't heard Danielle's chatter inside my head.

*Inside my head?* The thought dawned on me: *I still have Grace's power.*

"Stop," I told her, my eyes flaring white behind my glasses. "Where have you taken me?"

It helped for me to vocalize rather than just mentally think through my questions and demands. And I still didn't know they had worked, not until Danielle's eyes glazed over ever-so-slightly, and she cocked her head to the side.

"We are in Sacramento," she finally said, a vein pulsing in her neck as she tried to fight my control.

"Where exactly?"

"At the facility," she said, her voice wavering.

"Stay with me."

"You have a power." Her face constricted as she tried to regain control of her consciousness. And having heard the phrase before, and realizing that its main point was confidence, I mentally steeled myself.

*Fake it until you make it,* I reminded myself as Danielle's hands started to shake.

"That's right. I am more powerful than the others. *Resistance is futile.*"

"I thought you were a normal..." Her throat quivered, and rather than think of another pithy quote, I focused on maintaining control over her mind. It wasn't easy, and the more we fell into our new roles, the more I noticed that her mind mirrored her ability, her thoughts zipping away as quickly as they came.

"Is Dorian here?"

"Yes."

"Is she alive?" I asked, my muscles tensing as I awaited the answer.

"She is."

"Far from here?"

"A few rooms over."

"And Ingrid and Fiona?"

"The other end of the facility."

We stood there for a moment staring at one another, Danielle still trying to break free from my grasp. In that time, I tried to skim the top of her mind to see what she knew about Ingrid or Fiona's conditions, but doing so seemed to take power away from my ability to control her, and I quickly cut that shit out.

For now, we would focus on Dorian.

"Take me to Dorian."

"They will recognize you. There are guards."

I focused on Augustin's image, his bald face, the features I'd seen several times now. The skin on my face shifted.

It took every ounce of strength and concentration I had to push forth the transformation *and* maintain dominance over Danielle's psyche, but once it was complete and she was mid-gasp at what she saw, I felt better, stronger, as if I had leveled up.

*I'm living in a video game.*

I smirked at my own thought, and turned to one of the reflective surfaces in the room. The polished metal cabinets allowed me to see my transformation, that it had truly taken place.

I was the spitting image of Augustin, who was all but dead for all I knew.

"You can shift too?" she asked, her eyes flickering as a bit of cognizance pushed its way forward.

"I am the most powerful of them all. I've already told you this. Now, no more talking, take me to Dorian."

We left the staging area, which was nothing more than a room that was cleared so Danielle could teleport with as many people as she needed. Danielle turned left, and I followed close behind her, focusing my power as best I could.

If I let my hold over her mind slip, she could simply teleport away, which would make this a lot more complicated. I suppressed anything that wasn't a targeted concentration on what should happen next. This included fear, nervousness in seeing how they'd been keeping Dorian, doubts in my own ability – my only goal was to move from point A to point B.

We moved into another hallway and I saw two MercSecure goons ahead. They stood before a metal door, weapons on their chests and their fingers on the outside of the trigger guard.

"Danielle, Augustin," the man on the right said as he gave us access to the room.

I purposefully didn't make eye contact with him, and as the door slid shut behind us, my focus turned to the sarcophagus in the center of the room, an object similar to what they'd kept Veronique in back in Austin, Texas.

I almost dropped my control over Danielle's mind when I saw poor Dorian, stripped down to her bra and panties, purple bruises adding to the tattoos covering her arms.

Her eyes were shut, her hair disheveled.

She was a fucking wreck.

Augustin's form melted away as my higher consciousness devoted my power to controlling Danielle and using Father's ability to heal Dorian.

"Guard the door," I told Danielle, remembering that she didn't have any ability aside from teleportation. I figured she had some combat training, an assumption proved right when

I briefly skimmed her mind, seeing that she was clearly thinking of a way to overpower me.

"If you try anything," I told her, "I will turn you into a goddamn vegetable. Stand near the door. No, come over here and undo her clasps first." I placed a palm on Dorian's head, my attention still on Danielle as she removed the clasps keeping Dorian pinned down.

There was no other choice: I had to do this, otherwise I'd die.

I felt my heart tense as my palm warmed, Father's healing ability spreading from Dorian's face and downward, healing her bruises, fixing her cuts.

Danielle was expressionless as this happened. Somehow, by the grace of God – or better, by the power of Grace – I'd been able to finally control her mind to an extent that she couldn't fight my powers.

"Gideon?" Dorian Gray whispered as soon as her vision blurred into focus. "How?"

"I'll explain later. We have to get back to the others."

"You have Grace's powers?"

"Yes, long story. I'll explain."

She stood in the center of the room for a moment, her legs spread further apart than normal as she stabilized herself. Dorian's training kicked in, and rather than spend any more time asking me questions, she hobbled over to Danielle.

"Dorian…" I began to say, watching as Danielle's eyes went wide.

"This ends now," were the words that came out of her mouth, mirroring what Veronique had said just ten minutes ago at the beach in Lake Tahoe.

"Before you do, I need to ask her a few questions. Danielle?"

"Yes?" she asked, trembling now.

"How did you know where we were?"

"Tracking… Chloe."

*Fuck me,* I thought as I realized that I'd never turned Chloe's GPS tracking off. "My God, I'm a fucking amateur," I mumbled as Dorian stood before Danielle, a single finger in her mouth.

"Not yet, Dorian. A few more questions."

"If you were tracking Chloe, why didn't you eventually rescue her?"

"Because she allowed us to find you. And besides, she is close to being retired."

"Gideon, please come stand next to me," Dorian said as she removed her finger from her mouth. "Make sure she doesn't move."

She wrapped the fingers of her free hand around my wrist. I felt Dorian's powers open themselves to me, but as I was getting more familiar with doing, I kept my current three abilities.

I closed my eyes, fighting Danielle's attempts at teleporting away.

"Goodbye, Danielle," Dorian said as she pushed her wet finger onto Danielle's forehead. A single tear fell from Danielle's face as purple energy moved to her skin, spreading rapidly.

We were gone before the enemy teleporter's head exploded, but our forms were there long enough for me to see it start to open up, slow motion, an image that six bottles of whiskey couldn't wash down.

Dorian and I reappeared on the beach to find the other CBGs gathered around Augustin's dead body.

Grace, whose face was puffy from fresh tears, put all the pieces together in a matter of seconds and spread the news to the others. I was nearly knocked over when Veronique wrapped her arms around my neck, hugging me.

"We didn't know what to do," she whispered.

*I was so worried...* Grace thought to me, sniffing and wiping her nose.

Next to hug me were Stella and Michelle, the young super damn near squeezing the life out of me. "Gideon, I thought you were dead!" Michelle wailed. "I thought we... we were dead too."

Even Stella's eyes were a little wet, even though she tried to cover this by not making eye contact with me.

Dorian, still in her bra and panties, took one look at the glistening lake and the mountains beyond. "Interesting location."

I knew instantly how she'd managed to teleport back to our party: she'd used her empath teleportation abilities to pinpoint them, and while I wanted an intimate moment with her, a moment that I could express just how much I'd missed her, I knew it could come later.

The CBGs had seen me disappear with one teleporter and return with another.

What in the actual fuck?

There'd be questions, even with Grace's briefing, but those questions could wait. For now, we needed to deal with Chloe, get out of Tahoe City, and I had a little news to share that would bring hope to Michelle and Stella.

"Okay, everyone, we have a little time due to the fact that Danielle is now dead."

"You killed her?" Stella asked.

"I did," said Dorian, taking in just about the biggest breath I'd ever seen her take. The air was nice here, fresh, much better than the stale air inside the Sacramento facility.

"So like I said, we just had a little bit of time. But we need to leave," I told the group. "First thing we should do – and this is on you, Veronique – is to encase Augustin's body in metal and send him to the bottom of Lake Tahoe. Let's get rid of the evidence for now. I'm going to plug into Chloe's neck and turn off her GPS tracker," I said, patting my pocket and feeling the USB key that Dr. Kim had given me. "The rest of you can pack up. We're leaving in ten minutes, and Dorian…"

"Yes?"

"We need a bigger ride. I'll go with you. I'm sure a neighbor or two has a large SUV around here."

"Sounds good. Let's get some new wheels," she said, sweeping her dark bangs out of her face.

"Finally, and we can discuss this later, but I want you two to know now."

Grace smiled, as the next words came out of my mouth.

"Stella, Michelle…" They looked to me, curiosity more evident on Michelle's face than Stella's. "Fiona and Ingrid are alive, and we will get them back tomorrow."

# Chapter Twenty-One: Don't GoogleFace Yourself

They say you're not supposed to GoogleFace yourself, but fuck all that noise.

This was the first thing I did once we hit the highway in our borrowed minivan – thank you, Tahoe soccer mom! – the vehicle in auto drive as I searched for articles about myself.

Sure, it was vain, but considering the fact that I was a freaking wanted terrorist or whatever they deemed me, it seemed like the smart thing to do. Plus I was coming down off some serious adrenaline from the Sacramento incident and seeing someone's head explode.

I needed a distraction.

As usual Grace was to my right, and the rest were in the back, Dorian and Veronique in my line of vision through the rearview mirror.

Chloe was passed out in the far back, and she was the least of my concerns at the moment.

As predicted, I'd made all the digital papers and popular news sites. They'd found pictures of me from various GoogleFace profiles I'd had, high school yearbook photo, and a few blurry ones from quick Internet searches. The headlines were clickbait worthy:

*Sci-fi Writer Turned Bomber*

*Mad Writer Attacks!*

*Stranger than Fiction: Reno on Red Alert with Sci-fi Bomber on the Loose*

*Reading Between the Lines: A Profile of the Reno Bomber*

There were other, equally sensationalist article titles, but I was curious how deep a profile could be if a journalist only had a few hours to write it up. So I clicked on the last one.

"First, I'm not a loser," I mumbled, continuing through the opening paragraph of the 'profile.'

Our vehicle switched lanes, and I looked up to see a car pass to the left of us. I returned to the article, a tingling sensation in my chest. Was this what it felt like to be a celebrity? I suddenly felt guilty for all the celebrity gossip I had looked up, the pictures, hell, even some of the porn.

It was strange to read about myself and know that ninety percent of the stuff I was reading was a lie. Sure, there were some kernels of truth, like the fact that I graduated from Connecticut Southern, and the titles of my books…

This got me thinking that I might actually see an uptick in sales on *Mutants in the Making* because of the media blitz.

"Don't believe everything they say," Grace reminded me.

"Oh, I'm trying not to."

"What are they saying, Gideon?" asked Michelle.

"Lots of bad stuff."

"Did they talk to your mom yet?"

My heart sank.

"Come again?" I said, looking back at her through the rearview mirror to see the young super.

"They said on the news earlier that they were going to talk to your parents later today."

"When did you have time to watch the news? We've been shopping, then we were attacked, and now we're in a minivan heading towards Sacramento."

Dorian snickered.

"What's so funny?"

"Nothing."

"I was watching while I was getting ready. You told us to get ready. They are going to interview your mom soon, it should be interesting! Have you met Gideon's mom?" Michelle asked Grace.

"You mean this woman?" Grace asked as her form began to change to my mother.

"What is the first rule, *our very first rule*, about shifting?"

"What if I stay in your mom's body, but speak to you in Ira Glass's voice?" she asked me in Ira Glass's voice.

Michelle burst out laughing. Even Stella and Veronique, the ones who usually laughed the least, thought this was funny. I caught another glimpse of Dorian, a look of amusement on her face.

"Oh, come on, Grace."

"It's *This American Life*, I'm Ira Glass, each week we take a look at Writer Gideon's life to see just how crazy it has become."

"My life isn't crazy," I told her. "Nope, yes, it is."

"And where do you think you will be staying in Sacramento with the beautiful Cherry Blossom Girls?" Grace asked, still in my mom's form and using Ira's voice.

"Am I a Cherry Blossom Girl?" Michelle asked.

"Everyone in this car is a Cherry Blossom Girl, well, aside from Chloe. We have to figure out what to do with her."

"You keep saying that," said Veronique. "Now that Dorian is here, why don't we just teleport her to…" She thought for a moment. "Where is some place very far away?"

"Canada is pretty far away."

"Maybe Luke wants her," Grace-as-Ira suggested.

"We don't just give people to people, that's not how this works."

"Who is your favorite Cherry Blossom Girl? Well, Writer Gideon?"

266

I gulped loud enough for the driver in the eighteen-wheeler next to us to hear.

"The one who doesn't sound like Ira Glass," I finally said.

"I'm pretty sure it's me," Dorian said. "I can tell that he really missed me."

"Please," Veronique said under her breath. As usual, my eyes met hers, the rearview mirror our meeting ground, and as I had countless times before, I got an uneasy feeling from her.

"Who cares?" Stella said, her arms crossed over her chest.

"Don't worry, Stella, we're going to get them out, if it's the last thing we do…"

"Yes," said Veronique, surprising us all. "If Fiona and Ingrid are alive, we will save them."

*What's with the change of heart for Veronique?* I thought to Grace. *Also, seriously, change into anything but my mom.*

*Changing.* She morphed into the Asian female she liked to take, the one that she'd stripped from the geisha on the wall of my bedroom back in New Haven.

*You should call your mom.*

*I know...*

*She doesn't know what's going on, and she's your mother, trust me when I say that your mother is better than mine.*

"Well, Gideon, which one do you like the best?" Michelle asked.

"Chloe, I like Chloe the best. Because she's the quietest, and that allows me to focus on driving and the fact that my fucking mom – pardon my language, Michelle – is going to go on national television today and talk about me."

Michelle laughed. "You can't like Chloe the best, she's not part of the group, and she's passed out!"

"Time for some music. Who wants to listen to music?"

"Not me," Veronique started to say.

"Great! Grace, find us something to listen to, some good driving music."

# Chapter Twenty-Two: Mom

It took us about two hours to get to the Sacramento area, Dorian doing a little research along the way, and finding us a pretty nice place near a country club in Davis, California.

It was a pretty sweet home, at least five bedrooms from what I counted, and we were able to send the owners off on a mission to, you guessed it, Asia. It was easier to do this, or at least it was for me. It made sense to put them far enough away that we would be long gone before they ever got back, or figured out what had happened.

*Breaking Bad* Gideon did not give a flying fuck.

At least this was the mentality I had to maintain to be able to exploit the general public to the best of my ability. And to think that I was once part of this general public; now I was an outsider, a stranger looking in, the apple that fell too far from the tree, the boy who desperately needed to call his mama and tell her not to go on nationally syndicated television.

But what would I tell her, how would I describe all that had happened?

"There's nothing you can do now, Gideon, except accept it. Once you accept it, maybe it'll be easier to explain."

"Thanks, Grace," I told her as we stepped into the backyard of our new HQ. We wanted to take a look at it, get a little fresh air, and see if there was room for training.

There was definitely some space here, but the homes were much closer together, which meant we would need to train at night. This brought me to my next order of business: trying to get a leg up on Mother by seeing who she'd use next.

I'd already accepted the fact that it was going to be a long night, a night that would start by talking to each of the CBGs to figure out if there was anyone they had trained with who might be one of these 'elite' supers. I still had Ken's app, and I could still see if there was someone who matched the description of whatever the CBGs told me.

We would also need to visit Father, which could be easily accomplished now that we had Dorian.

All this and more (my God, reader, there is always more) was swirling in my mind when Michelle appeared at my side, telling me excitedly that my mom was on TV.

I didn't want to watch, but curiosity killed the cat and has since killed at least one writer.

So I followed the speedy super into the den, saddened by the fact that this was what my life had become.

All I really wanted to do was write. It seemed I was going nonstop, and I'd finished *Mutants in the Making III*, yet I hadn't had the time to actually sit down and do the final edit.

But with Michelle's power, this would be a possibility for tomorrow.

But then again, no it wouldn't, because we were planning to rescue Ingrid and Fiona tomorrow.

So time management, I really could have used a personal assistant by this point.

"Aww, Mom," I said as I saw her on the television screen.

"I just don't know why he did it," she said, dabbing at her eyes. My mom looked the same as she'd looked for the last ten years or so: curly hair, slightly frumpy, but with my same eyes, and hell, similar glasses to me.

I don't want to say that she looked like a heavier version of me with a wig on, but that would be one way to describe her.

"Go on, tell your story," the female news anchor said. It was a pretty big interview, on MS-CNN of all places, and I didn't recognize the anchor interviewing her. Maybe I should have, but my generation stopped watching cable TV a decade ago.

"He was just such a sweet boy, you know the type, and I swear he never, never did anything that would make you think that he would one day become a terrorist. And all those countless lives, just doesn't seem like him. Gideon was a quiet boy. He played the clarinet when he was in middle school. He wasn't strong, always a little bit weaker than the other boys, but they didn't pick on him. People usually like him."

*Dammit, Mom,* I thought as she continued.

The CBGs had gathered around to watch my mother's interview. Hell, even Chloe was there, still passed out.

"Did he ever exhibit some behavior, or maybe, because he is a self-published writer, did he ever *write* something that made you think that this would be his path in life?" the news anchor asked, emphasizing the 'self-published' part in a snide way.

"Not that I can recall. He always read sci-fi books, and I think he wrote some sci-fi books, but no one cared about them, I mean he maybe had a few readers, and his father was one of them. I believe his last one was about a transgender dwarf if I remember correctly..."

"A transgender dwarf, huh? Do you think he was dealing with any suppressed sexual feelings?"

"My Gideon? No, he was always straight as far as I knew. Well, he could have been gay. He never said anything about it though. He did have some male friends growing up. A few of them even spent the night."

"You said that he was writing about a transgender dwarf. Maybe there was something there," the shitty news anchor suggested, "and that something triggered the response in him that later led your son to take it out on all those people."

"He would never do something like that," my mother said. "He was a good boy. I don't think he even knew how to shoot a gun. He'd never been in a fist fight or anything like that. Only one little scuffle in middle school, if I'm not mistaken. He didn't know how to build bombs, at least, he never told me if he did."

"I see," the female anchor said. She had some fake sympathy in her eyes, but not a lot. She was clearly fishing for a soundbite, and unable to get the one she wanted. This made me wonder where my dad was, a question that came up next.

"And is his father in the picture?"

"Gary? Yes, Gary and I are happily married."

"And where is he today?"

"He didn't want to come out of the house. He's very ashamed of our son."

Now this one I actually doubted. My father was pretty savvy, smart enough to become a pretty hardcore stoner after New England legalized it. He was retired now, and he spent a good number of hours researching various strands, partaking in whatever he could get a hold of, and even dabbling in the hydroponics.

He was probably stoned right now, which was why he didn't come out to the interview.

I couldn't take it anymore.

Seeing my mom on TV was giving me all sorts of strange feelings, from past memories, to shame, to an urge to call her and tell her that I was about to do something that was important, that this wasn't all for naught, and that she shouldn't believe the news anyway.

But rather than say anything, or stand there and watch as my mother described intimate details of my life together, I headed upstairs to one of the bedrooms.

Like I said, the house had five bedrooms, maybe more, and definitely a study. The bedrooms were nice, spacious, with high ceilings and arched entrances, which kind of made me feel like I was living in a castle. I fell on one of the beds, definitely a guest bed by the decor of the room, and relaxed for a moment, feeling a nap coming on.

It had been a long day, and even thinking the word 'nap' got me yawning, my eyes fluttering as sleep came over me.

"Don't sleep," a voice said, a voice I recognized immediately as Dorian's.

I force my eyes open to see Dorian sitting on the bed next to me, her dark hair swept over to one side. She wore some of the extra clothing we'd picked up from Zara: a tight black T-shirt, and a pair of black jeans. Her tattoos were on display, the cherry blossoms she had added in Nashville, the ones that matched the typewriter with cherry blossoms on my own shoulder.

I hadn't really thought about my tattoo lately, there'd been too much going on.

"Let's go somewhere," she said, her eyes filling with adoration as she looked at me.

"I have work to do."

"Don't be grumpy. Besides, it looks like you were about to sleep."

"Well, consider that my work." I cleared my throat. "My best stories have come to me in my sleep."

"I doubt that." She placed a hand on my leg. "Where is a place that is near here, a place that is interesting and beautiful? I'm sorry, I don't know as much about America as you do."

"A place that's interesting and beautiful? Well, let's see, we are in California, so, I don't know… Malibu?"

"Can I see your phone?"

"It's in my pocket."

Dorian stuck her fingers in my pocket, which definitely woke my little writer. "What is this tube?"

"Father's blood, I carry it with me wherever I go. Father being, well, kind of your Father, not mine. Yeah, I'm going to catch you up on all that."

"And you also need to catch me up on all this…"

"Instead of explaining it to you, let me try something."

I closed my eyes for a moment and focused on all that had happened over the last couple of days without Dorian. I then imagined myself blowing this information into her mind, and when that didn't work, I sat up and physically touched her head, the information extending from my fingertips into her brain.

"Got it," she said. I opened my eyes to see Dorian staring at me, her head cocked slightly to the side, her brown bangs sweeping against tops of her eyebrows. "You finally became one of us, didn't you?"

"That's what this means," I said as I tapped on my modifier. "And I'm able to take your abilities, only three at a time, though."

"We will have to explore that later, for now, let's go…" She performed a quick search on my phone and found a resort in Malibu. "How's this?" she asked, turning the phone back to me. "We will be back within an hour or two, just tell Grace and she'll tell everyone that we went out. Also, we'll bring back food."

I nodded, unable to say 'no' to Dorian's cute face. "Yeah, all right, let's do this."

*Grace,* I thought aloud, *I'm going to relax with Dorian at a hotel in Malibu for an hour or two. I will return with pizza.*

*Have fun, and we'll have fun learning all about your childhood. I won't tell the others you've left, unless they ask. I'll just say you're napping upstairs with Dorian.*

*We'll bring back food too.*

*Can't wait!*

Dorian placed her hand on my leg and we were gone before I could send another reply.

# Chapter Twenty-Three:
# Malibu Vacay

Dorian and I appeared in a hotel room with an incredible view. There also happened to be a couple in the room, the woman undressing and the man on the bed, stroking his cock.

The man cried out, and stopped mid-scream as I took over his mind. I took over the woman's mind too, knowing that I wouldn't be able to hold them for very long. Grace's power was weird, and sometimes I felt I had a good grasp over it, and other times I felt that my grasp was constantly slipping away from me.

How I'd been able to best Danielle with it was still beyond me.

There was a mirror on the dresser, and I caught a glimpse of myself, my eyes white behind my glasses, the scar on my face, my handheld in front of me like an idiot.

For some reason, acting out the powers helped. I didn't know if the actions were necessary, but it felt right doing them.

"Throw your cellphones on the ground," I told the couple. Once they did this, I turned to Dorian. "Teleport them away from here."

"Where should I teleport them to?"

"How about Davis? It'll take them a little while to figure out what happened and get back to the hotel."

"We can hear you, you know," said the man, his erection rapidly shrinking. I still held his mind, barely, and his last statement was able to break through my control.

A thought came to me as I smiled at the couple. "You will forget that you were staying in this hotel. You lost your phones, and you are in Davis for some shopping."

"There's no good shopping in Sacramento," the woman said to me.

"Shit, lady, are you being serious right now?"

"I'm just saying that I don't want to go shopping in Davis. I used to go shopping there, when my sister lived there, and her husband worked over in Sacramento."

Rather than argue with the woman, I nodded at Dorian and she approached the two. It struck me that the man didn't have pants on, and that the woman was also partially undressed, her fun bags hanging low, nipples pointing to the ground. I told him to get dressed quickly; luckily, the woman didn't give me any shit this time.

Once they were dressed, Dorian vanished with the couple, and appeared again a few moments later. She came into my arms and kissed me, and I held her there for a moment, feeling the channel open up in my field of vision.

I took Dorian's energy power, and still had Grace's psychic and shifter abilities. I didn't want Dorian's teleportation ability, so avoided that channel. I had no idea how I would control it, nor did I feel like accidentally teleporting my ass out to the Pacific Ocean.

And rather than voice it, I just let things take their natural course.

Sex.

Or the closest thing we could have to sex that involved both of us getting our jollies. She could help me, but I couldn't really help her aside from kissing her nipples or the insides of her legs.

*Or could I?* I thought as I felt her power surging within me.

We took all the covers off the bed, mostly because I didn't want to think about the last guy's sweaty ass on that top comforter. I was now in my boxers, and Dorian was in her bra and panties. She had high waisted panties, something Grace had picked out.

I watched as her breasts spilled out of her top. She didn't have any tattoos over her chest. Her sleeves ended at pretty much her shoulder joint, and as I had done before, I took a moment to admire the juxtaposition of ink on her pale skin.

The idea came again, and I figured I'd vocalize it.

"I think we can do more than we did last time," I told her, as I pulled my boxers off.

"How so?"

"I have your abilities now."

She looked at me curiously for a moment.

I suppose I hadn't shown her that I had her abilities, nor had I tested actually using them. "Hold on," I told her as I rolled off the bed, my half-erection flopping against the side of my leg.

I grabbed an ink pen from the desk, and as I put its tip into my mouth, I imagined myself spreading energy into it. It started to turn purple, but my fingers were unaffected by the blistering power.

Like I was auditioning for a role as Gambit, I tossed the pen into a sofa chair and it exploded. I should rephrase, the chair did not explode, but the pen did, and it left a pretty big burn mark on the seat, and a small amount of fire, which I doused with water from the tap.

Even though Dorian had seen me use Grace's power, I don't think she'd truly understood what my new ability allowed me to do.

She was in my arms in a matter of moments, kissing me, her legs wrapped around my waist. I pressed her against the wall, feeling my hard-on pressing against her wet mound.

"We have to test it more," she said through her kisses.

"I know, I know. But how?"

"Your toe? My toe?"

"Which toe?" I asked as she kissed me again.

"Little toe?"

"It's still important!"

"If we're going to do that, we have to *at least* test it out," she said firmly.

"I'm not disagreeing there, I just don't know *how* we should do it."

"We'll touch each other's little toes and try to charge them. If they blow off, you can heal us, right? Didn't you say you have the healing ability?"

I gasped. "That's right! Worst case scenario, we can teleport to Father, which is something we need to do later anyway, and he'll be able to heal us up."

"So the worst thing that can happen is we both blow our little toes off in an act of lust." She giggled. "That's so stupid."

"Stupid is as stupid does, err, something," I said as I got down on the floor. A new problem arose. "How are we supposed to actually do this?"

I supposed that we could lay in a sixty-nine position and lick or suck each other's toes, but that seemed a little ridiculous. Well, all this seemed ridiculous, but people had done way stupider things just to get a bit of tail.

"Are you worried about how we're going to do this?" Dorian still hadn't sat down on the floor. In fact, she was looking at me with her hands pressed against her sides, not quite a disappointed look, but definitely an 'I thought you were smarter than this' look.

"A little."

She started to laugh again. "Stand up first. Okay, put your fingers in your mouth, and we'll both bend over and charge each other's toes. If they blow off, shit, we need to be careful not to have them explode in our faces."

I glanced around the room and saw the woman's purse on the dresser. The man had his car keys next to her purse, and sure enough there were a pair of sunglasses. All I could do was hope that there was another pair inside the purse.

It turned out that there were two pairs of sunglasses, which we gladly put on, mine cool and sleek and Dorian's large and tinted amber.

"Our eyes are protected now," I told her, as I put my finger in my mouth and imagined myself spreading energy to it.

I felt a tingling sensation at the end of my finger, and when I pulled it away from my mouth, I noticed that there was just a slight bit of energy whirling around.

Dorian had done the same thing, and after looking at each other, both of our eyes shielded by sunglasses, we bent over and latched onto each other's pinky toes.

I winced, waiting for something to happen, and as I did, an Oliver Sacks quote came to me: "The study of disease and identity cannot be disjoined."

*Seems apropos,* I thought as I waited for my toe to blow off.

And luckily for both of us, we weren't going to need new toes.

I looked up at her, and she practically tackled me with a kiss. She was going all out now, sucking my face, my nipples, kissing my neck, and I was trying my best to respond but Dorian had clearly taken charge.

"Let's do it outside," she said suddenly, nodding towards the balcony that overlooked the Pacific Ocean. I forgot to mention just how sweet this hotel was. It literally sat on the coastline, the sea reflecting bits of tangerine and grapefruit as the sun set in the distance.

We burst out the balcony doors, and I quickly laid a blanket down. I got on my back, and Dorian took her panties off and got on top. There was a moment of hesitation, I'm not going to lie about that.

There was still the potential that I would have my dick blown off, but it was a risk I was willing to take.

Dorian was already wet, so there was no reason to do much aside from slip it in easy, which I did, trying my best not to wince when I felt a tingling sensation spread up my shaft.

She was tight, and once we both got used to our new position, and I was sure my little writer hadn't burst into flames, Dorian began moving her hips back and forth, finding a rhythm.

Once she got accustomed to it, she started going faster, her hands now on her breasts, her fingers pinching her nipples. I placed my arms behind my head, feeling just about as lucky as a man can feel.

Still thrusting her hips forward, Dorian started to turn sideways, until she had some reverse cowgirl going. I still felt the tingling sensation, but nothing had exploded, and this was way too hot to notice a little detail like that.

Besides, I had some of Father's blood in the room, and I could give myself a quick heal down afterwards, just to be sure.

My last thought threw me off guard.

*I may have to use another man's blood to heal my own proof of manhood...*

I let go of this thought as Dorian began twerking, her ass cheeks moving up and down.

Fuck were women beautiful.

And I tried to hold on. Dammit I tried my best, but seeing her ass move, and seeing her look at me over her shoulder caused me to have a *sexual eruption* that would have done justice to Snoop Dogg's 2007 song of the same name.

Except I didn't take my time, nor did I take it slow, but I'm pretty sure she got hers because Dorian was moaning along with me, her head tossed back, her eyes closed.

So we both came early, who cares?

It was still a good time, and a much-needed distraction. After all, the next twenty-four hours were going to be a doozy. And even though I had just orgasmed, I started to worry about what would happen tomorrow.

"Your smile is gone…" Dorian now lay next to me, resting on her side with her hand on my cheek.

"Just got hit by a wave of thoughts. It happens. Let's go get cleaned up. We really don't want any super babies."

She laughed. "Yeah, that would be troublesome. Grace would be so jealous."

"I'm more worried about Veronique."

"What about Stella? Anything happen with her?"

"No, no," I said, recalling Grace's Stella trick from the previous night.

"Good, I think three is plenty."

"Trust me, if I add anything else to my situation, I'll have to register as a member of the Church of Latter Day Saints."

"Who are they?"

"Doesn't matter. Let's get cleaned up, dressed, and then it's pizza time."

# Chapter Twenty-Four:
# Fighting Jules is Going to
# Be a Pain in the Ass

There are heroes in this world, and then there are people who show up with pizza. I've learned long ago that the distinction between the two is fuzzy at best.

"Pizza!" Michelle cried out, as Dorian and I reappeared in the dining room area of our borrowed home.

I'd bought four pies, well, "bought" may not be the right word, but I did at least tip the guy at the front counter. Karma was important to me, and judging by the fact that I usually had to manipulate the general public to navigate my way through the world, I needed all the good karma I could get.

Chloe came to the table, Veronique at her side. She was awake now, and I couldn't quite read the look on Chloe's face.

*How much of what happened back at the beach have you told her?* I thought to Grace.

Everyone's favorite psychic shifter was sitting in the living room when we appeared, in her base form, her eyes locked on the television as a married couple renovated a home in Vermont. I knew it was Vermont because of some of the shots of Burlington.

It was unfortunate that Vermont was practically a dying state, and that they were trying desperately to bring young people in because the population was kicking the can. It was a pretty place, full of trees and rolling hills, an extension of Western Massachusetts that held a unique beauty.

*She knows we were in a fight, she doesn't know the results of that fight.*

*How has she been behaving?* I thought back to her.

*She's been fine, actually. She hasn't shown any signs of animosity, and there haven't been any malicious thoughts in her mind. Most of her thoughts revolve around just how comfortable she now feels, even though she's under house arrest. She doesn't really like Veronique, though, but...*

*I know, most people don't like Veronique.*

293

*Dorian likes Veronique, Stella not so much, Michelle thinks she can be grumpy, and I'm fine with her too. You seem to like her as well, especially her body.*

I looked over at Grace to see that she was making a funny face at me, her eyes squinted shut and her mouth making a pouty kiss.

"Pizza, pizza, pizza," Michelle said, as she whipped around the table. She had found a happy medium for moving quickly, a speed that didn't ruin her clothing.

The first box open, she went for a slice, the cheese still connected to the main pie as she yanked the slice away.

I felt my stomach grumble and I went for a slice as well, cupping the pizza so it resembled a taco, a pro move, one designed not to let the goodies fall out.

"It's so good," Chloe said after she took her first bite, her eyes widening with pleasure.

"You should taste the pizza in New Haven," I said with my mouth full. "New Haven has like three of the best pizza restaurants in the country. Seriously."

"There was a training facility there, correct?"

"Yep, the past tense version of that sentence is even more poignant," I said while chewing my second bite. It was hard to say the word "poignant" while eating.

Veronique sat next to Chloe, a look of hunger on her face. It was too bad we didn't have Angel in a backpack; having that little head around allowed Veronique just to top off the tank every now and then.

"Later," I told Veronique. I glanced over at Dorian, who confirmed this with a nod.

"Good, then I'll make some coffee now," said the metal vampire. And showing just how much the two had trained when it came to hostage management, as soon as Veronique stood, Stella sat down next to Chloe.

*Hostage Management,* I thought as Stella casually took a slice of pizza. *Now there's a course not available at Southern Connecticut.*

*They are doing a great job of watching her,* Grace thought back to me.

"So after we eat this pizza, we will need to figure out what we can do to prepare for tomorrow. I am serious when I say we will get Fiona and Ingrid out."

Sure, I said my last sentence with a mouth full of pizza, but I wasn't lying: by this time two days from now, I expected that I would have to buy another pie next time we had pizza.

"So they are actually alive?" Chloe asked.

"Yes, that was the intel I was able to get when I freed Dorian."

Chloe had been given the Cliff Notes as to what had happened back at the Tahoe beach, but she hadn't been awake when I told the CBGs that Fiona and Ingrid were actually alive.

"Then I want to help in any way I can," Chloe said after swallowing her last bite of pizza.

"Absolutely not," said Veronique from the kitchen.

"We think it would be best if you stayed behind," Grace said, her eyes white as she sat at the table.

"Sure, I will stay behind," Chloe said, her eyes glazed over just a bit; Grace's powers weren't as strong with other supers, but she was able to affect some of them, and it appeared Chloe was one of the ones easily affected.

"I'm going too," Michelle announced. "If anyone is saving my friends, it's me!"

"I need to figure out more about the facility before we decide who's coming or not. And I want all of you to tell me as much as you can about the elite supers that Mother may be bringing in. What do you know? And have you ever trained with them? Maybe we can find some connections, especially because you, Chloe, are from the West coast, and the others are from the East."

"I'm actually from the west, but trained in the east," said Dorian.

"That's fine, but are there any people you have trained with that particularly stand out to you? I'm not talking about someone with normal-ish powers, like Angel, I'm talking about someone that impressed or frightened you with their abilities."

The CBGs exchanged glances. In this moment, Grace accessed all of their thoughts, at least their thoughts at the surface level, and she was the first to speak.

"It seems as if all of you, aside from you, Michelle, have trained with Jules."

Dorian bit her lip, nodding. Stella, who had been chewing a slice of pizza, swallowed it before she spoke. "I only met him once. His power is that other people's powers don't work around him."

"Hmmm, do you mean he has like power negation?"

"Yes," Chloe said to me. The brunette reached for another slice, and placed it on the table. I realized then that we hadn't set plates out, but before I could act, Grace had already telepathically brought some plates from the kitchen. She even lifted Chloe's slice with her powers, and placed it on a plate.

"Please continue," I told the sound manipulator.

"Victoria, Augustin, and I all trained with Jules. We did so several times. Our instructions were to all attack him at once. It really didn't matter what we did, as soon as we got within his sphere of influence, our powers stopped working. We were only able to beat him once."

"What about a projectile? Like throwing something at him?"

"I tried that," said Veronique. "It is almost like Stella's power. Everything that got close to him suddenly lost its energy. My consumption power doesn't work either. Believe me, I've tried."

"Okay, so we can all agree that Jules is probably one of the guys that Mother will bring. It makes sense." I placed my phone on the table. I wasn't about to go at it with greasy fingers, but as soon as we finished eating, I was going to look this guy up and see what I could discover about his abilities.

"Is there anyone else that you guys can think of?"

"They have trained with a lot of people, but no one else seems to have left as big an impact as Jules," Grace said. "Each of them individually has their own memories of an opponent that was difficult, but Jules is the one that no one could beat."

"Except for the one time we beat him," Chloe added.

"Well, that at least gives us a leg up," I said as I considered another slice. The eternal question. "We'll need to do several things tonight and tomorrow. For one, Dorian and I need to visit Father. He may know more about how we can take Jules down."

"I need a paintbrush."

"Done, we'll get you a paintbrush."

"I need to feed."

"Yes, Veronique needs food. And as we have done before, we will need to prepare frag pouches and other projectile weapons we can use against the private military men that will likely be waiting for us when we arrive. I really wish they would quit sending these people after us, because it is clear that they have no effect. But I think what Mother is going for is distraction. I'm guessing Remy will be there as well: he was injured in the last fight, but it was likely just a flesh wound."

"So we need to take a trip to the store," said Grace. "That's always fun. We'll need armor again as well. Most of it was left back in the Reno hotel."

"Yep, armor too. Damn, we should really consider getting a lot of armor and putting it in a stash somewhere, so we can just teleport there, grab it, and go. Anyway, regarding our plan of attack, I prefer to get Fiona and Ingrid out; I don't know who else may be held at the Sacramento facility, so it might be important for us to see about that, especially before we destroy the place."

"So we're not destroying the place?" Michelle asked.

"I don't think that this mission should be about bringing the facility to the ground; that can wait until later. We still have a few more to take down anyway, and I'd rather know who is being held there before we really kick things into high gear."

"The mission is to get Ingrid and Fiona, that's it," Stella said with finality. "I really don't care who is in there."

"Pretty much what I just said…"

"Except mine was more to the point."

I offered Stella a toothy grin. "That settles it. We have a plan, and we're going to stick to this one."

As the CBGs hung out in the family room, I retreated to the study so that I could go over Jules' abilities without distraction. I sat behind a mahogany desk, feeling like a goddamn CEO as I leaned back in the chair, my feet propped up.

I opened Dr. Kim's app, and found the search bar, where I typed the name Jules and his info came up:

## Jules, Subject J.

Build: 1.069

Base height: 179 centimeters

Base weight: 70 kilos

Strength: 3

Intelligence: 9

Constitution: 8

Wisdom: 8

Dexterity: 5

Charisma: 6

## Main: Power Negation

* Negation Control

* Power Suppression and Redistribution

* Elemental Negation

* Temporary Power Erasure

* Obsolescence


He only had five listed abilities, and I only needed to look up two. I found "Negation Control" on a site dedicated to superpowers used in animes. Maybe this wasn't the best source, but after reading what it meant, I figured it wasn't far off. Negation Control gave Jules the power to nullify any mind attacks, so Grace's abilities were all but useless against him.

The other one I didn't know, Obsolescence, gave him the power to create a dead zone around him, which checked out with what the others had said.

After jotting down Jules' make number, 1.069, I closed the app and went to the computer. Luckily, there was no password, and once I was in, I took a little time to make sure that my usage here wouldn't be traced. There were websites for this, and I used one of those websites as a jumping off point, eventually accessing Dr. Kim's files that I'd saved in the cloud.

I went to Videos and found what I was looking for.

05052028AEFL#1069, or in layman's terms, *filmed on May 5th, 2028, Agency of Enhancement and Future Logistics # 1.02287.*

I clicked on the video and was surprised to see Dorian and Veronique. They were wearing all black MercSecure clothing, and Dorian's hair was in pigtails. Veronique looked pretty much the same, just a little bit younger, same sharp features and dark eyes.

The two were in what I assumed was one of the underground facilities outside of New Haven with high ceilings and padded walls. Bars of steel were to Veronique's left, a metal wrecking ball to her right.

Standing before them was a tall man with a side part. Jules wore glasses, his cheeks were gaunt, and a scarf was tucked into the front of his body armor.

Dorian's purple energy spread up her arm as she came in to punch him. Her fist stopped about two feet away from his body before she was blown backward.

I thought the wrecking ball would take him out, especially when the camera cut to a different angle showing Veronique lifting the ball with her powers, her eyes blazing red.

No such luck.

The wrecking ball flew through the air, missed, and left a crater in the floor.

Jules was relaxed the entire time, as if nothing had happened. Hell, he could have been reading a book while they were attacking. And it didn't matter how many energy creations Dorian cast in his direction, or the steel bars that cracked against his protective outer shell, the dead zone surrounding him kept Jules safe.

There was nothing they could do to touch him.

And I kept watching the video as they tried. One thing that I noticed about Jules' ability was that he really had no attack power. He just continually blocked everything until they lost the will to fight.

Had this changed?

While it was an incredible power, it seemed faulty that he couldn't attack them.

"I get it, I get it," I said as I watched another video, this one of Chloe and Victoria attacking Jules. They weren't able to get a hit in, and the scarfed man continued to flash that bored look of his.

This got me thinking about Chloe, and I turned on the app to check out her abilities.

**Chloe, Subject C**

Build: 17.169

Base height: 185 centimeters

Base weight: 56 kilos

Strength: 4

Intelligence: 7

Constitution: 7

Wisdom: 5

Dexterity: 7

Charisma: 4

**Main: Acoustokinesis**

* Sound Sculpting

* Acoustic Acceleration

* Sonoluminescence

* Rhythm Manipulation

* Sonokinetic Combat

* Sound Detection

* Sonic Stimulation

* Overcharge

*Will she actually join us?* Her abilities were clearly useful, but I didn't know if now was the time to be recruiting a new member, especially with what we had to do the following day.

So I came to the same conclusion that Grace had already come to: Chloe would stay here for the attack.

*Grace, are you and Dorian ready?* I thought aloud.

*Give us just a few more minutes. They're doing the big reveal on the house that they renovated.*

*Got it, I'll watch a few more videos in the meantime.*

# Chapter Twenty-Five: The Father, The Spirit, The Buried Trailer

I played a little Duck Duck Goose before we left, going around the room and resetting my powers.

In order, I now possessed Stella's vector ability, Father's healing power, and Grace's telepathy. I even plugged into my neck to double-check that I was right:

(1) Vector Manipulation

* Kinetic Energy Manipulation

* Vibration Emission

* Inertia Negation

* Telekinetic Regeneration

* Velocity Manipulation

* Aversion Field Creation

* Overcharge


(2) Cell Regeneration

* Regenerative Healing Factor

* Regrowth

* Cellular Activation

* Flawless Restoration

(3) Psychic

* Second Sight

* Psychometry

* Telepathy

* Psychokinesis

* Hypnosis

* Nightmare Sight

Since we were teleporting to the middle of nowhere Nevada, I wasn't too concerned about concealing my face.

I had considered taking Father's other power this time, a Pandora's box if there ever was one. But as I promised him, I kept to one channel. I didn't know if I would ever take his ability to manipulate the future; I had enough problems dealing with the present.

It was Grace who helped Dorian understand how to get to Father's trailer.

This was harder than I'd thought it would be, and actually took Grace physically touching the side of Dorian's head so she could clearly transmit as much detail as she could about his location.

Once Dorian had it, we appeared there in a flash.

I almost cried out when I saw a crater where Father's trailer used to be.

With a dark sky overhead, the moon hidden behind a cloud, the coldness of the desert creeping into our bones, Dorian kept her hand on my wrist, her other finger in her mouth.

"There's no one," Grace finally said, the perimeter secure. "I'm not sensing any mind activity."

This did little to calm my nerves.

I had just read about Jules' ability to negate the powers of a psychic; I too was ready to attack, or at least create a shield around us using Stella's power.

But Grace turned out to be right.

Even after Dorian felt it was safe enough to let go of my wrist, we still continued to check the area.

Nothing, no tire tracks either signaling he'd driven away.

"Are you sensing anything else?" I asked Grace, referring to her psychometry ability.

"There was a struggle, and that's all I can sense. There was also a shifting... Gravity? Is that the right word?" she asked, mostly to herself. "That crater was caused by gravitational pressure, in fact..."

The three of us moved over to the crater where Father's trailer once stood.

Dorian cast a ball of light over the crater, high enough to provide enough light for us to see what had actually happened.

"Damn, that's some pressure," I said, as I looked down at the top of the trailer. It had been completely buried, likely struck from something above.

"This is in Jules' power, isn't it?"

"No," said Dorian.

"Do you think Father is in there?" I raised my hand to the side of my mouth. "Father, I mean, Jim! Jim! Can you hear me?"

"If he is, he's dead," said Grace. "It has been like this for... I think over a day now. And I'm not getting any mind activity, but then again, I never got activity from Father."

"Do you sense that he escaped?"

"I really can't tell. There aren't any tracks that seem strange, or..." Grace began searching around again, this time touching the ground every now and then. Dorian cast another ball of energy that followed over Grace, providing light.

The two searched for quite some time like this, enough time that I was getting antsy, afraid that someone would return. I didn't know what was giving me this fear, but with supers, you never knew when you'd be attacked.

"Let's go," I told the two. "This place is giving me the creeps."

Was Father alive? Was he dead? I had no way of knowing, and aside from the fact that his trailer had been buried, there were no signs of struggle.

We appeared in Davis, back at our borrowed estate.

Damn, it would be nice if the CBGs and I could finally have a place to call our own. There were times when I felt like a traveling businessman, always a stone's throw away from home, constantly being called to another assignment.

One day, if this all worked out, we would have our own place, a base of sorts.

And of course, even thinking this spawned a series of mental images featuring famous superhero bases, from the Justice League to Batman's man cave, *but you aren't a superhero, and neither are they.*

I had to keep reminding myself of this: the things we had done had made us practically villains.

In the eyes of the government, we were terrorists. My growing group of readers aside, anyone who stumbled upon our story would assume immediately that we were the bad guys.

I'd been deemed a terrorist, and now the goddamn public was weighing in. And even if this truth was nuanced, the damage had already been done, proof of the true reach of the FCG, the Federal Corporate Government; they had much more control of the media after the series of fiascos over ten years ago.

What they said was law, what they said was truth.

And anyone saying anything different was the enemy.

So it would be an uphill battle, that much was true, and as I explained to Stella, Michelle, Veronique, and Chloe what had happened back at Father's place, this thought was at the back of my mind: *a pyrrhic victory is the only victory you'll ever have against the powers that be.*

"I don't think they killed him," Veronique finally said. "He was a clever man. And I'm still hungry, if anyone's wondering."

"We really don't know, and I didn't sense anything," came Grace's reply. She was by my side as always, her hand looped through my arm.

"Father probably disappeared, and he will reappear again when we need him," said Stella.

"I barely met the guy, but he seemed nice," Michelle chimed in.

Chloe merely shrugged. And for some reason, this shrug made me want to come clean with her, to tell her what was really going on.

*Honesty is the best policy,* said someone who hadn't discovered the power of a lie. I was naïve enough at the time to think that honesty would always be our best way forward, which in a way was lying to myself.

"I will bring someone for Veronique," Dorian said.

Grace squeezed my arm again, and I noticed that I was being presented with two options. It was a strange sensation, and very subtle, but whenever one of them touched me or I touched them, it was something I definitely noticed.

*Why don't you do the mind wipe? It's good practice. You'll need to conceal your identity too,* Grace thought to me.

*Got it.*

I let her shifter ability move to me, and for the first time, I decided to try something new.

I mentally *forced* Stella's power out, instructing myself to keep Father's healing capability. It was pretty easy to visualize the power switch in my head. I simply imagined pool balls clinking together and the ones that were there before leaving.

Since I already possessed one of Grace's powers, her telepathic ability, this one stayed put.

Just to be sure, and without plugging in, I tried to form a vector shield and failed, proving that I'd mentally forced Stella's power out.

"Good work," Grace said, immediately sensing what I had done.

"I can't believe that worked." I tried again, this time patting Michelle on the head, taking her power, forcing out Grace's shifter ability, and then retaking Grace's shifter power, forcing Michelle's back out.

"I no longer need to think of the powers as lining up," I whispered.

It was a bit of a revelation for me, because trying to keep the powers in some particular order made it so I had to do the Duck Duck Goose scenario whenever I wanted to reset.

What I'd just discovered was that I had more control over my abilities than I had previously thought. I didn't need to absorb them in any particular order anymore, I could mentally arrange things.

"This power just keeps on giving!"

"Let's do this," I told Dorian and the metal vampire.

The three of us walked down the hall to one of the guest bedrooms. I flipped on the light and sat on the bed next to Veronique, who scooted closer to me, her thigh pressing against mine. It was a smaller space, but there wasn't any furniture, so it made the room seem bigger somehow.

A poof of purple energy and Dorian was gone.

"If I could get sustenance a different way, I would." Something softened behind Veronique's dark eyes as she turned to me. "You know that, right?"

I raised both hands. "No judgment here; I have experienced your power now and I understand the hunger that you have. I only wish you enjoyed pancakes and pizza for your own sake, because a life without either is a life I don't want to live. And speaking of which, I'm so sick of shitty pizza, I really feel like I was spoiled in New Haven."

"Sometimes it feels like you were spoiled most of your life," she said with a playful grin on her predatory face.

"Hey, just because I'm a New Englander, who was born and raised in America's dying middle class, doesn't mean I was spoiled. You want to see spoiled? Go to Greenwich."

"Greenwich. I know that place; we watched them remodel one of the mansions there last night. It looks really nice. Maybe we can get a home there one day."

"Connecticut is out of the picture when it comes to a future base. It's a beautiful state, don't get me wrong, but it's a small state, and most of the free space is wooded, and we need room to train. High taxes in Connecticut too – state, income, property – not that this matters, considering our line of work. Hold on a second."

I focused on my features and melting them away. I felt a shift in my face, but not in the rest of my body, as I was trying to only change my facial features. My hair grew a little longer, my jowls thickened, and I felt the skin over my cheeks stretch downward.

I still wore my glasses. Grace's ability made little sense to me, most notably her power to actually form clothing and accessories. I did not possess that part of her power, so whatever form I took, I still had to wear my glasses.

"How do I look?"

Veronique stared at me, her eyes wide. "You are getting better at that."

"So I look all right? I was kind of going for a Provincetown fisherman."

"I have no idea what that looks like."

"Hopefully like this!"

Dorian appeared, her hand around the elbow of a thin man. The man wore a faded shirt that said Scandolf the Orange in bolt letter. He had a ratty beard, and was in a pair of board shorts and tattered leather sandals.

"What the..."

I took over his mind, telling the beach bum to relax, that this would all be over soon. His eyes didn't turn as white as when Grace took someone's mind, but they did glaze over, and he obediently dropped to his knees and waited for Veronique to approach him.

Veronique held her glowing red hand over his head, and his skin immediately started to shrivel, then to turn purple. Once she was finished, and color had returned to her face, she nodded to Dorian.

"Wait, I want to try something," I told them both.

I approached the man, who had since slouched over, and lightly placed my hand on his arm.

With a deep breath in, I activated Father's healing ability. A wave of warm energy spread out of my fingertips, and the man, whose eyes were closed just moments before, began taking short breaths. Soon, his eyes were open, and the purple tint to his skin was fading away.

"Can I feed again?"

"That's the plan," I told Veronique. "And if this works, we don't have to get innocent people any longer. As long as we have a volunteer within our group..."

Veronique lifted her hand and the guy began to quiver. His skin wrinkled, and the purple tint returned. Once she was done, and breathing heavily, like an animal that had just gorged itself, I healed the man for a second time.

"Your turn, Dorian," I said, and without a word, the punk rock teleporter zipped away with the guy, reappearing less than thirty seconds later.

"I'll volunteer to be drained next time," Dorian said. "As long as you can heal me."

"You don't have to do that," said Veronique, a rare sense of shame coming over her.

"If it prevents us from taking random people, then that's probably a good thing."

"I agree. And with Father's ability, I can just heal whoever Veronique feeds off. That said, for tomorrow, I think we should do things the old-fashioned way. I don't know if there are any side effects to being consumed and then replenished, but we should probably play it safe."

"Or just drain Chloe," Veronique said.

"Yeah, or just drain Chloe, which would kill two birds with one stone, and you two know how much I like killing two birds."

They both looked at me funny.

"Sorry, that came out kind of strange. Anyway, it's research time for Writer Gideon, so relax, enjoy some television, and we will talk later."

Dorian cocked her head to the right. "Are you going to change your face back to your normal face? Because your current face is starting to melt a little bit."

"Whoops! Grace's shifter ability takes a crapton of concentration," I said as my normal features reformed. "How's that?"

"Cuter," Dorian said.

"But only just a little." Veronique's hand flared red; she zapped just a small amount of my lifeforce.

"Hey!"

The two left the room, both of them giggling.

"Wait," I called after them. Only Veronique peeked her head back in. "Can you send Chloe in? I believe it is time that she *gets woke*. Sorry, that last sentence sounds way stranger in third person singular."

"Gets woke?"

Dorian also peeked her head back in. "You aren't thinking of giving her powers back, are you?"

"No, nothing like that, but I do think I should be up front with her."

"As long as either Stella or I are here, I will let you stay alone with Chloe," Veronique said firmly.

"I'm fine with that," I said, a little offended that she thought so poorly of me that I couldn't hang out with a hostage alone.

Then again, maybe Veronique was right.

"I'll send her then."

"To the office," I told them as I left the spacious bedroom.

"Hi, Gideon," said Chloe as she stepped into my borrowed office. She was with Stella, who looked slightly annoyed at the fact she couldn't watch her television shows.

Chloe's voice always had a hint of melody to it. She looked cleaner too, and I wondered if she'd taken another shower while Dorian and I were on our Malibu vacation.

I gestured for them to sit at the two chairs in front of the mahogany desk. I felt like Michael Scott, long-time manager in *The Office,* as I leaned back in my own chair, contemplating how I was going to frame this.

"Chloe, you trained and were close with Augustin and Victoria, correct?"

"Correct. Why? I know you have fought them. If you're asking for weaknesses…"

I paused, seeing just what she'd reveal.

"I don't really know any aside from the obvious."

"The obvious?"

"Augustin uses ranged attacks, and isn't as good with close combat. He can do fire fists and stuff, but it's not his strength. Victoria's only ranged attacks are if she picks something up and throws it. She has trained extensively in hand-to-hand combat."

I winced, not ready to tell her of Victoria's fate.

"What's wrong? I don't really know what else to tell you other than that. Augustin has also used ice bombs before. Like I said, he tinkered with explosives, and one thing he'd do is place an explosive and cover it in ice."

"What good would that do?"

Chloe grinned. "It looked cool when it exploded."

"What about Danielle? What do you know about her? Did you train with her or anything?"

"Off and on. She was mainly just a mule, but I liked her. Too bad all she can do is teleport, not like Dorian. Danielle is pretty tough, though, and she throws a mean punch."

Stella and I exchanged glances. The vector manipulator's facial expression was hard to read.

"I'm going to be completely honest with you," I said finally, "because honesty is a foundational policy for the CBGs."

"Okay..."

"We killed them, all three of them. Well, I didn't kill them, but I am partially responsible for Danielle's death."

"You what?" Chloe's happy-go-lucky expression was gone, replaced by something that looked as if she was trying to chew on a piece of leather.

"Victoria died while you were out, back in the desert of Nevada. Veronique ripped the metal from her body and used it to impale her. Augustin was also killed by Veronique, on the beach in Tahoe."

"She killed them both? What about Danielle?"

I noticed that Stella's hand was curled, a translucent energy already charging just in case she needed to use it.

"That was Dorian's doing. She exploded her head. Probably one of the more fucked up things I've seen, but then again, I see something messed up every day now. My point is: I want you to know what is going on, to be in the loop. And I hate to frame it like this, but we have to figure out what to do with you."

God, it felt awful saying that. Regardless, I continued.

"If we let you go back to them, you'll become an immediate threat to us. So we don't want that. We also don't want to kill you."

"Are you sure about that?" she asked, glaring at me now. "It sounds like Veronique would love killing me."

I almost said, 'she loves killing everyone,' but stopped myself just in time.

"Don't let Veronique fool you, she's a softie at heart." I swallowed hard, trying not to taste the flavor of my own bullshit. "She's the strongest of us, or maybe Stella is, but she shows more mercy."

"No, I don't."

"Stella," I said, leaning my elbows on the mahogany desk. "Trust me, you show more mercy than Veronique. And that's not a diss, that's a compliment. Shit, I'm getting off track here. Chloe, let's focus."

"I'm focused," she said, her expression finally relaxing.

"Good, it's time to start thinking of how you want this to end."

"I don't have a say in the matter."

"Do you want to join us?" I asked point-blank.

"And if I don't?"

"There are other options," I finally said, feeling like a goddamn mob boss. "We could have Grace wipe your mind and send you far away."

"How is that an option?"

I felt bad for her, I really did, but as the self-proclaimed 'Decider Guy,' I had to figure something out, and figuring that something out required me to be a hardass.

And quickly realizing that I was running out of shit to say, I fired off a message to the CBGs' CFO.

*Grace, what do I tell Chloe?*

*It sounds like your desire to be honest has put you in a tough spot,* she thought back to me.

*What do you think we should do? What does everyone think? Aside from Veronique, well, get her opinion anyway, but I'd like to not kill Chloe. I can't believe this is a conversation I actually have to have.*

Stella's eye twitched ever-so-slightly, which told me Grace was pooling the group. It only took a moment for everyone's favorite psychic shifter to get back to me.

*Dorian, Michelle, Stella and I agree that we should keep her around, that nothing should change, and that we should gradually let her into the group. Veronique was against it, but said to tell you that she doesn't want to kill everyone, and that there are some people she likes, including you.*

*Sorry to pigeonhole her.*

*You've done more than pigeonhole her.*

*Is that a sex joke?* I thought back to Grace.

*She thinks very fondly of your experience in the minivan in Colorado, at the mall. I believe she likes the risk of doing things in public, an exhibitionist.*

An image stretched across my mind's eye. Veronique was going down on me while we waited for the others to shop.

*Well, this conversation just got interesting. But back to the topic at hand: what do we do with Chloe?*

*I already told you what to do.*

*You're right.*

"So we're just going to keep you around for now," I told Chloe. "Not that you are some object that we can just keep around and do whatever we'd like with. Nothing like that. I just wanted to tell you what's going on, and about your teammates. Even though I'm directly responsible for their deaths, I'm sorry that they died, especially if you liked them."

"It's not your fault, and did you just bring me in here to tell me nothing is going to change?"

"Sort of," I said, shrugging at Stella, who offered me a cute shrug back.

"Can we end this now?" Chloe asked.

"Sure."

She stood, and Stella followed her out. I was surprised to see Veronique at the door. She stepped in after they left, and came over to me.

"I was just about to start research. Then…"

"Then?"

"I need to finish editing my manuscript."

"Can I be in here with you?"

"How about we meet later?"

"You're blowing me off?" she asked as she sat on my lap.

"Not quite. We can spend some time alone tomorrow."

"Doesn't have to be alone." And for some reason, I could tell from the way she said this that she meant with her and Dorian.

"Okay, raincheck. How's that? We have to focus on rescuing Ingrid and Fiona."

# Chapter Twenty-Six: Published!

I did my research first. Sure, it wasn't the coolest part about my job as CEO of the CBGs, but it was up to me to cobble together a strategy for tomorrow.

The facilities folder in Ken's documents didn't have everything that a guy could want, but it came close. There wasn't a schematic for the Sacramento facility, as there had been for the others, but it did have some information about the types of walls they'd used, oddly enough, and various entry points.

And yes, reader, I wish I were better at planning these things.

And hell, maybe I was getting better, but the point remained: I was a special type of amateur, an amateur's amateur, the noobiest noob, a nincompoop even, and looking back, I really wished that Southern Connecticut had had some coursework on urban warfare and military invasion strategies.

With this in mind, I did a GoogleFace search revolving around classic invasion techniques.

The only problem was finding a good search term for building invasion strategies. Every time I typed in any word that involved 'military' and 'building,' I got articles about *How to Build a Better Military*, or *How to Use Military Strategy to Build Better Habits*, or *Developing an Army Strategy for Building Partners* from the goddamn RAND Corporation.

There was a wiki on military strategies and concepts, so I figured this would be a good place to start. After clicking it, I was presented with a list of options, and I wondered which brave soul had compiled all this stuff.

None of the options really applied, as most of them were about people with guns, and while the other side would have guns, we had supers. Hell, they had supers too, especially the one that was going to give us the most hell, Jules.

Did I know he was going to be there?

No, but I had a good feeling, and so I figured we should develop a strategy around dealing with him.

And the more I thought about it, the more I realized that we were not going to be able to do shit.

Grace's powers wouldn't work; Stella's powers wouldn't work; Dorian's powers wouldn't work, nor would Veronique's; and Michelle should probably stay here, but I didn't want her staying alone with Chloe, so she'd probably end up coming, and she couldn't do much either.

*That's it,* I thought as an idea came to me. I didn't want to say it out loud, because that would ruin the whole "show, don't tell" schtick popular with fiction. And it wasn't a great idea, but it was an idea, and sometimes the best idea is the only idea that's not going to get you killed.

With a strategy in place, and the World Wide Web available at my fingertips, I did what Kanye West's kids must do every day: I GoogleFaced myself.

Yep, I was a terrorist of the highest degree, vilified by the right-wing media, and despised by the left; hell, there had even been a fatwa issued against me, so I was hated by that side too.

What hurt the most was a subreddit dedicated to not only finding me, but posting poorly Photoshopped pictures of me with dicks in my mouth, which just goes to show you what happens when you let an entire generation be raised by South Park.

It was disappointing, and checking my books on Amazon I saw that I'd been hit with a good number of one-star reviews. So the trolls were out in force, the pundits, hell, even the White House had issued a statement condemning the attack.

What can I say? Whenever there's something tragic, everyone who's anyone has to condemn it.

Why the hell does everyone have to condemn it, we all know it's bad, why do we need to make our official positions known? I was close to responding to one of the bottom dwellers that had posted in my subReddit, when I thought otherwise: Even if the entire world is trolling you, never feed the trolls.

"The only thing you can do is get the third book out," I told myself, and with that, I went to the living room to find everyone gathered around the television.

"Michelle, I need your power."

"Okay," she said as she lifted her hand into the air, not taking her eyes off the TV.

I didn't know if there would ever be a day when I would have to limit the amount of television the CBGs watched, but I was seeing firsthand just how much time it took out of their lives. They had their shows now, which, when we weren't kicking ass or assaulting secret government facilities, they made sure to watch.

On the other hand, it kept them from distracting me, so I could do important things like work, which I was supposed to be doing right now.

Only thing was, the show they were watching had already caught my attention. In the show, they were converting a Brooklyn warehouse into a mixed usage space. It made me miss the East Coast, and all the times I've been to New York. Hell, it was only a ninety-minute train ride from New Haven to Grand Central Station, and maybe after the drama died down, Dorian and I could teleport there and do the old Times Square thing.

Oh, to be a tourist again.

"Are you going to touch my hand or not, Gideon?" Michelle asked.

"Sorry, I should probably get to work."

Edit, edit, edit, edit, edit, edit, edit, edit, edit, edit, edit, edit, edit, edit, edit, edit.

Edit, edit, edit, edit, edit, edit, edit, edit, edit, edit, edit, edit, edit, edit, edit, edit.

Edit, edit, edit, edit, edit, edit, edit, edit, edit, edit, edit, edit, edit, edit, edit, edit.

Edit, edit, edit, edit, edit, edit, edit, edit, edit, edit, edit, edit, edit, edit, edit, edit.

It took me a few hours of heightened concentration to turn my word vomit into an appetizing word salad. It was three in the morning by the time I finished. I got the cover ready, something that I had created on the fly and felt had a certain vibe to it. The cover was black, and it had a heart pattern that was repeated several times, something meant to provoke mystery.

I uploaded the cover, and then went back to the blurb.

*Damn the blurb!*

Even with Michelle's caffeine-laced power searing through my veins, I still didn't have the willpower to work on the blurb.

"Come on, come on, come on," I whispered as I added the other information I needed to the EBAYmazon upload page. This included the title *Mutants in the Making 3,* the search keywords, copyright shit, the basic categories.

Everything else was set, but the blurb was like a haunted void before me, inviting me in with the knowledge that I might lose myself in its construction for hours, days if I'm not careful.

*You must fight the blurb!*

All the advice I'd read about blurbs came to me, from leading with a hook or a question aimed at the reader, to ending with somewhat of a cliffhanger.

*Dammit, Gideon, defy convention!*

But convention is convention because it is convincing, and while I wanted to maintain some artistic freedom, I also wanted the book to be read by as many people as possible. I wanted to convince them that they couldn't live without it.

*Think of the children!*

"I am thinking of the children," I told the voice in my head. "Ingrid, Fiona, Michelle: this one is for you."

After a deep breath in, I began pouring my soul into the keyboard, my fingers practically flying off my knuckles.

It took me thirty more minutes, but I ended up with something that I thought perfectly described how I felt at that moment in time. I read it again, making sure it was perfect:

*Some say my story is fake.*

*Others say I am a terrorist.*

*Neither of these things are true.*

*I was just a normal guy until the night that the psychic shifter showed up at my doorstep. A sci-fi writer, but a normal guy nonetheless. The* Mutants in the Making *series is a true account of what has happened to me since Grace showed up, since I took it upon myself to take on the Federal Corporate Government, since I broke bad and became what I am now.*

*A changed man, a man on a mission to expose a terrible conspiracy, a boiled down Generation Z muckraker hellbent on bringing the truth to the public.*

*Some say my story is fake.*

*Others say I am a terrorist.*

*I wish it were that simple.*

# Chapter Twenty-Seven: Pillow Talk

My book on its way to the EBAYmazon store, I stumbled into the hallway, nerves a-firing due to Michelle's speed powers. I wished that I had the ability to adjust the powers that I had absorbed, but I didn't, and it was clear that the overcharge that had affected Michelle when I first met her also affected me.

My fuck was I hungry.

Late-night munchies on the brain, I pilfered through the cabinets in the kitchen, putting everything on the island that I would like to eat. By the time I'd finished raiding the place, there were granola bars, cereal, chips and a stash of candy that I found.

"Hi, Gideon," said Michelle, who now stood next to me in an oversized shirt that read UC DAVIS AGGIES.

*How many teams in America are named Aggies?* I thought as the super teen went for the candy.

"Feeling hungry?" she asked, bouncing from heel to heel. Her hair was down now, and the pink streaks down the side caught my attention. I wondered what kind of permission she had to get to first bleach a swath of her hair, and then dye that portion pink.

"Starved," I told her. I went for the granola bars, and ate two of them quickly. "Everything going okay with you? Shouldn't you be asleep?"

"I can't sleep very well, you know that," she said as she stuffed some chips into her mouth.

"You should at least be resting, because tomorrow, hell, *today*, is a pretty important day for us."

"I can't wait to see Fee and Ingrid."

"We don't have them yet," I reminded her, "and we will need to be very careful in how we go about this. Which means we need to prepare."

"I'm sure we'll be fine, you always have a plan, right?"

I looked her over twice. No, she wasn't being sarcastic, she actually thought that I knew what was going on. But like any good upper management, I simply nodded, letting her believe the lie.

"Who is still awake?"

"Chloe was awake an hour ago, but I think she's asleep now on the couch. Stella is awake."

"Got it, it's time to switch out powers."

I moved towards the living room to find Stella yawning.

"You should really get some rest," I told her.

"Veronique should be down in a few minutes. I told her I would take this shift, and she's going to take the next four hours."

"Do you mind if I touch you?"

Stella looked from the TV to me, the blue lights zipping across her eyes.

"You know what I mean, and I'll work on a better way to ask that question, so it doesn't sound creepy."

"You do that." She patted the place next to her, indicating I should sit down. As Michelle had said, Chloe was on the other couch, asleep, her knees curled into her chest, looking cute with some of her hair in her face.

I sat next to Stella and she offered me her hand.

"It will only take a second."

As soon as our hands touched, I cast Michelle's power aside and brought Stella's into the mix. From what I could recall, I now had both of Grace's powers as well as Stella's, which was a pretty comfy place to be.

"Are you going to bed?" Stella asked.

"For sure," I said with a yawn. "I could really use some sleep; I just published the final installment of *Mutants in the Making*."

She shrugged.

"That's it?"

"I don't read books."

There was a point in my life where this would have been a combative thing for me to hear.

I would've told the person the beauty of reading, and what you can discover about yourself and about the world when you open a book. I might even have quoted Aldous Huxley and told her that, "Words can be like X-rays if you use them properly – they'll go through anything. You read, and you're pierced."

But I was in no mood to argue, and no one liked a guy who continually quoted from books to defend his arguments. Now that Michelle's ability was out of my system, exhaustion had seeped in. Hell, I was afraid I wouldn't even make it to a bed, so rather than turn up the *Reading Rainbow* act, I told Stella goodnight.

I walked back to the kitchen and also told Michelle goodnight. The young super now sat on the island, amidst the food, gorging herself. She looked up at me, embarrassment spreading across her face.

"It's fine," I told her.

"Goodnight!"

I took to the hallway, and from there up the stairs to the second floor. I didn't know where everyone was sleeping, so I figured I would just find an available space.

And that's when I felt a tug at the center of my chest. I stopped, knowing all too well that that feeling was Veronique using her ability long distance.

"We are in here," she told me.

I turned to see her standing at the end of the hallway in a silk robe. The front of the robe was partially open, and no, I couldn't see her perky nipples, but I did see more skin than she usually showed.

"I have to go watch Chloe now, so come in here and sleep with Dorian."

"You got it," I said.

She stepped aside and let me pass into the dark room. I practically fell into the warm space she had left on the bed. Dorian was curled up in a little ball, wearing a black nighty and a pair of black boy shorts. She reacted as soon as I got into the bed.

"I was wondering when you'd join me," Dorian said softly. "Veronique is a good cuddler, but not as good as you."

"I highly doubt that you and Veronique were cuddling."

"We were waiting for you."

Normally, a statement like this would've blown the front of my pants off, but I was exhausted; hell, the fact that I was still wearing my jeans showed just how tired I was. I briefly recalled the time that we had had back in the hotel in Austin, Veronique and I going at it while Dorian watched. We would need to do that again.

But real life kept getting in the way.

"What are you thinking about?" Dorian came into my arms, and kissed me on the cheek.

"You wouldn't want to know. More importantly, how are you?"

"Better."

"You never told me what happened back in Sacramento," I said, recalling the conversation we'd completely glossed over. "I was really afraid that you were dead, you know, or that you had somehow turned to their side."

The darkness surrounding us had made me feel vulnerable. It wasn't possible, but I wished there were a way for us to get closer, so I could just bury myself in her skin, hide myself away from the world.

"I wish there were something I could tell you. I was out for most of it, and that thing that they had me in prevented me from using my powers."

"I was wondering what that sarcophagus was for. Makes sense, but I wonder how it prevents you from using your abilities."

"I really don't know. After the fight, Mother just knocked me out and I woke up in there. That's that. I wasn't interrogated or anything. I don't know what they were planning to do with me."

"I should check your drive tomorrow, just to be sure nothing has changed."

"Good, please do that." She smiled softly. "Are you ready to sleep?"

"Is that an invitation to do something else?"

"That could be fun…"

"No, let's just sleep," I finally told her. "Tomorrow's going to be one hell of a day and we need rest."

# Chapter Twenty-Eight: In Which the CBGs and One CBB Enjoy a Nice Breakfast

"If a man had stolen a pound in his youth and had used that pound to amass a huge fortune how much was he obliged to give back, the pound he has stolen only, or the pound together with the compound interest accruing upon it, or all of his fortune?"

The quote from James Joyce's *A Portrait of the Artist as a Young Man* would have sent my middle school grammar teacher on a rant the likes of which the Nutmeg State hadn't heard before. Regardless, it fit a future scenario I would have to deal with.

After all was stolen, exploited, destroyed, and/or killed, and I was able to somehow scrape my way out of all this to come out on top, what burden would society place on me?

What burden would I place on myself? How could I ever repent for some of the things I'd done?

I suppose there were more interesting things to be thinking about at nine in the morning. As I waited for another pot of coffee to brew, my head buried in my phone as I looked at new stories I'd find about 'America's Sci-Fi Terrorist' on GoogleFace, but that's where my mind had settled, taken root, and started to sprout.

There was an article in the Washington Post about me publishing the latest installment of my manuscript, and a more conservative op-ed piece about how pricing my books at ninety-nine cents had proven I was guilty of terrorism.

I found this last one pretty funny, especially because the guy who had written it was a famous TV pundit who liked to write "nonfiction" novels that re-envisioned slavery's role in the Civil War.

Politics aside, the man had never been an independent writer, so he wouldn't know what it's like to upload a Word doc that later becomes a book in someone's hand, or to see your sales on a daily basis, hell, an hourly basis, or deal with all the extra crap that us indies had to deal with.

I could definitely see the benefits of having a real publisher, from the legal aspect to the advances. I mean, if I ever wanted to set up a book tour, I would have to actually book it on my own, and if I wanted to get in an actual bookstore, I would have to go through a lengthy process of setting up my books to be printed on demand.

This was one reason why I so readily jumped at EBAYmazon's offer. They were sort of a hybrid publisher, and considering they owned the industry and all the places that books were sold, they were pretty much the only publisher that still mattered.

I read a few more articles, watched the TwitchTubeRed video of my mom's interview, finished another cup of coffee, hated my situation and then accepted it for what it was. The CBGs and Co. were hungry, and Michelle and I had pretty much eaten us out of house and home last night.

Well, that was mostly Michelle, but I had contributed.

Dorian entered the kitchen, in a shirt that showed off her stomach and a pair of tight jean shorts. As I normally did when I saw someone, I did a compulsory scan of their entire body, from the black shoes she had borrowed from the owner of the house, to her tatted arms, to a little locket she wore around her neck and the red bandana she'd tied on her head.

"We need to find a good breakfast restaurant," I told her, "and all of us are going to stuff our faces until we can no longer eat."

"I don't know if that sounds as appealing as you may think," she said as she approached me.

"Well, you know what I mean. We're going to eat a lot. I'm looking forward to it. And I'm sure Michelle, Grace and Stella are also looking forward to it. I think we should bring Chloe too, I did say everyone should go, and if she does anything you and her can just zip out of there and Grace can fuck with everyone's brains."

She pulled at the hairs on my arm for a moment. "Can I pick the place?"

I eyed her skeptically. I had no doubt that she could use my phone and find a place to eat, but would it be a good place?

"I know how to read reviews, Gideon, and I know how to understand and interpret star ratings," she said smugly.

"Right. I'll make the announcement."

I stepped into the living room area to find Veronique, Stella, Michelle and Chloe watching television. Grace was still in bed, but she had already sent me a few mental messages, so I knew she was up.

"Attention all superpowered people."

"That's us!" said Michelle.

"We're going out for breakfast."

"Chinese food!"

"No, Michelle, that's not considered breakfast food in this part of the world. Back to what I was saying. We're going to some type of diner, so change and put on whatever you want to wear. I'm talking pancakes on top of pancakes, sausage, gravy, biscuits, fruit plates if that's your thing. That kind of diner. Eggs any which way you can have them, scrambled, boiled, poached, over easy, you name it. Everyone's coming, Chloe too."

Stella raised an eyebrow at me. Her hair had been braided again, and she looked clean, refreshed. "Are you sure this is a good idea?"

"I'm sitting right here, you know," said Chloe, a hint of annoyance in her voice.

"We'll handle Chloe," Dorian said, as she came around and stopped on my right. "I will sit next to her, and if anything happens, you and I will disappear. And don't make me miss breakfast, I will be very unhappy if I miss breakfast."

I felt a small wave of tension move between the two.

Focusing on it, I noticed that I could hear soft chatter in Chloe's head, calculating how she should react. Chloe was surprised that Dorian had turned so bitchy, as she had always assumed that Veronique and Stella were the worst.

What I didn't notice by scanning the top of her mind was any thought about our operation, or if she wanted to stay or go, or anything of that nature. She was, however, slightly interested in going out in public, being normal for once, because as a member of AEFL, she was never allowed a modicum of normality.

*I'm getting better at this,* I thought, as I watched Michelle zip away. There was really no watching Michelle zip away, she was simply there and then she was gone, but I got the hint and felt the slight breeze as she passed.

*Yes you are, Writer Gideon,* thought Grace from upstairs. *I think this'll be a good time for us to get closer as a group, and have a nice, delicious meal. I want French toast this time. I saw a TV show last night about French toast. You never told me about French toast, and I want some with cinnamon and possibly some powdered sugar on top and maple syrup. But not imitation maple syrup. I want some real maple syrup. It's healthier and doesn't have high fructose corn syrup.*

I started to laugh, and everyone in the room looked at me like I was crazy.

"Psychics," I said pointing at my head. "There's a lot going on up here."

"Is your uncle a shapeshifter like Grace?" Michelle asked.

We were in the waiting area of a popular diner in Davis. Even with our psychic abilities – Grace's and mine – we weren't able to get a seat because of the size of our party. This was something we would need to work out in the future, especially if Chloe stayed with us and we rescued the Super Teens.

We had our core members: Grace, Veronique, Dorian, and the Cherry Blossom Boy, a.k.a. me. We had our newest member, Stella, although I didn't know if she was as into the mission as the others. We had our possible future member, Chloe, and currently we were with one super teen, Michelle, with two more on the way, Ingrid and Fiona, who were basically members and I really needed to stop classifying them as anything but.

Nine people, nine mouths to feed, and nine bodies to transport wherever we went next. I had an idea of how we could handle this, but it was something we could explore later. What we really needed was a base, a meeting place that we would always be able to travel to.

"My uncle?" I asked Michelle, following her finger to the TV screen on the wall.

Any thoughts I had of changing the structure of our organization were shattered when I saw my crossdressing uncle on one of the morning talk shows, explaining how I was a good boy, but he always thought that I was a little troubled.

"He's not a shifter," I told Michelle, who was looking up at me with astonished eyes as usual. For some reason, I got the feeling that the young super looked up to me, which was not great, considering the fact that I was just about the worst role model a teen could have.

We had to wait outside, but it was California, and the weather was pretty decent. A drought was probably coming, but it was California, and droughts always came. An earthquake was probably coming too, but we would be gone long before that struck, and besides, if this was the last place a person saw before getting buried in a pile of concrete, well, I could think of worse places.

We stood outside the diner, looking in through the glass where Michelle had caught my uncle on the mounted TV. I could also see my partial reflection, an older man with bushy white eyebrows and a sick handlebar mustache. The mustache wasn't as handlebar-y as I'd hoped it would be, but it was still pretty badass.

Since I was going for an older man disguise, Grace went for an older woman, a GILF if I ever saw one.

She wore a tight tracksuit, which accented her grandmotherly curves, clearly showing off that this granny had been going to Pilates classes every day for the last twenty years.

Anyone looking, and we were definitely getting a few second glances, saw a pair of grandparents and their granddaughters and possibly one of their granddaughter's friends, Dorian, or maybe Chloe was the friend. Or maybe Chloe and Dorian were the sisters, Veronique was the friend, and Michelle was a grandkid from a different marriage.

It didn't matter, and if anyone asked, I would set the record straight.

What kind of old man would I be? That thought was on my mind as I looked at my reflection, secretly wanting to pat myself on the back for taking the form and keeping it.

I wouldn't be the type of old man that would yell at you to get off his lawn; nor would I be the type of old man sitting on the front porch waiting for the rapture, a rifle across my lap; I also wouldn't be the old man at Burning Man with armpit dreadlocks trying to hook up with twenty-somethings hoping to find themselves; I wouldn't be the old guy at the country club in Massachusetts golfing daily.

The rate I was going, I probably wouldn't make it to old age. It would take a goddamn miracle for me to get out of all this shit, but I wasn't so focused on the future anymore, and the couple thousand dollars I had in a 401(K) wouldn't be worth that much in thirty years anyway, especially if I died in ten, and even if I lived that long, inflation was going to do some nasty things to the little nest egg I'd already saved.

"Wait, if he's not a shifter, why is he a woman?" asked Michelle. "Does he just like dressing like women? Is that it?"

"That's right," I told her. "There are tons of terms and definitions about gender choices that you can learn later. My uncle's situation is so complicated: he doesn't want to be a woman, but he likes the way women's clothing feels. He also likes makeup. But he's not gay. He's actually pretty straight, sorry, 'pretty straight' doesn't really mean anything these days."

"What does he do for a living?"

"He lives in Vermont, and he does whatever people in Vermont do for a living, which is questionable at best, and usually revolves around selling maple syrup, marijuana, cheese and apples."

A couple looked over at me as I said all this, nodding, appreciating that a grandfatherly fellow was explaining intricate information about the Vermont economy to his granddaughter.

If you figured that Veronique was on high alert, you would be right. Not only did she have one hand aimed in Chloe's general direction, but she was also looking for anyone and anything out of place. Before we left the house, she'd gone to the garage and filled her pockets with metal, so she was technically doing a little open carry too.

I watched my uncle talk for a little bit longer, remembering that I had dedicated *How Heavy This Axe?* to him. He never read it, not many did, but maybe after the audiobook came out, I would make sure that Jake sent him a copy.

For a guy with a smartphone, I hadn't really been paying attention to my emails. Real life was much more interesting than whatever digital existence I had cobbled together. I was sure my inbox was filled with letters from my fans, people threatening to sue me, letters from Jake, and information about my recently released book.

I hadn't even checked the sales. That was what this had come to, to the point that I wasn't even checking my sales.

Whereas before, two days after releasing a book I would have been on EBAYmazon every hour, tracking my sales and my page reads.

And it wasn't that I didn't care, it was just that I was tired of it.

I was tired of having part of my day-to-day revolve around checking if people actually cared what I had to say. Because I knew that people cared now, and whether they read it to find discrepancies, or to know more about who they assumed was a terrorist, or they actually believed what I had written – my words had infiltrated the masses.

And this was something I hadn't processed yet: as long as I remained persona non grata, my story would reach more and more readers. Many of them will think I was full of shit, or hate on my writing, or solidify their assumption that I was indeed a terrorist.

But there would be some who thought I was telling the truth, that it couldn't have been me, and if it had been me, there must've been a reason.

"Edward, party of six," a pretty waitress with a lip ring called out.

I waved, and she held the door for us while we filed in, one at a time.

We were led to a booth that had another table added to it so that it could fit more people.

"Coffee," Veronique said, as she took her seat.

"I always order you coffee," I reminded her.

"You're a good grandpa, Edward," she said, stiffly, "but I wish you would give us more money."

"You want money? I can get money." It was about this time that I noticed the waiter was still listening to us. Rather than try to explain myself, I just told him to get everyone coffee except Michelle, who would have a glass of orange juice.

"I'm just playing with you," Veronique said. "I wonder what it would be like to be a granddaughter."

The metal vampire sat next to me, and sitting next to her was Chloe. Across from Chloe was Stella, then Dorian, Michelle, and across from me was Grace.

"I bet it would be nice to be a granddaughter," Grace said as she looked over the menu. She found her French toast, pointed a finger on it, and looked up at the waiter, her eyes glowing white.

"No powers in public," I coughed, and she quickly apologized and just kept her finger on the French toast picture.

"We would have to have a mother to have a grandmother, and I don't think Mother is really our mother. I really didn't like her. I only met her a few times. But she seems angry. Father was better."

Dorian laughed at Michelle's statement. "It would be nice to have grandparents. From what I've seen in movies, they're usually pretty nice, plus they give you things."

"From what I've heard, when your parents won't give you something sometimes your grandparents will," Chloe added. "I mean, that's like the best way to do it, right? Ask your parents, and if they say no, then move to the grandparents."

In the end, Grace went with her French toast; I chose the eggs benedict with a short stack of banana chocolate pancakes; Veronique chose two cups of coffee; Dorian and Michelle split the Mondo breakfast platter, which contained just about everything that the place made in some shape or fashion; Stella got oatmeal and a caramel crêpe; and Chloe got the sausage and biscuits as well as a short stack of ginger pancakes.

"Do you guys always eat breakfast like this?" Chloe asked.

"Ummmm, it really depends on where we are," Michelle answered. "We didn't have breakfast like this when we were in Colorado. We ate Chinese food instead. I want to go to China one day. Food there seems very good."

"We've had some pretty good breakfasts," said Grace, "but mostly those have been the ones that Gideon cooked."

"When you were passed out in Austin we went to a pretty good breakfast restaurant," Veronique told Dorian.

"I wish you had brought me something."

Veronique and Dorian shared a laugh, Dorian's nice and light, Veronique's slightly stilted.

"I love it when we eat pizza," said Grace. "We've eaten all types of pizza, and if you don't eat the crust, then you will save some of the carbs."

"There's healthy pizza too," said Michelle. "We had one of those one time. Do you remember that, Gideon?"

"Grandfather," I reminded her.

"Can I just call you Grandpa?"

"That works for me."

"We should really have something fancy one day, I don't know what it should be, but something interesting," said Veronique.

"Yeah, but you don't even eat food," Stella reminded her.

"But I want to eat with you all somewhere where there are tall buildings. We saw the property brothers doing a special where they renovated a house in northern Chicago. It looked like a very interesting city."

"A trip to Chicago would be awesome," Dorian added. "The windy city."

"There are things we have to do first," Stella said, bringing us all back to earth.

"You aren't wrong, Stella, but it's nice to dream about a simpler future," I told her as I sawed at my English muffin.

"I don't know how that's going to play out for us, but I sure hope it's nice and easy."

"And we really need a place we can call our own," Grace added.

"I was just thinking that outside, well, sort of."

"I know you were," she told me, and yet again I realize that it was hard to distinguish her thoughts from mine.

"It'll happen one day," said Dorian. "I don't know when that day is, but I'm pretty sure it will happen. I'm confident we will have a base."

"You guys want to get a house somewhere?" Chloe asked.

"That's right," said Stella, surprising all of us. "Just like those homes we see them build on the TV shows. We want to do something like that. I don't know what it would be like yet, but it would have a room for everyone."

# Chapter Twenty-Nine: Take Me Shopping and I'm Yours

*And You Will Know Us by the Trail of the Dead* is probably one of my favorite band names.

Did I ever think it would describe my life? Of course not, even serial killers aren't born serial killers, well, maybe they are, but I'm not up on the psychology of murder, and I don't plan to write a thriller any time soon.

My point? There weren't any other band names I could think of off the top of my head that would describe our evening plans, which was something I considered as Dorian, Grace and I tasked ourselves with finding some wheels in our Davis neighborhood.

The vehicle needed to be rather large, capable of fitting nine people. We also needed shrapnel supplies, armor, and a paintbrush for the punk rock teleporter.

The vehicle was easy. It was California, and no matter how high the gas prices were, people liked to drive, and people further away from the bigger cities liked to drive bigger vehicles. I didn't quite get the appeal of this, considering my birthplace and the proximity of our cities in New England, but aside from the carbon footprint, I had no complaints.

They were definitely comfier.

It literally took us, and by "us" I mean Grace and me, a few minutes to find a nice vehicle near the diner. The owner handed over the keys, finally paying off that "debt" that she had had for so long, and I gave her a little cash, but not that much, because I liked to keep some on me just in case.

We returned to the restaurant to collect the others. Michelle actually sat up front this time, Grace behind her next to Dorian and Stella. In the backseat of the large suburban, Chloe sat next to Veronique, who was always within arm's reach of our sort-of hostage.

"Are we going shopping again?" Michelle asked.

"Yeah, that's right," I told her. I put the vehicle in drive and started heading out to the nearest shopping area, GoogleFace assisting me with prompts on the center console.

"Let me get this straight," Chloe said. "You guys pretty much just travel around stealing money, borrowing people's homes and switching out cars. This is how you live until something happens with AEFL, or MercSecure, and then you are forced to start up again. Correct?"

"It's not incorrect," I told her, making eye contact with Veronique. As usual, she was staring at me through the rearview mirror, her dark little eyes piercing and somewhat sexy. I didn't know when they'd become sexy, I would've never described her eyes as one of her sexy features, but like anyone you get to know, the more you get to know them, the more interesting and appealing certain aspects of their features become.

"I also have to feed," Veronique said.

"But I've figured out a new way for us to do that," I said.

"It's definitely going to be easier on my teleporting," said Dorian.

"That's right," I told her. "As long as we have a volunteer."

"I want to volunteer."

I looked from the rearview mirror to the front passenger seat. Michelle had a big smile on her face, and was nodding in an encouraging way, her ponytail beating against her upper back. She sat on the edge of the seat, which seemed unnatural in a vehicle, especially one with padded heated cooling massaging leather seats like the one we were currently in.

"I don't know if you want to volunteer for that," I told the young super. "It's definitely not so pleasant."

"Have you thought about showing Veronique what it feels like to drain someone's power?" Chloe asked me.

"Not fully. But if you're game, Veronique, I think that would be interesting."

"We'll see," came Veronique's reply.

"It probably won't work," said Dorian. "Just like how last night…"

I glanced at Dorian in the rearview mirror, recalling how I'd been able to have sex with her last night in Malibu without any issues.

"What happened last night?" Michelle asked.

"Yeah, what happened?" Grace asked, her eyes white as she looked up at me.

"When we were getting the pizza, Gideon took some of my power and we tried to charge each other's toes, and it didn't work."

I cleared my throat. "Yep, what Dorian said."

The young super snorted, and this was followed by laughter from Veronique and Grace. Chloe didn't know what to make of Dorian's last sentence. Stella simply shrugged it off.

"Why were you guys charging each other's toes?"

"For science!"

"That is the stupidest reason I've ever heard, Gideon," said Michelle. "But, if you say so, well, I believe you."

"The point I'm trying to make is that it may not work for Gideon to really use Veronique's power against her," Dorian said. "It's something we should try, but it may not work. Just like Grace's power. I don't think Gideon could use Grace's power against her, do any of you?"

"I don't know," said Chloe. "I don't know enough about this ability that Gideon has to make a judgment call on it. But I do know that Grace's power is... something else entirely."

"I seriously doubt it," Grace said as we pulled off the main road.

Who doesn't like shopping for improvised explosive devices?

And where better to get them than the Home Depot, which was a couple miles away from the breakfast joint. Even though I'd now seen a good portion of the lower and western half of America, I was still getting used to the fact that everything was far away and required a good amount of driving.

*You have that look on your face, Writer Gideon,* Grace thought to me as we pulled into the parking lot.

*What look?*

*The 'your thoughts are running wild' look.*

*Sorry, I'll think about more important things.*

"Now if you don't mind," I said aloud, "it's morphing time."

I snapped my fingers – dramatic, I know – and my face turned back into my old man disguise. "Now see here, grandchildren, go into the Home Depot and get a ton of shit we can use to fight private security operatives and other supers. Don't forget your paintbrush, Dorian, although Michael's, next door, might be better for that."

Maybe it was breakfast, but I was feeling *cray*.

"Okay, Grandpa Gideon!" Michelle cried out.

"You got it, Gramps," Dorian said in a cute voice.

"Just call me Papi, young lady."

"Okay, Papi."

"Well, now I don't like the sound of that one bit."

"What about Grampy?"

"Don't like it, but it'll work."

I glanced in the rearview mirror to see Dorian, Veronique, Chloe, and Stella getting out of the vehicle. If you thought that having a nice breakfast would somehow relax Veronique and Stella's guard around Chloe, you'd be wrong.

If anything, they were going even harder now, one on either side of the sound manipulator. And she was pretty cool about it too, not acting like a hostage or anything, which was what she technically was.

I hoped she figured out what she wanted to do soon, though; otherwise, we would have to decide, and I really didn't want that decision being for Grace to mindwipe her and then Dorian teleporting her to the Midwest or some shit.

We had some cash, but I figured Jedi mind tricks would be the easier way to go, especially with the fact that Grace and I could double up.

Veronique and Dorian knew what to get, so they went one way, while Stella, Grace, Michelle, Chloe and I went the other.

Keeping the sales associate who first approached us engaged was easy, considering Grace had been watching so many home improvement shows, and she really was interested in customizing a place for the CBGs.

Hell, I loved the idea, I just didn't know how feasible it was.

First of all, where would we get property that we could pay cash for? And sure, we could brain sweep someone, and have them leave and take their home and use it as ours, but eventually that would come back to haunt us in some way.

No, we would need a lot of documents to make this work, from IDs, to land deeds, to what-the-hell-ever. Not gonna lie, I'd never bought a house before, nor had I purchased property. I knew fuck all about the process; it would probably end up with me screwing things up somehow.

Then again, we could just find an abandoned home and set up there, kind of go for those squatter's rights.

Probably wouldn't work though.

"I like this toilet," Grace told me. She stood in front of a Japanese wonder that played music, spritzed your bunghole, had built-in air freshener, and speaking of spritzing one's bunghole, it had different settings for buttholes and vajajays.

"It's not bad, out of our price range though, honey," I said as she sat down on it, showing me and the associate waiting on us what it would be like to use it.

"Doesn't it just look right under me?"

The associate laughed, Grace's GILF act having an effect on the young man.

"So, it cleans you?" asked Stella, a curious look spreading across her face. She didn't normally break form, but when she did, it was usually for a clarifying question.

"Yes it does, and moving right along, follow me, grandchildren, to the light fixtures."

"Wow, they're all your grandchildren?" the sales associate asked me. He was a thin dude, with an Adam's apple that made it look like he had swallowed a dinosaur egg.

"Yes, they are, but they have different mothers. Fathers too. And believe you me, they are trouble, especially the one with her hair braided."

"Hey," Stella called up to me.

"Yeah, and the youngest one, well, she's a little bit jumpy as you can tell, but not too bad. I usually give her tasks to do outside, just so she can burn off that youthful energy. Boy, do I miss being young."

"You don't look so old to me," the sales associate said. "In fact, you look a bit familiar."

I stopped dead in my tracks.

The sales associate continued like all the color hadn't just drained from my face. "Yeah, do you go to the Methodist Church? I think I've seen you there."

"Ha! Guilty as charged! I'm a big fan of God, love the guy, especially the Methodist interpretation."

"Yeah, God is a great guy."

"Who's God again?" Michelle asked.

My eyes went wide, but by this point the sales associate was already distracted by Grace, who had lightly touched his arm to get his attention.

"What would you recommend for a postmodern farmhouse that has a veranda that overlooks a hill and which has a vineyard at the bottom of the hill?" asked the psychic shifter. What she had just said made no sense, but the fact that her chest was bulging out the front of her yoga-ish outfit had the man caught hook, line and sinker.

I cycled back to catch up with Michelle. "I'll explain God to you all later. Wait a minute, no I won't. You can read, right?"

"Yes, I can read, and I was just trying to be stupid. I know who God is."

"Why are you trying to be stupid?" I whispered to her. Chloe stepped past me, snickering at the conversation I was having.

"You get to be a grandpa, Grace gets to be a grandma, and I want to be a stupid grandchild. Just a little stupid though, not like completely stupid, just the type who asks tons of questions. I want to play roles too, you know. *Stupid cute*, that's probably a thing."

"Got it, let's catch up with Grandma Grace. I'm pretty sure your cousins, Dorian and Veronique, will be done getting supplies soon. We'll have some time for arts and crafts later when we make our frag pouches, and then it is training time."

"I want to be helpful this time," Michelle said, seriousness moving across her face.

"Let's just take care of this facility first. And besides, I might have a little side mission for you and the others when we do it."

"Side mission?"

"Show, don't tell," I reminded her as I caught up with Grace.

"What's that even mean?" Michelle whispered.

"Ask a writer."

"You're a writer?" the sales associate asked.

"No, no, unless you consider someone who writes their congressman on a weekly basis a writer. How about that drought, huh?"

"There hasn't been a drought this year..." he said.

"Moving along, moving along," I told him as I spotted Dorian and Veronique, their cart full of an assortment of metal goodies. "There you two are," I called over to them.

"Hi, Grandpa," said Veronique with a thin smile on her face. "We're ready to go."

# Chapter Thirty: Level Up

We weren't quite veterans of assaulting these facilities, but we had done it a few times now, enough that I'd been able to recognize firsthand what worked. Usually, things went south when enemy supers showed up, and that was one thing that was hard to prepare for.

The perennial amateur.

I knew that there was a person who could manage the CBGs better than I, who had the tactical training, the sheer wherewithal, and the patience to lead the small troop of hotties to victory in any battle.

But I was trying, and the fact that I now had some power of my own made me more formidable than I'd been before.

The first stop after the home supply store was a smaller shop that sold guns and ammunition. "Your grandparents are sustaining members of the NRA," I told my granddaughters as soon as we entered the store, "and it's time you kids get body armor. We'll get guns later."

Somehow, this statement worked. Then again, I was surrounded by pretty women, which seemed to sway the doubt of any sales associate, including the blue-eyed vet who worked at the gun shop. He kept going on and on about how the VA was a pain to deal with and how they weren't giving him the pain meds like they used too. I went along with it, cursing the FCG, telling him to hang in there, sympathizing with the poor fellow.

In the end, we knew it would be bad optics to have some guy see a couple grandparents outfitting their grandkids with body armor, so Grace did her thing, her eyes turning white, and the guy forgetting we were ever in the store by the time we'd left.

We had ballistic helmets as well, helmets that looked way cooler than the ones we'd had in the past.

Our new brain protectors looked like sleek motorcycle helmets, with an attached visor that was just about the thickest yet clearest piece of plastic I'd ever seen. Mine also had a night vision mode that was turned on by pressing a button on the side of the helmet. And sure enough, my glasses went under there as well, so I wasn't sacrificing vision.

I imagined us now, all in gunmetal gray body armor and super dark green full cut helmets with night vision capabilities. It would make a hell of a movie poster, but we were going for the visual here.

This was the Cherry Blossom Girls upgraded, actually prepared for once.

After a quick stop at WalMacy's to get black underclothing and frag pouch supplies, we headed back to the hacienda by way of teleporter. From there, we changed into our black clothing and body armor.

"What about the helmets?" asked Grace, who was now in her base form, her eyes light blue, her hair bleach blonde and pulled into a tight ponytail.

"Wear them too," said Veronique, who sat on the couch already in her full battle regalia. Even funnier was the fact that she was watching one of her home improvement shows with her visor on, Chloe sitting next to her simply in her normal clothing.

Michelle appeared at my side, a flash of black. She was also in her combat clothing, her helmet too. Last to join us were Stella and Dorian, both of whom weren't wearing their helmets yet.

"As Veronique said, we're going to do some serious training this afternoon, and we should do so with all of our gear on. I want all of us to get used to the bulk of our equipment." I placed my helmet over my head, and pulled down the supervillain-esque jawline protector.

"It's not too bad," said Stella, moving around in her vest and testing its flexibility. "But it's not as breathable as the stuff they gave us at the facility."

"I wish we could get our hands on some of that stuff. Unfortunately, we don't have our own private military supplier, so we have to go with what they have on the market. At any rate, let's make the best of this." I stepped over to Dorian, and she wrapped her hand around mine.

I noticed the two channels open up, but I didn't take any of her abilities. I would be sorting out the abilities I needed for tonight in just a few moments, no in point doing it here.

"Let's go, people," I said, as everyone approached Dorian.

The CBGs and our captive appeared in the desert.

We could've been anywhere, and there was no way for me to tell our location via landmarks. All I could see in the distance were heat waves and a few ridges a couple miles away, indicating to me that we were possibly in a valley.

It was hot, Texas hot, sweat already forming on my brow. The thought came to me that while this would be a quiet place to train, it wasn't actually that practical. There would be obstacles at the military installation, buildings, walls, not just an open space.

So with this in mind, I asked Dorian to make a brief check on the warehouse in Nevada that we'd fought at a few days ago.

I figured that AEFL and MercSecure would be done with cleanup by now, and all that would be left would be the ruins of the warehouse, which was a better environment for us to train in. Dorian flashed away, a poof of energy indicating her departure, and she appeared mere seconds later.

"No one was there," she said, and all of us gathered around her for quick travel to Nevada.

Our forms took shape on the western side of the warehouse.

I could see the impact point from our attack, the vehicle that we had filled with explosives and driven into the exterior wall. There was fire damage everywhere, debris, and shadow coverage on the southern quadrant of the warehouse.

While our attack had decimated the front right end, the back of the warehouse was pretty much intact, aside from the blackened stains on the wall, and the smell of burnt lumber.

"Try not to destroy the place too much," I said as a joke. "Also, I need to touch some of you."

Yep, that came out wrong, evident in the gawking stares from Stella and Chloe, the tilt of Michelle's head, the crooked smile on Veronique's face, Dorian's raised eyebrow, and Grace's smirk.

"You guys know what I mean."

"We're not guys," Michelle reminded me.

"Let's not make this difficult. Even though I have superpowers, I'm still the weakest link, so a lot of today's training will be dedicated to me getting my ass kicked. Luckily, and this is going to sound as strange as my last statement, I have Father's blood. So, give me your all, but try not to do something like cut my arm off, or blow a hole through my body. Let's keep it civil. Speaking of civil, did you ever notice that calls for civility are always made by the people in the position of power? Sorry, something I was thinking about recently. Where was I?"

Stella smiled. "You really don't know when to shut up, do you?"

"I thought that was part of my charm, I say what's on my mind, and leave it to others to pick up the pieces. Besides, what I just said about civility was true, really, think about it after we've trained and rescued Fiona and Ingrid. And my chattiness makes it hard for telepaths to read my mind. Isn't that right, Grace?"

"No," the psychic shifter said, her eyes flickering white.

"We can debate this later. Also my name's *Writer* Gideon, and I'm an idiot. Hey!" I yelled at Grace, once she gave me my mind back.

# Chapter Thirty-One: American Idol

They came at me full-on, Grace wielding bits of stone and debris with her telekinesis, Veronique shooting metal bars at me, Stella on defense. Michelle was also in the melee, but she hadn't struck yet. Chloe was with Dorian, the teleporter tasked with keeping an eye on our captive.

Their attacks came at me in slow motion due to the fact that I'd borrowed Michelle's power.

It was as if I could see into the future and catch a glimpse of where they were planning to strike next. There was something almost prophetic about it, something that made me feel as if I were a step ahead of time itself.

Veronique cast a series of nuts and bolts in my direction, and rather than try to dodge them, I simply stopped them midair, using her own abilities to fling them back in her direction.

A giant wave of energy cut through the concrete of the warehouse, and I pressed it into the air, suspending the concrete with Stella's vibration emissions.

I knew I couldn't hold this particular power combination long, especially since I was heating up, my heart slapping against my rib cage due to Michelle's manic power, but I held it for as long as I humanly could.

For at least five minutes, the three of them continued to pummel me, including Michelle, who kept trying to punch me in the kidney. Grace took me off my feet a number of times, my arms barely coming out in front of me to stop my fall. Veronique continued berating me with projectiles.

"It's not sustainable," I said as I raised my hands, an agreed-upon white flag. I quickly moved over to where I'd placed my various items, and went for Father's blood. The top came off the plastic test tube, and I took his healing ability over Michelle's enhanced speed.

"Anyone need healing?" I asked, out of breath, my helmet coming off. It was hot, the damn helmet, and I wasn't the only one who'd decided to take it off for now.

Veronique came forward, scratches up the sides of her arms where I'd struck her with her own nails.

A thought came to me and I went for it, knowing all too well that she'd be pissed once I stopped. My hand glowing red, I attempted to fully drain Veronique, which as it turned out wasn't as easy as I had hoped it would be.

I was on my knees moments later, my hands at my sides as she counter-drained me. She was much stronger than I, and even as I tried to heal myself while she was draining me, I could see the veins starting to bulge on my arms, my skin turning purple. "Enough," I told her. "You win…"

"You will never be as strong as a person who originally holds the power, don't forget that."

The metal vampire crouched next to me, and placed a hand on my cheek. Carnage flashed behind her eyes as she lightly slapped me a couple times, and told me to get back to my feet.

"You should try some of my powers," Chloe suggested.

I looked over at the shapely brunette, remembering the video I had seen of her exploding an inmate's head using her acoustokinectic powers.

"Let me check out your stuff again," I told her as I went for my smartphone. I had installed Ken's app on the phone, and a quick search brought me to her power listing.

### Main: Acoustokinesis

* Sound Sculpting

* Acoustic Acceleration

* Sonoluminescence

* Rhythm Manipulation

* Sonokinetic Combat

* Sound Detection

* Sonic Stimulation

* Overcharge

One of her powers that I wanted to play around with was her Sonoluminescence ability, which was a fancy way of saying that she could turn sound into light. We had seen her do this before, back at the facility in New Mexico when we first encountered the Super Teens. Remembering that encounter forced Adam's image into my head.

I wondered where the young telepath was, and hoped for his sake that he wasn't at the Sacramento facility, because if he was, we weren't going to hold back. But I could feel that out later, after I was finished 'leveling up,' as it were.

"Sure, let's give it a shot."

Chloe approached me, her arm out, her hand bent at the wrist. I touched her hand and felt the channel open up within me, her powers moving Father's out of the way.

It was hard to describe power replacement with my newfound ability, but it made sense, and I didn't question the feeling of pushing a power out, and choosing which one I wanted to take in.

I felt this strange sense of auditory understanding come to me. I had retained Chloe's powers before, but I hadn't really explored them. And now that I had them again, I wanted to see if they were worthy of coming with me tonight.

After all, I had to make three power choices, three important choices for the success of our mission.

"Because I'm not able to take all of a person's powers, I'm just going to try to do a few of the things that you're capable of based on the list of your abilities that I have on my phone." I showed Chloe my smartphone, as if it contained the secrets of life.

"Let's see what you can do."

An arc of light was cutting through a hole in the ceiling, into the warehouse. Focusing on it, I was able to move the light, vibrate it, and with a little more focus, I was able to form it into a blade.

Bringing my hand back, I shot the blade into one of the standing walls, where it burnt a baseball-sized hole as it passed through the surface. I took a deep breath in, surprised I was able to do something so utterly badass.

"Can you sing?" asked Chloe. "Part of my ability allows me to use sound waves to stimulate someone's emotion. Since I don't know very many songs, I have trained myself over the years to tap into the frequencies. But you probably know a lot of songs. Of course, I can now use targeted melodies directed at a single listener, a tune that others can't hear. But I don't expect you to be able to do this."

"I know a few tunes, a couple raps too."

I almost started up Kendrick Lamar's "Bitch Don't Kill My Vibe," but went instead with an emotional hit from my childhood, a real tearjerker.

By the time I had finished the famous tearjerker by Bright Eyes, all the CBGs aside from Veronique were tearing up; hell, I had even got to Chloe, who was sniffling, trying to act tough like the song wasn't just about the saddest damn thing she'd ever heard.

"This is so awesome!"

I thought of another song, a song that would make them all want me.

I didn't have the greatest singing voice; no, my voice was little too baritone for that, and I was never really confident in my singing ability. But with Chloe's power, I was like the love child of Beyoncé, Robert Plant and Ed Sheeran's ginger ass. Shit, I was good enough that they could name a color after me, and because I experienced high levels of stage fright, I particularly liked the ability to sway people through pop songs, "SexyBack" by Justin Timberlake being especially powerful.

"Please keep singing," Dorian purred, her hand pressing into her lady parts.

I looked to Veronique to see her unclipping her bulletproof vest; Grace was having trouble holding her form, her face going from thin brunette with glasses to Scandinavian beauty on fleek; Stella just had one eyebrow raised at as she licked her lips; Michelle was looking at me in a way that I hoped a thirteen-year-old would never look at me again; and Chloe was gyrating her hips, a single finger in her mouth as she stared me down.

"It works!"

"You don't want to sing some more for us, sweetie?" Grace asked, the middle point of her face pressing together as she tried to hold her form.

"Definitely not that song, although I will put that in my repertoire and we will see about it later. Okay, I want to try some new tunes, something that would make you scared. Know what's a scary song?"

The thing was, I didn't really listen to scary music, which I'd classify as metal or any other type of hardcore industrial double bass pedal-driven rock. What would be a scary song?

Maybe I could evoke fear through something like a monsterish growl…

"That's not working," Michelle informed me, as I clawed at the air and made a horrific sound with my throat.

"Yeah, I can see that. Okay, I want to try to force you all to fear me, that's the sound I'm going for. I mean, maybe I should just stick to sexy and sad, because that will stop most people, but fear could also be helpful. I'll have to play around with it. At least sad is easy, and I could use it against MercSecure soldiers. I could use sexy too, but I'd like not to see some *Brokeback Mountain* shit spontaneously take shape."

They exchanged glances, unfamiliar with my reference. I decided to keep it that way.

"Let's see what else I can do. Come at me, ladies."

Veronique pointed from Stella to Chloe, indicating that Stella was on guard duty.

Stella shrugged and lifted her chin as she walked over to Chloe, letting Dorian take her place. We moved back to the area of engagement, which was loosely defined as the quadrant of the warehouse that hadn't yet been completely destroyed.

As it stood, I had some of Chloe, Veronique, and Stella's powers.

Part of me knew that they had been going easy on me, that I hadn't actually been holding my own against them. But this was all part of the training.

Regardless, I was a secret weapon.

Or at least I used to be. There would be video evidence of me using powers at the Sacramento facility. My cover was blown, which meant I needed to up my game.

Grace was the first to attack, going with the old Nightmare Sight trick.

I was suddenly standing in a field of bodies, fires burning around me, my arm broken, a storm whirling above me, a gun pointed at me, pressed into the back of my skull.

Lying before me was Dorian, her head separated from her body and her face staring out at me; Grace, her mouth agape and her arms and legs missing, slashes across her face; Veronique, struggling to stand, coughing up blood and eventually falling over; Michelle, impaled by a sharp pole, her head to the side, tears of blood streaming down her face;

Stella, lying before Michelle, also impaled, her hands still trembling.

I gasped, and the image went away.

A sharp spear of metal floated before me, an inch away from the center of my forehead. Gasping for breath, and still not able to fully comprehend what I had just seen, I took a step back, only for Dorian to appear behind me, her hand wrapping around my neck from behind.

"All it would take is one simple charge," she said, even as two channels opened up, allowing me to select which of her powers I wanted to take.

She held her hand there for a moment, giving me enough time to notice that there were soundwaves vibrating between us, soundwaves that, with my eyes closed, I could see.

Soundwaves I could use.

I blew Dorian back into the wall, where she teleported away before she could collide with the steel frame.

I sent a wave of vector force hurtling in Grace's direction.

Pressing off from the ground, I hovered in the air where I blocked an incoming steel beam from Veronique. Her power was much stronger than mine, and as I held my hand out before me, the metal started to wrap around, forming a horseshoe-shape with pointed ends, both ends aimed at my throat.

Feeling the vibrations again, I zipped back to the ground and pressed them upwards, sending the sharp horseshoe into the ceiling, where it got lodged before falling to the ground. I didn't see her, but I definitely felt Michelle stop behind me and bring her heel against the back of my knee.

She was around me a second later, her fists coming back ready to strike me.

Just like Veronique had done, the young super stopped an inch away from my face, a little smirk cutting across her cheeks. She disappeared in a flicker accented by the pink stripe in her black hair.

Back to my feet, I brought my hands together and told them to try again. "I know that I'm not going to become an expert in one long afternoon, but by the end of this, I hope I'll be more helpful than I used to be."

Grace's eyes blazed white, and the nightmare returned.

It wasn't fair, she was exploiting my weakness, but it was good for me to experience it, to fight through it. Rather than cry out in shock this time, or feel like curling up in a ball and disappeared from the world, I began humming a song I hadn't heard for years.

Leonard Cohen's "Hallelujah" could be sung multiple ways, but the way I hummed it was sad, and as the song played out, and I watched the CBGs die before me on the twisted battlefield dreamscape that Grace had created, her power began to waver, until it was gone again, and I was in control.

# Chapter Thirty-Two: Life's a Gas

We had to get another vehicle for our scheme, and it only made sense to do so on our way to get dinner for everyone.

This task would be left to Dorian and me, while the others prepped at our borrowed home. Later, she would be responsible for teleporting everyone, which meant that I would also need to adjust her Tele-Sphere Radius.

Since I didn't want the food to have a chance to get cold, we took care of the vehicle first.

My abilities were as follows: telepathy, shifter, metal vampire.

I'd chosen these powers for this leg of our mission due to the fact that we were going to have to purchase things like gas canisters, fire logs, butane, anything that was explosive, and Grace's abilities were pretty much required to go out in public. If we ran into trouble, then I'd turn to Veronique's power.

We needed a vehicle with a large gas tank, so as we'd done before, Dorian and I found an SUV. The man filling the vehicle up at the gas station in Davis watched as Dorian and I approached, quickly came under my spell, and handed me his keys without saying a word.

I wore a baseball cap now, and some of the clothes I'd found at our borrowed home, and for the face I gone with Grandpa Gideon, which seemed to be a good disguise.

I was thrown off guard for a moment when I noticed a small television screen on the gas pump showing my image. The news media was still focusing on my story...

Our vehicle secure, a Lincoln Navigator, Dorian and I headed to WalMacy's in search of fuel canisters and other assorted explod-y things.

As I drove, I remembered the layout of the facility in our plan. We would be divided up into two teams, linked by mental messages between Grace and me. Besides, the installation was too large for us to search as one group, and one group was clunky.

"Are you sure you can drive?" I asked Dorian as we finished purchasing our gear at WalMacy's. I had pay for it using cash, not feeling like using Jedi mind tricks. We were now parked at the WalMacy's gas station, and I'd just finished filling up a five-gallon canister of gas.

"I already told you I could. You never asked."

"All right, just don't get our asses killed." I tossed the keys to her, and after we loaded the vehicle, Dorian took the wheel.

"Finally." She slammed down on the gas pedal and skidded onto the street, narrowly clipping a Toyota Prius.

"You think you're a better driver than me?"

"I hate to be the one that tells you this, but you drive like an old man. Which is telling considering the form you decided to take."

"I thought you liked when I took my older, distinguished gentleman form. You know, if it's your thing, we could have fun while I'm in this form…"

"Oh, please," she said, laughing. "That's the last thing I want."

"All I'm saying is that cosplay can be pretty fun in the bedroom, just ask Grace."

"I should ask Grace, huh?"

"That came out wrong," I told her as a convertible Sebring zipped around us and took off.

Dorian pulled up to a light, and drummed her fingers on the wheel as she waited for it to turn green. "I'm guessing a shifter can be pretty fun in the bedroom, I'll admit that."

"*Pretty fun* is an understatement, but it can also be pretty scary. I probably shouldn't be talking about these things with you."

"You know I don't care." She glanced at me. "But would you care?"

"What I care about what?"

"Would you care if there was another man in our group and we treated him the same way we treat you?"

Dorian had me by the balls and she knew it. Of course I would care, I was only human, a stupidly introspective human, which led me down a harrowing thought path about gender roles and double standards.

407

"Yeah," I finally said. "I would care."

"Well, we don't care, because we have evolved past you."

"Evolved? I have superpowers now too, remember?"

Dorian laughed. "Don't take this conversation so seriously."

"I just get what you're saying, though, and it's not something I've really thought about because I'm the person getting to enjoy the situation. Does that make sense?"

"It does. You're a lucky guy, you know that?"

"I tell myself that every day, seriously. And if I could be lucky for just one more day, I would hope that it was tonight, because I really don't like the fact that Fiona and Ingrid were taken. They were sweet girls, well, not Tulip, but sweet. I'm sick of all this kidnapping, by the way. We've got to stop getting jacked by AEFL."

"Have you ever wondered why it is that all of our members are women or girls?"

I shrugged. "I'm not complaining about that fact. Wait, does that have something to do with your previous statement about there being another guy in the group and promiscuity?"

"No," she said, as she hit the left blinker. "I would say seventy-five percent of the supers we trained with were female. I don't know why that is, but there were men, too. Just more women."

"We'll have to ask Father next time we see him. But hey, if there are ever enough men in our group, we can officially change our name."

"Cherry Blossom Boys?" Dorian's hand came up to press her dark bangs to the side. "We haven't seen cherry blossoms in quite some time."

"I'm sure Grace can make some appear in your head if you ask her."

"I'm the type of girl that wants the real thing."

Dorian pulled into a parking spot in front of Panera Chip, the Panera Bread Company and Chipotle merger that offered fresh and healthy food, burritos included, which seemed just a step up from the normal swill you could get at this price range.

"I'll keep that in mind," I said, not really knowing what she wanted to hear from me.

"I know, it's not a possibility right now, and I'm fine with that. I mean, it's pretty hard to compete against Grace, because Grace can become me."

"She can only look like you. She can't actually become you. It doesn't mean she has your sense of humor, the lightness I feel when I'm around you, your aesthetic? I think that's the right word. I wouldn't compare myself to anyone, if I were you."

"I have one request." Dorian took the keys from the ignition and turned to me.

"Anything."

"I want to go somewhere with you, tomorrow, once we successfully complete this mission. Just you and me. A big city, somewhere interesting."

"Any particular place in mind?"

She thought for a minute. "Chicago. That looks interesting. We just saw the city on one of our shows. Just you and me, for an entire evening, and hotel stay too. A nice hotel."

"Chicago, huh?" I considered this for a moment. "Yeah, sure, we can arrange that. I've never been there, actually."

We got out of the vehicle and met at the entrance to the Panera Chip. I knew that Michelle wanted pizza, because who didn't want pizza? But we had a mission tonight, and I didn't want something heavy in our stomachs.

We ended up ordering a bunch of vegan burritos, soups, bread, pastries, and they gave us a couple apples too. We weren't far from the military base, just two miles, so Dorian drove the vehicle up the street another mile and parked it next to a fried chicken place.

One purple flash later, and we were back at our borrowed home in Davis, California. The television was on, and the CBGs and Chloe were gathered around it.

"Pizza!"

"No, Michelle, we are having something healthy today. Tonight's very important, and it's good for you not to have a heavy stomach. Although, I guess you could consider a burrito a little heavy, but at least it doesn't have a bunch of cheese. Wait a minute, yes it does. At least it's vegan?"

The speedy young super narrowed her eyes at me. "This better be good, Gideon."

"Or what? What will you do to me?"

"I'm going to jog back half a mile, and run towards you with my fist out."

I laughed. "I can hardly imagine you jogging."

"I like this soup," said Stella as soon as she opened the container with corn chowder inside. She ate directly from the container, and handed it to Veronique after she'd had some.

*So that's how we're doing this...*

I wasn't expecting our dinner to become a communal thing, but it did, all of us sharing our food, from the burritos to the soup. At some point Grace sat down on my lap, an apple in her hand, which she also shared with me.

There was nothing we could do at this point aside from eat, be merry, and wait for the night's operation to start.

"Is there such a thing as a pizza burrito?" Michelle asked me, her mouth full.

"I believe those are called calzones."

# Chapter Thirty-Three:
# Operation Ball Tap

Operation Ball Tap was well underway.

And no, it wasn't the best name for what we were trying to do, but I felt it was apropos, as our mission was to get in, get out, and leave them reeling upon our departure.

Dorian reappeared to grab my group.

We'd gone with a red team and a blue team, the red team consisting of Grace, Veronique, and Michelle, and the blue team consisting of Dorian, the Gidmeister, and Stella. For her part, Chloe was playing the passed-out victim on the couch, her wrists and ankles cuffed together using clothes hangers.

I didn't feel so great about putting her in that position, and watching Veronique drain her was as uncomfortable as usual, but what other choice did we have? Even if she had promised to join us and never do us dirty, now was not the time to make new alliances.

Tomorrow? Sure, but as it stood, we need to keep her captive, and we didn't want her aiding the enemy in any way.

"Bye, Chloe," I said to the curvy brunette.

Dorian snorted. She placed her hand on my arm, her other hand wrapping around Stella's wrist. "You want to give her a kiss on the cheek too?"

Boom. It wasn't a far distance, which meant we weren't traveling in the weird vortex that was Dorian's far travel teleportation ability. So no stomach problems on my end, but I did notice Dorian's hand was a little warm, likely because of the way I had modified her stats.

We needed the teleporter to be able to transport a lot of people, which meant that her Tele-Sphere Radius needed to be kicked up a notch.

It currently looked like this:

### Main Second: Teleportation

Tele-Sphere Radius: 6

Conscious Spatial Awareness: 9

Recharge Speed: 5

Restoration Speed: 6

Teleportation Rapidity: 5

Teleportation Distance: 9

Empathetic Teleportation: 6

Banishment: 3

Overcharge: 2

For a moment there, I was glad that Luke wasn't judging me on my story. It was true, I had neglected their stats as of late, and if this were actual gamelit or LitRPG fiction, the reader would probably be angry by now.

But fuck the reader.

Just kidding, if it weren't for the readers, *Mutants in the Making* wouldn't be a bestseller. And sure, they never gave me respect when I published *How Heavy This Axe?,* but holding grudges is for partisan voters and grumpy cats.

"Focus, Gideon," Dorian whispered as soon as our bodies appeared behind a black vehicle.

Her spatial awareness was good, and I'd used as much as I could from GoogleFace Maps to give her images to associate with the military base. Not a lot, but she'd got the gist of it, and her power to sort of paint a place into existence meant that we'd spawned behind cover.

"How do you know I'm not focused?" I asked her, my voice slightly muffled by my ballistic helmet. It was dark out, a slight breeze blowing through the air.

"You have that look in your eye..."

"Are you reading my mind now?"

She smirked. "Wrong Cherry Blossom Girl."

*Ouch.* Rather than start this argument up while we were in the process of infiltrating a military base, I got down, waiting for a message from Grace.

It came just a few moments later.

*We have started exploring the northwest quadrant of the facility. Veronique has already taken out one guard, and we've hidden the body.*

*How's Michelle?*

*We have her going ahead to do reconnaissance. Her speed makes it so that she doesn't even trigger motion-activated lights.*

*That's fast.*

*We will update you as soon as we find something, or run into trouble.*

*Good luck, Grace.*

*Same to you, Writer Gideon.*

Feeling just about as cool as I'd ever felt, I gave Dorian and Stella the "let's move out" sign, which I'd seen people do in movies. So basically a peace sign, and a wave of my hand as if I were hopping a little rabbit.

Dorian figured out my gesture, the smirk still on her face; Stella simply rolled her eyes.

We crouched behind the military vehicle and looked around the hood, immediately spotting a motion-activated floodlight. I clicked on my night vision and saw the outline of several men standing guard, just past the spotlight.

We would have to take out the light and then the men. Or we could use the light to distract the men and go from there.

I pointed at the light.

"My power is too visual," Dorian whispered. "Stella, can you take out the floodlight?"

The vector manipulator nodded.

"Will it make a lot of noise?" I asked.

"It'll make some, but we can use that to distract them. There are three men over there, correct?"

"That's right," I said, my night vision making Stella's features a crazy color red. This shit was trippy.

"Gideon, you move over to that wall there and hang in the shadows, Stella will block the light, I'll teleport over to the soldiers, bring them here, and we'll take care of them. I would banish them, but I'm trying not to overheat."

"You got it," I told Dorian as I crouched into my best *Metal Gear Solid* impression.

I got over to the other side, feeling like an utter badass, especially because I was able to stop the butterflies fluttering around in my stomach from going too crazy, and causing me to do something like fall, make noise, or fart, or anything else that they could have done that would've drawn attention to me.

And I had to fart too, likely because of the damn burrito I had eaten earlier.

So once I was in position, I tried with all my might to squeeze out the poot without making any noise. I ultimately failed, but luckily for all of us, my little bit of gas coincided with Stella blowing out the flood lamp.

We were in the clear, and my embarrassment quickly faded as Dorian disappeared and reappeared with three armed men. Stella and Dorian went to work immediately; there was a little commotion, but no one seemed to hear it.

"You have to help," Stella said after she rejoined me, her nose twitching at the peculiar smell wafting around me. "What's that smell?"

"I think we're near the sewer line," I told her.

"Makes sense. Anyway, we can handle this."

"I didn't have my ass banished all the way to the desert of Nevada, only to run into a guy named Father after carrying you for a couple miles, then to receive some pretty badass superpowers, *not* to participate."

She chuckled. "Just follow our lead."

I let them go ahead as I mentally sent a message to Grace, letting her know that we had taken out three MercSecure guys.

Our bodies partially hidden by the shadows, we made our way to the front of the building to find two more guards. The front was lit, which was going to make this a little more complicated, but not much.

"Remember," Dorian whispered to me, "we don't want them seeing us and radioing their counterparts."

"Well, eventually someone's going to find the bodies," I said, "but we'll be out of here by then."

"Exactly."

We had chosen this area of the base for a reason.

From the info I'd been able to uncover, it seemed like one of the more logical places where they could keep people, which I mostly got based on the architectural breakdowns of the base. This particular building had a ton of rooms, all separated by a single hallway, and while it wasn't labeled as such, it did look like a place where one could keep inmates.

The building Grace and the others were clearing was similarly designed. If Ingrid and Fiona didn't happen to be in here, we would have to fan out more, which could prove troublesome.

"I've got these two." Stella lifted her hand at a pair of soldiers about fifty feet away. Just as one was turning to us, she cut them down with a blast of energy that forced them to throw their weapons into the air. Luckily, Dorian was there in a flash to catch their weapons, set them down, and drag both men over to us.

I did my part as well; I was the one that took out the camera that was facing the front right before all of this took place. It felt good too; I can't emphasize enough how awesome it was to be useful.

Just as we were about to go into the building, I received a message from Grace.

*We found them. It's time for part two.*

We joined Grace and Veronique almost immediately.

"Where's Michelle?" I asked.

"We have her circling the building to make sure there's no activity coming our way," Veronique said. The two stood before a long row of cells, a row that appeared to be empty aside from the bright lights at the end of the hallway.

"Confirmed?" Stella asked.

Veronique merely nodded.

"We believe it'll set off alarms if we open the doors," said Grace, who wore her body armor and helmet now. Not fake armor either, armor that she could've just conjured up, this was the real deal, and it didn't hug her body as well as some the stuff she'd had before, but she still looked hella hot.

"Can we disable anything?"

"We already tried that, or Veronique did, by stripping some of the wires off the electrical box. The lights didn't even waver. They're being kept on by some other force, and I don't believe we have the time to figure out what's keeping it running."

I considered our options for a moment. "Veronique, take off one of the doors. Stella, take off the other. They've got them in sarcophagi, correct?"

"Yes, same thing they had me in before," said Veronique.

"Got it. Dorian, go in with Veronique; Grace and I will go in with Stella. We'll get them out, Grace can call Michelle back, and we'll be gone before anyone arrives. We have to time this perfectly. I don't know what their response time is, but I'm going to guess that it's pretty fucking quick."

The five of us moved down the hallway, stopping in front of the doors in question. It only took a second for Veronique to blow off the handle. Stella did something similar, using her powers to bring the door crashing down into the hallway.

Alarms sounded immediately, and lights flashed on the ceiling.

Father's vial of blood in my hand, I quickly dabbed my thumb, giving myself the healing ability and mentally replacing Grace's psychic power.

We moved the sarcophagus to find Fiona in a hospital gown, her eyes closed, and a troubled look on her face. I placed my hand on her shoulder, and life instantly came back to her.

I felt a twist in my stomach as this happened, as confusion stretched across her brow. "Where am I?" she asked, coughing.

"I have to help Ingrid now," I told her hurriedly. "Just know that we are here to rescue you. Grace, Stella, please help her out."

Stella lifted Fiona out of the vat, hugging her in the process. As the alarm sounded, I moved to the other cell to find Dorian and Veronique, the metal vampire holding Ingrid over her shoulder.

"You might want to set her down for this, just in case she transforms."

Veronique did as I instructed, and I quickly healed Ingrid, whose face came alive almost immediately, her teeth elongating and her eyes filling with terror as she took in her surroundings. She didn't transform completely to Tulip, thank fucking God, and the first question to come out of her mouth was similar to Fiona's. "What happened? Where am I?"

"We'll explain later," I told her, as I waved everyone into the hallway. "Grace, have you called back Michelle yet?"

"I have," she said, her eyes filling with concern. "She's not responding."

Grace staggered forward, falling to her knees with her hands pressed tightly against her skull.

"What's happening? Hey! What's happening, Grace?"

"They're here," Veronique whispered, her hands flaring red.

"Shit!" Dorian went for her paintbrush, placing it in her mouth.

"They have Michelle," Grace whispered. She was still wincing, as if she were having a migraine. "And Mother's here too."

Stella turned toward the wall, brought both hands back and blew through it, revealing a literal army of Remy clones, MercSecure soldiers, Mother, Angel, and two new supers, one of whom I recognized as Jules.

We were in for one hell of a fight.

# Chapter Thirty-Four: And That's When the Screaming Started in My Head

"Were you looking for someone?" Mother asked.

She stepped aside, allowing Angel to show us Michelle's limp body. He held the young super by her ponytail, the rest of her body on the ground. Rage boiled inside me as I watched him drop her, Michelle's chin cracking against the pavement.

All of Remy's clones pointed their guns at us at the same time. The clones were interspersed with MercSecure paramilitary soldiers, men and women, also with weapons trained on us. Jules was in a bowtie, and next to him was the unknown super, a thick redhead in a black MercSecure bodysuit.

"You know, Gideon, Sabine, the rest of you, I told you in Austin that this has gone on for far too long. Now, you have made it a national issue, and you've brought attention to us, attention we never wanted in the first place."

"That's too fucking bad," I told Mother.

"Let Mother speak," said Angel, flexing his muscles. He wasn't quite his full size yet, but he was close, and he would have resembled a teenage Angel if it weren't for the aged skin on his face and his long greasy hair.

He no longer had any of the scars from the fire back in New Haven, but you could tell the difference between his face and body.

"It truly is a pity that it has come this far. You should've been killed long ago," said Mother, a hint of melancholy in her voice. "If only Veronique were smart enough to actually see to the completion of her mission."

I glanced to my left to see Veronique with her hands charged red, bits of metal floating beneath her fists.

"And Dorian, what a disappointment you have become. True, you never were as good of a teleporter as Danielle, the *late* Danielle, but your energy abilities made up for that. It's a pity."

"You guys killed Danielle?" Fiona asked.

"And Augustin," said Stella under her breath.

"And Victoria," I whispered.

"I'm ready to fight," said Ingrid, her voice tinged with rage.

"I'm sure the fight is coming; just don't change into Tulip yet."

Ingrid looked to me and nodded, allowing Mother to continue her supervillain-esque diatribe.

"Ah, and then there's Stella, our only vector manipulator. Well, not really. Jules also has an ability similar to yours, more powerful, more useful really, so you're not our only one. You too are expendable. In fact, all of you are expendable. *Kill them,*" she said suddenly, nodding to Angel. "Do not take any of them alive. I want all of them dead."

Mother placed her hands on her slight baby bump and stepped back.

Angel was the first to come forward, flying over her with his fists clenched, cracking them into the vector shield Stella had formed around us. The Remy clones came too, exploding on contact, firing their weapons even though Veronique was able to stop most of their bullets.

Jules simply hung back, waiting for the fight to come to him as the other super brought her hands up, the parked vehicles starting to shift toward us, MercSecure men gathering behind them.

As everyone moved to fight, and Ingrid began her terrifying transformation into Tulip, I took a deep breath and projected my voice forward, belting out Adele's "Someone Like You" with all my heart.

All of the MercSecure men began to sob as I continued Adele's famous earworm of a song, Chloe's power on full display.

It was a momentary distraction, and I was lucky that it didn't affect anyone in our group. It didn't affect any of the supers in Mother's group either, but the MercSecure people were quickly out, which gave Veronique and Grace a unique opportunity.

Grace focused on the group of mercs at the right, taking over their minds and turning their weapons on Remy's clones.

Veronique turned her attention to the mercs on the left, stripping them of all the metal they had, and bringing the metal into the air as projectiles aimed directly at Mother. Joining these projectiles were a dozen of her frag pouches, each ready to deliver a small but brutal payload.

Jules stepped forward, his power stopping all of Veronique's projectiles from hitting Mother. It seemed as if he had about a seven-foot radius around him, preventing anyone from using a superpower in his vicinity. This was further proven when Dorian conjured up her patented T-Rex with gun arms, the prehistoric beast firing purple plastic blasts at Jules, all of which did absolutely nothing.

The unknown super rose into the air, and brought her hands to her sides, palms facing up, like she was charging.

"Whoa!" I shouted as a column of water sprayed past me, veering into some of Remy's clones.

Fiona was on top of the column of water, and was blasting some of Remy's clones as they exploded, mitigating their damage.

431

By this point, Tulip had already torn off from the main group, trading punches with Angel. The aunt-fucker was holding his own, and there were a couple instances when I thought he might overpower Tulip.

Dorian teleported away, only to appear behind the fight, where she kicked into action against more clones.

Literally.

While she usually chose ranged combat, Dorian had gone full Karate Kid against Remy's increasing number of clones, many of whom were trying to bludgeon her with the butts of their guns.

But that's not what I focused on.

I was focused on the fact that the redheaded super in the air looked like she was about to bring something down upon us, and I quickly realized what it was, or at least I felt it, when my chest was pulled forward and I slammed into the pavement, stopping myself just in time from faceplanting.

*Is her power gravity based?* I thought, feeling the strain on my skin as it pushed further into the pavement. It was like something dense was now sitting on my shoulders, and try as I might, I couldn't stand, couldn't move.

Some of the others were still fighting, but those who were close to me, including Veronique and Grace, were in the same prone position.

Rather than fight it, Veronique locked her dark eyes on the woman in floating in the air and drained her from afar.

The woman was not able to resist this power, and since it was out of Jules' sphere of negation, the drainage didn't stop until she dropped to the ground, again protected by her teammate's dead zone shield.

The screaming started up in my head.

I was still pinned down; the mysterious super had kept up her attack even with the fact that Veronique was draining her, and the ear-piercing scream inside my skull gave me the feeling that my brain would rupture soon.

Damn if Jules wasn't a cocky bastard. Or at least it helped me to visualize him as cocky, considering he simply stood there in a bowtie with his arms crossed over his chest, a bored look on his face as shit hit the fan all around him.

I glanced at Angel and Tulip, who were still trading punches.

Tulip was twice the size of Angel, with a face that was part-velociraptor, part-werewolf, with jagged teeth and beady, rabid eyes. His sheer rage looked as if it could overpower Angel, if given just a little bit of help.

And that was where I came in.

Even though I was pinned down by the mysterious super's gravity power, I was still able to lift my hand, as Veronique had done, and use Stella's power to *sweep* Angel's feet out from underneath him.

He cried out in anger as his back slapped against the ground. Tulip hopped on top, his claws coming down on Angel's shoulders, his mouth foaming as he started chewing at Angel's face.

*Gruesome...*

Bullets plinked all around us, Stella's vector shield still preventing any chance of metal unhappiness reaching the pinned CBGs. Stella was behind us, focused solely on keeping us protected.

We needed to find the real Remy, that was clear, but there were so many clones, clones battling Grace's turned

MercSecure guys and clones going against Fiona's water attacks, that it was impossible to figure out the real one.

And even though I had some of Grace's power with me, and I was able to suppress it some, Mother continued to scream inside all of our skulls. It was excruciating too, I'm talking nails on a chalkboard amplified in an arena. The point of her attack was clear: disrupt us from using our power.

Dorian appeared in our sphere, bullet wounds on her arms, fear splashed across her face.

"Where's Michelle?" I shouted back to her, my jaw heavy, tongue practically falling out of my mouth.

"I can't get her," she said, staying far enough back that she wasn't affected by the gravity still pressing the three of us to the ground. "Michelle is in Jules' range of influence, I can't do anything about it, my powers stop when I get too close!"

"We need to take out the one that's pinning us down!" I called over my shoulder to her.

"I'll take her out of the sphere," Veronique cried over her shoulder. "Dorian, banish her!"

The weight still pressing her down, Veronique managed to twist to her side, where she saw one of Grace's mind-controlled soldiers. She focused all of her energy on taking his weapon from him, stripping the metal out of it, and any metal in the vicinity, which came from bullet shells, armor, fillings in people's mouths, you name it.

The metal pressed together, melting, taking in new parts, forming a basketball-sized sphere of jagged shrapnel.

The sphere floated for a moment, as Veronique locked eyes on her target, knowing all too well that her power would cease to exist as soon as she reached Jules' sphere of influence.

But if she flung it fast enough, momentum would take over by that time.

"Stella, Grace, help me throw the metal ball!"

"Got it!" Stella said.

"I'm ready too," Grace told Veronique.

"I can help!" Dorian called over to us.

"No, pull her away as soon as you can," I told Dorian. "We need that one banished."

The teleporter was gone in a purple flash, the ball of metal zipping through the air towards Jules, and ultimately, towards the mysterious super.

As we had predicted, the power propelling the ball of gathered metal dissipated it soon as it reached Jules' sphere of influence, but momentum took over from that point, and it was going so fast that the female super was unable to stop it from cracking her in the chest, and sending her flying backward, out of Jules' sphere of influence, where she met a waiting Dorian, who placed one hand on her shoulder and disappeared in a purple burst of energy.

The weight on our shoulders disappeared instantly, the fight now turning in our direction as the three of us stood, ready to finish this.

If only it'd been that easy. If only Mother hadn't placed her foot on Michelle's neck.

Angel roared as he lifted Tulip into the air and body slammed the muscled beast into the pavement, causing a fissure that quickly led to the sidewalk.

"Ingrid!" Stella shouted, bristling as Tulip whimpered, the monster turning to its side, not able to lift itself.

Satisfied that he'd finished off Tulip, Angel wiped his hands together, grinning like an asshole as he again approached Jules' sphere of influence.

The ground lit up as helicopters beamed their lights onto us, the wind from their blades ruffling the shrubbery. MercSecure goombahs appeared, their red beads trained on our chests.

"Keep the shield up," I reminded Stella.

I was standing now, the pressure gone thanks to Dorian banishing the gravity-wielding super.

"Get Tulip," Veronique told Dorian, who disappeared in a flash and reappeared, Tulip in the same position that Angel had laid her in.

The beast snapped his jaws, frothing at the mouth, but Tulip couldn't seem to get to his feet, and within seconds, he began to morph back into Ingrid.

*Fiona,* Grace thought aloud, *return to us.*

The water-user dropped behind me, as just about the stupidest idea I'd come up with yet made its presence known.

"Get ready to grab Michelle," I told Dorian.

"Where are you going?" she asked, surprise airbrushing across her face.

"Don't worry about me; just worry about getting Michelle."

I felt Grace's hand wrap around my wrist.

"Are you sure?"

"I've never been more sure of anything in my life. Well, maybe that's not true. Anyway, now isn't the time to try and sort that out. You know my plan. Inform the others," I said, wincing as Mother's mind scream knifed through my psyche. "And don't do so telepathically. In fact, don't tell them; just tell them to get ready."

With that, I stepped out of our protected bubble and glared at Mother, whose heeled foot was still pressed onto Michelle's neck.

My chest lit up with red beads from the MercSecure guns. I naturally lifted my arms, having seen one too many episodes of *Live PD*.

"Pretty sad that a group with actual superpowers has to resort to aiming their guns at me," I said, locking eyes with Angel. "It's like they're not strong enough to actually take me on."

"Is that a challenge?" Angel asked, his fists curling at his sides.

"He's trying to bait you, dear," said Mother.

"What can he possibly do to someone like me?"

"Stand down, Angel."

"No," he said, glaring at her. "You wouldn't let me end this back in Texas; now look what he's done. Two of ours are dead; Chloe is pretty much gone as well. He's humiliated us, and he's exposed our program to the nation!"

Angel stepped out of Jules' sphere, practically seething with animosity.

"Finally," I told him, loosening my shoulders. "AEFL's little bitch finally comes out from his Mommy's wing."

Angel stopped, his face contorting.

"Are you going to attack me or not, Angel? I'm sick of waiting around…"

Angel flew at me, and I just barely managed to bring my arms up to block his attack. Instinct had taken over by this point, Stella's vector power forming a shield in front of me.

It still hurt like hell, but Angel bounced off and I stood my ground.

He approached me on foot this time, swinging as I tried desperately to get into position.

A guy with military training versus a dude with video game training?

My ass would have been handed to me right away had Angel used his legs rather than his arms to try to take me down. He just kept pummeling me, trying to break through the shield I'd formed.

And the bruises.

I knew they were coming. Stella's power absorbed his hits, but it didn't absorb them completely.

But there was a goddamn method to my madness, and once I was in position, with my back now facing Mother and Jules, I mentally dropped Stella's power and braced myself for Angel's true punch, watching the aunt-banger pull his fist back, connect with my forearms, and launch me into Jules' sphere of no power.

And even though Angel had shattered my right forearm, I managed to land right next to Jules, stick my left hand up and grab his wrist before he could pull it away.

That was all it took.

Jules' power now mine, I activated it immediately, causing Mother to cry out and the real Remy, who stood behind her, to start losing his clones. I could feel Jules' power fighting mine, and I knew that his was much stronger, but I'd done what I came to do – provide a momentary distraction.

Mother stepped away from Michelle as she gathered her bearings. Dorian appeared, slapped her hand against Michelle's back, and threw her other hand in my direction.

My hand outstretched, I was nearly touching Dorian's fingers when Angel grabbed my ankle. One look back and I gave the fucker a kick he wouldn't soon forget, my heel connecting with his nose.

Dorian flashed to the other side, all of us touching her in some way or fashion, and we all disappeared together.

# Chapter Thirty-Five: Regroup

"I've got to go back," said Dorian as soon as we all arrived. "We still need to explode the vehicle at the entrance." A vein was pulsing on the side of her head, she'd carried quite a load back to our borrowed home in Davis, but I knew that the mission wasn't complete.

I also knew that my fucking forearm was shattered, and it hurt like a bitch. But adrenaline was a hell of a drug, and even though I was reeling from the pain, I was also reeling from the chemical rush inside my body.

"Yeah, that should definitely add just a little more chaos to an already chaotic situation," I said, ignoring the pain.

"Heal yourself!" Grace told me, noticing the way I was holding my arm.

I hadn't really tried healing bone before, but focusing on Father's power, I ran my other hand against my forearm, feeling some movement beneath my skin. Bones reattached, and meshed together, my muscles cushioning them. As I fixed myself up, an idea came to me, a way to heal instantly, but I suppressed it for the time being.

By the time I'd finished, my arm was still sore, but at least it was no longer shattered.

"Dorian, before you go." I reached out for her and placed my hand on the side of her head, standing as I did so, focusing my healing power on her. Her skin lightened at my touch, the redness of her face dissipating, the vein beating at the side of her head slowing.

She nodded, knowing exactly what she needed to do.

"Wait, I'll go with you," said Stella, "you shouldn't be going alone."

"And I'll take care of these three," I promised the vector manipulator.

Something softened behind Stella's eyes as I immediately moved to Michelle, and healed her up. The young super practically bolted off the floor, leaping into the air and moving at lightning speed for just a moment, actually passing through the wall, and stopping in the kitchen.

"I feel great!" she cried out from the kitchen.

Stella nodded, and vanished along with Dorian.

As part of the plan, Grace helped me move Ingrid onto the couch. I healed her, and as soon as her eyes opened, her face began to transform.

"No, Tulip, you're safe now, we're here to help," Grace said. Ingrid's transformation wavered. "No, Tulip..."

"Gideon, run the GPS device." Veronique stood behind us, ready to bring Tulip down if necessary.

I plugged the GPS device into Ingrid's neck, careful as she snarled a bit, and Tulip disappeared back into wherever the damn beast came from.

"Fiona," I called over to the water user. She sat on the couch, next to a recovering Ingrid. I plugged into Fiona's neck, immediately running the GPS device. "Michelle, get them some clothes." Michelle was immediately gone, upstairs, and returned just moments later with some spare clothing.

"Come on, Dorian," I said as I started to pace. "Come on..."

"Where did she go?" Ingrid asked as she pulled an oversized T-shirt over her chest. She stepped into a pair of house shorts, pulling the waistband tight.

"Little surprise for our friends at the military base."

"We've got to get a new vehicle, and get out of here," said Grace. She was still in her ballistic helmet and her bulletproof vest. For her part, Veronique had already removed the helmet, but she still wore the vest. I was also in my helmet and vest, the face protector moved to my forehead.

Realizing I no longer needed this bulky shit, I removed the helmet, and instructed Michelle to find us a large bag upstairs.

"I saw a gym bag," she said excitedly.

"Great, bring that. We're going to keep our body armor this time if we can help it."

"And about the vehicle?" Grace asked.

"I know, we need to get something, just in case they're able to track us here. You and I can go out and quickly find something in the neighborhood. And yes, we should have gotten a vehicle before. Mistake on my part. Dorian should be back any moment now, and…"

"What's wrong with her?" Fiona asked as she looked down at Chloe, who rested on one of the couches.

"She's with us," I said.

"Why she sleeping? And who is she exactly?" asked Ingrid.

"Well, that's a long story. I suppose I could wake her up; it would be easier if she were awake."

I looked to Grace and Veronique for confirmation. Once they both nodded, giving me the go-ahead, I moved over to Chloe and placed my hand on her, her skin immediately returning to its normal color.

"You're all right," she said, gasping awake. Her next reaction was to sweep the brown hair out of her face.

"Yeah, we all made it back in one piece. And now we need to get out of here."

"How can I help?"

"You can stay here with me," said Veronique, a thin smile on her face.

448

Having your life force drained by Veronique is one of the more unpleasant things a person can experience. As she does it, you feel increasingly helpless, your energy leaving you, ennui setting in, and to add insult to injury, the look on her face as she does it can be just as unsettling as the act, the hunger behind her dark eyes.

So that was behind the almost fearful glare Chloe leveled at Veronique.

"Let's get a car," said Grace as we turned to the door.

"Michelle!"

The speedy young teen appeared before I could finish saying her name. I took the body armor off, and Grace took hers off, both of us handing the armor to Michelle.

"Again, what's the plan? I can't go looking like this."

Grace nodded, her form changing to that of a black woman with braided hair. "Touch me, take my shifter ability, and don't lose Jules' power."

"I did good back there, didn't I?" I asked, a genuine grin spreading across my face.

"You did, Writer Gideon, and I knew you had it in you. But Jules' power is one that you likely won't be able to get again, so I want you to make sure you don't lose it; I think it will come in handy."

She placed a hand on my cheek, allowing me to take her shifter power over Father's healing ability. I couldn't help but bring her in and kiss her.

"Gross!" Michelle said.

"Hey, you were supposed to go back to the living room," I told her.

"No way, I'm coming with you two. I want to be helpful."

"The most helpful thing you can do is just hang out here and get all our stuff packed. The night is far from over."

"Fiona and Ingrid can get ready to go, I have everything I need."

I turned to Michelle and placed both hands on her shoulders. "They haven't been here for the last few days, and they are probably a little disoriented. I don't know. I would be after all that. My point is, you know where everything is, right?"

She nodded.

"Then you're in charge. Get our clothing, make sure we have the armor and all that together, and we'll be back with the car soon as we can. Okay? Dorian and Stella should be here in just a moment too. I don't think they're gonna screw this one up."

"Fine, fine."

Michelle moped for a second, looked up at me, winked, and was gone in a flash.

# Chapter Thirty-Six: Not-So-Grand Theft Auto

Even though we had been outside for our fight against Mother and her minions, it wasn't as nice as being outside at the moment, away from the melee, in a nice residential neighborhood as a California breeze blew through the palm trees that lined the streets.

Lots of trees here too. I'd never been much of an arborist, but my crossdressing uncle considered himself somewhat of an enthusiast, and he could name most of the indigenous trees of New England, specifically New Hampshire and Vermont.

He lived in Manchester when I was a child, but later moved to Brattleboro, seeking a more liberal city. He appreciated the New Hampshire Live Free and Die attitude, but not with the strange conservatism that came with it.

And thinking of my uncle and Vermont made me realize just how far away I was, the sheer size of America.

There really was nothing else like it. Hell, it was almost a pity that the government had become my enemy, but I was the type to stand up for what was right, disregarding the casualties I left in my wake.

*Writer Gideon, you're going to a dark place,* Grace thought to me.

"Sorry," I told her aloud as we locked hands. "You know how my mind is."

"Yes, I know," she said as we made our way down the street. To better disguise myself, even though Grace was with me and she could just wipe anyone's mind anyway, I went for my old man form. Grandpa Gid. Grace stayed in her cute black girl form as she looped her arm through mine.

My phone buzzed, and I pulled it out to see Luke was calling me. The famous *Star Defacer* writer had already called me several times while I'd been battling Mother.

"Gideon," Luke said, instead of hello. "I was wondering what was going on with you. Have you checked your sales data recently?"

"No, I've been, um, a little busy. Let's call it that. A little busy. Why? What's going on?"

"You're not going to believe this, well, you may believe it considering that your face is now plastered all over the American media, but all three of your novellas are in the top 100."

I stopped dead in my tracks.

*The top 100?* It was every independent writer's dream to get into the top 100 on the EBAYmazon store. Breaking the top 100 meant that you were moving a fuckton of books, thousands per day. Having three books there only went to show the series read-through, and how popular my books were.

"I really wish I had the time to enjoy it," I finally told him.

"What's going on?"

"Oh, you know, the usual. Rescued some people from a military facility, fought some supers, nearly had my ass handed to me, somehow managed to escape, still surrounded by beautiful superpowered women."

"Doesn't seem like a bad life…"

I laughed. "You always are positive, aren't you?"

"I believe that is a Canadian trait, not that I buy into that stuff."

"So you're saying that all Canadians are positive, but you don't believe that, but you're still positive, right?" I asked as Grace and I turned down a cul-de-sac.

"Something like that. There has also been some trouble in the indie community, some things you should know about."

"What's going on?"

"A couple people's books are disappearing from the EBAYmazon store, Dustin Broner's being one of them. The ones that are like your series."

"Just disappearing?"

"That's right. It's pretty suspicious, if you ask me. And they seem to only be targeting books that are like yours."

"Wait, you think because I have a contract with EBAYmazon, that they are taking down books that are like mine?"

"That's what it seems like."

"I didn't approve of anything like this!"

Luke laughed. "What good would your approval do? You've signed a contract with the number one book publisher."

Grace squeezed my hand, nodding at a minivan about two blocks away. It was dark outside now, but the street lights were well-maintained in this neighborhood, so much in fact that I felt like it was a little too bright.

"Maybe I can talk to my rep about it. I don't want people's hard work being banned just because they read mine and got inspired."

"But some of these writers are *copying* your work, not word for word, but the whole premise."

"I've always been of the mindset that the cream will rise to the top, and even if others are copying my work, it'll just bring more eyes to what I've created."

"Yeah, maybe."

"I don't like the idea of a ban hammer, and it seems a little bit shady to me that EBAYmazon is doing it in preparation for promoting my work. I don't know when they're going to release the entire book, but that must be what they're trying to do. I mean, it makes sense. Limit the competition, and then when they release my book, it becomes a number one bestseller. I'm not talking about the top 100."

"You know, for a fugitive, you are pretty concerned about the livelihood of others."

I stopped for a moment, considering what Luke had said. He was right, I had bigger fish to fry. "I'll give you that."

"I'll poke around in some of the groups I'm in, see what others are saying. No one has raised torches and decided to come after you yet, but since the copycat books are down, people will be wondering why, and it could blow up. EBAYmazon are technically selling the book of a terrorist – I know, you're not really a terrorist, but just follow me here – and they are suppressing other books written in the same style as yours. Seems sketchy, right? Bad optics, too."

"I didn't think about that. I'll have to talk to my agent, but not right now. Anyway, I've got to go, so keep me up-to-date and we'll talk soon."

"All right, Gideon, talk later, and stay safe out there."

Grace let go of my hand. "How do you want to do this?"

"As quickly as possible. The family looks like they're home, so let's just knock on the front door and you can do your thing. Crap, I wish I had more cash with me; I'd like to pay them for the vehicle."

"The less you worry if what you're doing is good or evil, the easier all this will become."

She turned to me, and placed both her hands on my cheeks.

"I know, call it my Puritan upbringing."

"Puritan?" she asked, her eyes shining white. "A Pilgrim? Your mind is jumping to an image of a Pilgrim. You definitely aren't a Pilgrim."

"I know, it's just the way I justify what it means to be a semi-decent American. And not doing things like we're doing now: stealing, exploiting, you get it. But at least we're doing it for a good cause."

"Relax," she said as she patted me on the cheek. "Let's just get the vehicle, and get out of here."

# Chapter Thirty-Seven: Siren's Call

Seeing Tulip smash out of the front wall, raging, followed by a column of water was the *last* thing we expected to see as we pulled into the driveway.

An explosion at the back of the house rocked our recently acquired minivan, my hand accidentally pressing against the horn. Tulip spotted us, dropped, and launched into the air, landing on the hood and bringing both hands into the window as I screamed like a little baby.

We wouldn't have made it out had it not been for the telekinetic shield that Grace had conjured last minute.

"Stop screaming, Gideon! Go! Go!"

"What's going on!?" I shouted, as Tulip beat his fists against the window.

I kicked out of the front door, catching his attention. The snarling beast dropped, its tongue sticking out of its mouth as it looked at me, saliva dripping onto the pavement and the destroyed hood of the vehicle. I tried to stumble away at this point, backpedaling, really having no idea how I was even moving due to the fact my legs had turned to putty.

Then I was gone, standing in the backyard with Dorian, who was out of breath, blood streaked through her hair.

"We came back, Ingrid and Fiona turned on us," she said hurriedly. "They have Veronique."

"What you mean they have Veronique?"

I heard Stella cry out inside the home; the wall gave way a bit, and the sound of metal zipping around reached my ears.

"Do you remember that ability you unlocked for Fiona, the intoxication ability?"

My mind was a jumble of panicky ideas and leading images, but I did briefly recall Fiona having the ability to intoxicate someone just by adjusting their fluid levels.

"Yes…"

"Let's just say that right now, it's Ingrid, Fiona, and Veronique versus the rest of us."

I gasped. "Veronique too?"

"Intoxicated by Fiona."

"Shit. Okay, I can stop this, I have Jules' power."

I didn't expect to see Stella fly out of a hole in the roof, stop herself midair, and blast back down into the building.

There wasn't much time; the cops would be here at any moment, and as a cyclone of water tore through the western side of the home, I knew we'd better do something soon.

"Gather everyone you can back here, away from the fight!" I told Dorian, fear again returning to me. It'd been less than hour ago that I was fueled solely by adrenaline, and now the adrenaline was back, propelling me forward as I ignored Dorian's cries.

*Grace!* I thought aloud. *We need to get out of here before law enforcement and the fire department come. I guarantee they will be here within the next two or three minutes. Maybe sooner.*

*I'm trying my best, Writer Gideon! Tulip is incredibly hard to influence.*

*I won't distract you then, get to the backyard as soon as you can, with Tulip, or better, Ingrid.*

I didn't know what had happened, all I knew was I needed to gather everyone, so we could all get to safety together.

The wall exploded outwards, Veronique appearing in the smoke that followed, her chest heaving up and down as she locked eyes with me.

I activated Jules' power, and even as red energy charged up Veronique's hands, *absolutely nothing happened.*

It was shaky though, and I could feel her influence pushing into me, which brought to mind an image of someone fighting off the Force, which then made me hate the fact that half of the immediate references that came to me were *Star Wars* related. Didn't our culture have anything else to reference and appreciate when it came to sci-fi?

Rather than go down that rabbit hole, I focused on suppressing Veronique's power.

It would only be a moment until she used her other hand to orchestrate metal death aimed in my general direction, and while I figured it wouldn't pass my sphere of negation, I wasn't as strong as Jules, and she had been able to break through his using extreme force.

And as it turned out, I was entirely right.

She dropped her head forward, her blonde bob falling in her face as any and all metal she could grab hold of flew in my direction. A few pieces broke through, slashing against my skin, one of the nails lodging in my shoulder.

I cried out in pain, and dropped Jules' dead zone, only to be protected by a bubble of vector power from Stella. She lowered to the ground next to me, anger and astonishment furrowing her brow as she caught me up on what had happened.

"We were just in the living room when Fiona and Ingrid attacked. Fiona turned Veronique, and…"

"It's fine, we'll figure it out, I'm pretty sure I know what it is… "

"What?" Stella asked, as she protected us from more of Veronique's shrapnel.

"It's Mother's ability. She did the same thing with Dorian back in Nevada. I'm sure Grace will be able to do something about it, but for now, we need to get out of here!"

Her eyes went wide. "Mother's ability… That's right!"

"We've just got to get everyone, and get them out of here, before the authorities arrive. Because believe me, this kind of shit doesn't happen often in a residential neighborhood. Now, where's Michelle? Have you seen her?"

"I don't know," she said, her hands pressed in front of her body as she took more of Veronique's attacks. "It all happened so fast."

"Michelle! Michelle! It's Gideon, come here! Michelle!"

As if she were Beetlejuice, Michelle appeared to my right, breathing heavily, terror writ large on her face. "I think I can help," she said. "I should be able to get Chloe…"

"Where's Chloe?"

Michelle nodded toward Veronique's destruction. "Somewhere in that direction. I don't know exactly."

"We can try to get her… No, I'll get her. You go help Grace. Distract Ingrid, I mean Tulip, run around him, jump off his body, do anything to wear him out."

"Got it!"

Michelle vanished, and my mission became getting Chloe, who was likely passed out, and then helping Stella take on Veronique.

There was also Fiona to contend with, but Dorian, who still stood at the back of the yard, had sent some of her energy creations in Fiona's direction, which busied the water user.

*Grace,* I thought, *I'm going in to get Chloe, I believe that Mother did something to them, the same thing she did to Dorian. I know you can't do Tulip, but maybe you can fix Fiona. Michelle should be there any moment to distract Tulip.*

*She's here, and I'll move towards Fiona.*

*Tell Michelle to be careful, her only job is to distract Tulip, so he doesn't destroy anything else.*

*Will do!*

Deep breath in and I turned to Stella. "Provide some distraction for me."

"You're really going in after her?"

"We don't leave each other behind, that's part of who we are! Grace is going to bring down Fiona, and then my guess is she'll help you take Veronique down. We can fix this, but we have to go now. We have like one or two minutes tops."

A stoic look on her face, Stella nodded, pressing forward, and with her eyes closed, she squeezed her fists together, enveloping Veronique in a vector sphere.

Well, I didn't know if it was a sphere or not, because I couldn't really see it, but Veronique was floating, trying to break her way out of it, some of these attacks causing energy sparks.

"Go, Gideon, I can't hold this for long!"

I raced past Veronique, ducking under that partially collapsed door. There was a fire in one section of the home; the other side was completely drenched with water. Various appliances and kitchen utensils were scattered everywhere, glass every which way I stepped.

"Chloe!"

I tried again, but I never got an answer.

I assumed Chloe had been the living room, but the house was in such disarray that it was actually hard to make out where that would be.

So I followed my gut, and headed towards the center of the home, yelling Chloe's name as I began moving away some of the debris.

My arms were bleeding, and as I moved some of the boards that had fallen from the ceiling, I sliced open my palms, blood dripping down to the ground.

"I'm here," I heard a muffled voice say.

I saw Chloe's hand, and immediately went to move the debris off of her. Once I did so, I quickly stuffed my shaky hand in my pocket, pulled out Father's vial, and dabbed a bit of blood on my finger, sending Grace's shifter ability away. I stuffed the vial back into my pocket and turned to the sound manipulator.

Chloe was pretty badly cut, and her eyes were glazed over with delirium, so I pressed my hand into the side of her face and healed her.

I can't stress enough how cool it is to actually be able to heal someone's wounds. And remembering that I could do so, because of course I could use Father's power on myself, I quickly healed up my own hands and arms.

"What happened?" Chloe asked, her ears twitching as we heard Tulip roar outside.

I caught her up in a single breath.

"And you came for me?"

"Of course I did, *we don't leave anyone behind.* That includes you."

"I can help," she said suddenly. "Give me my power back; I can help calm everyone and we can get out of here!"

"Your modifier is broken…"

She rolled her eyes at me. "No it isn't. Look, Gideon, I'm trying to help here. Let me help."

I bit my lip for a moment as I looked the brunette over, feeling the intensity in the way she was looking at me.

"I don't remember what your stats were originally at," I finally said, "but I can adjust them and even you out later. How's that?"

"Works for me…"

I heard the house creak, dust falling onto our heads. "Okay, this is going to sound a little bit awkward, but get on your knees for a moment."

Chloe got on her knees in front of me, not a foot away from my little writer. Even in a situation as tumultuous as this, sex still crossed my mind, which just goes to show you what kind of horny bastard I really am.

I disregarded the thought and plugged into her neck where I scrolled to her abilities, the dials instantly appearing. The sounds of sirens met my ears. I noticed that the gushing water had slowed, but I could still hear snarls and barks from Tulip in the front yard as she tried to take on Michelle.

"Okay, I'm going to make some temporary adjustments…"

"Just hurry!"

"Yep," I said as I adjusted everything up.

**Main: Acoustokinesis**

Sound Sculpting: 4

Acoustic Acceleration: 4

Sonoluminescence: 3

Rhythm Manipulation: 4

Sonokinetic Combat: 4

Sound Detection: 4

Sonic Stimulation: 6

Overcharge: 2


Once I was through, I yanked the cable out and stuffed it back in my pocket, along with my phone.

Light came into Chloe's eyes as she lifted into the air, everything around us moving as if she were at the center of a nuclear explosion.

We were suddenly floating above the house, a soft smile on her face as she began to hum a beautiful melody, light radiating from her throat, which now had an orange glow to it.

The police that had already showed up, the ones kicking out of their doors with their guns aimed at the house, fell to the ground, overcome with drowsiness. Tulip fell as well, her body reverting back to Ingrid's small form almost instantly.

Chloe, a golden light bathing her face, simply nodded as she focused her song to the street in front of the home.

I could see Grace on the western side of the home, Fiona in her arms. Dorian appeared next to her, the teleporter instantly moving both of them to the back of the yard.

I glanced the other way and saw Veronique slumped forward, Stella kneeling before the metal vampire, lifting her over her shoulder and moving toward the meeting point. Another poof of magic energy and I saw Dorian with Ingrid, the young beast-morphing super stirring ever-so-slightly as she was teleported away.

"Time to go." Her throat still glowing, Chloe floated the two of us down to Dorian. As soon as we landed, Grace ran to me and threw her arms around my neck.

"Don't thank me…" I started to say.

# Epilogue: The Magnificent Mile

*Manchester Rich's breasts ache like someone is boiling water behind her nipples. She knows this is a sign; she figured out weeks back that whenever her breasts ached, something bad was coming.*

*Will there ever be closure for her? Will she ever come to grips with the fact that she has destroyed her childhood home, that the village she grew up in is now defined more by its ruins and fallen bodies over those who once lived there?*

*"I am not the enemy here, I'm the victim," Manchester reminds herself, recalling the other dwarves chasing her with their sharp, heavy axes, fury in their eyes because of her transformation, that she'd dare to show her ugly, bearded face in her childhood home.*

*"I did what I had to do."*

*She moves through the rubble, searching for things she can sell later in her journey. Manchester isn't stupid; she knows good loot when she sees it.*

"Are you almost done?" Dorian asked, looking up at me. I paused the newest audition for *How Heavy This Axe?*, from a narrator named Justin Jeffrey Ellicott-Winkel, who was by far, *by far,* the best narrator for the project.

I had to hear more. Then again, Dorian and I were at the famous Allerton Hotel on Chicago's Magnificent Mile, in the Superior Suite mind you, with a view overlooking the vast shopping district below.

"Just another minute," I told her, moving my hand to Dorian's nude ass. I drummed my fingers against her skin and returned to the audio audition.

*"You there, Manchester!" a voice calls out from the rubble.*

*Manchester readies her axe, knowing dwarves never back down, even if they've had their arms and one of their legs cut off.*

*"Decided to tuck your willy wacker between your legs, eh?" the dwarven man wheezes. He has already lost one leg*

*and both arms. Standing before him now, she remembers the man running toward her with a staff, and being one of the first dwarves that she cut down. "Well, you may have killed the entire village, but you haven't bloody killed me!"*

*Manchester turns to the fallen dwarf, her blood-stained axe at the ready.*

*"Even after coming back to the village with the Lamp of Lampshire, which would have granted us infinite lamps made out of gold, which we could have then melted down to sell and become the richest dwarf village this side of Dwarfington..."*

*"Ha! You know damn well we'll never be as rich as Dwarfington! They have an amusement park!" the man shouts. "A simple village like ours wouldn't even know what to do with that kind of money."*

*"There is plenty we could have done with the money," says Manchester. "What about education?"*

*"Screw dwarf children! I mean that literally, best ass I ever got!"*

*Manchester gasps. "You're sick in the head."*

"You're the one who had his pecker cut off, not me, Manchester. I'm just telling it like it is!"

"Okay then, what about hospitals? We could have used the gold for healthcare!"

"I'll be damned if the money we receive through the theoretical selling of this gold goes to helping the sick and the elderly," the old man coughed. "Like my grandfather before me who died of black lung before I was born, and his grandfather before him, who died of black lung before he was born: if you can't get over a cold, or for that matter, black lung, then you don't have the right to call yourself a dwarf! Being sick is for pussies. You should know, you have one now!"

"What about public works?" Manchester asks. "Better sewers, streets, parks, monuments?"

"By the cursed name of Odin's Puckered Anus, Manchester, what socialist concepts are you trying to stuff down my gullet? If a rich person needs any of those things, he can buy them for his home. How would the general public ever benefit from any of the horse crap you've just mentioned?"

*Manchester stops before the old dwarf, looking down on him with disdain.*

*"Awww, did I hurt your liddle feelings?"*

*Manchester's breasts ache yet again. She knows something is coming, she senses its presence, but whatever it is, it hasn't made itself known yet.*

*"Who's there?" she calls out.*

*The old man coughs, his eyes bulging out, snot flying onto his beard. "Who the fuck are you talking to? I'm here, you neutered twat!"*

*Manchester lowers her axe and steps away from the rambling old man. He'll die soon enough; something to the north has piqued her interest, a large form moving through the clouds, a dragon.*

"Done," I told Dorian, popping my earbuds out. "Sorry it took me so long."

The punk rock teleporter kissed me on the cheek. "This is our day, our evening, really; we really should enjoy as much of it as we can."

And what a day it had already been. Dorian stood, her hips swaying as her nude ass moved away from me. A great view if there ever was one. She turned, placing a tattooed arm over her cleavage.

"Am I the only one getting ready?"

"No, just give me a second."

Man, had a lot of shit gone down since Ingrid, Fiona and Veronique's random attack last night.

My assumption regarding the origins of their attack had been right: Mother had done something to the two girls' minds, Fiona had affected Veronique's psyche, and Grace had quickly fixed all of this after we'd teleported to Malibu, to the same hotel room that Dorian and I had hooked up in the previous day.

If you're thinking we encountered the same couple we'd discovered boning there the first time, you'd be right, and they were legitimately confused this time when my ragged ass showed up with eight superpowered females.

I had to appreciate their expressions. One minute, they're in their hotel room, and the next, a guy shows up with eight women of varying age, all beautiful, three of them incapacitated.

Grace immediately put the couple out, and they stayed that way until we found a new place to move to, which just so happened to be the room a single floor up. Big enough for nine people? Hardly, but we made it work.

So to get to the question everyone is probably wondering by now: did I get to sleep in the bed with a bunch of beautiful supers à la every harem anime ever?

Sadly, no, but I did get to cuddle up next to Veronique on the floor, who was very apologetic for unleashing the metal vampire back at the home in Davis.

Talk about a wild night.

Long story short: after securing a home in one of Malibu's richest neighborhoods the next day, and leaving Grace in charge, Dorian and I teleported to Chicago by way of Denver, Colorado, to give her a moment to recharge.

Once in Chi-Town, we took a room in the Allerton mostly due to the fact that the Moscow Mule was invented here, had sex, and then found ourselves taking a much-needed nap.

"Are you really going to watch me get dressed?" Dorian asked as I mentally recapped my day.

"Is that a problem?"

"I guess it's not." Dorian already had her boy shorts on, and she was in the process of slipping into the fishnets she usually wore.

"You can watch me get dressed too, but that might not be as appealing."

Dorian laughed. "Maybe not. What's on the agenda?"

"There's a little art function at the Art Institute of Chicago, so I figured we could sneak into that. Then maybe check out Millennium Park, and finish the night on the top floor of the Allerton, having some cocktails. Or we could play it by ear a bit. I know you told me not to, but I'm a bit worried about everyone back in California."

"You think we really need your leadership that badly, huh?" she asked, as she put her bra on. She adjusted her breasts, and stood just a little taller, sucking her stomach in for a moment.

"Well, I still have to organize our next plan of attack."

Dorian shrugged. "We've already decided that."

I nodded, relaxing back onto the bed for a moment. I felt a wave of exhaustion roll over me and let that bitch pass. Now wasn't the time to be tired. Another nap would be nice, but it was already past six, which meant I might as well wait a few more hours.

"I know," I finally told her, steeling myself by getting out of bed. "We need to train more as well. I realize I'm bad at leading these training exercises, so whenever one of you wants to step up…"

"Maybe Chloe would be into it."

"You think?"

"You could ask her."

"Sounds like a plan."

I grinned at Dorian, a toothy grin, but a grin that told her I was happy how things had worked out. Chloe had joined us; I'd trusted her by giving her power back and she'd been a member of the Cherry Blossom Girls ever since, a good member to have around, too. Her powers were ranged, like most of the CBGs, but we had our strongman in Tulip, and really, how many strongman-types does a superhero team need?

"Took you long enough," Dorian teased.

I finished tying my boots, looked up at her, and smiled. My next stop was in front of the mirror in the bathroom, where I mentally adjusted my features.

I was still persona non grata when it came to the American people, so it was best to keep my disguise going. I'd gotten a little better at using Grace's power, and was actually able to make myself look pretty handsome this time around: blond hair, blue eyes and some beard stubble. No scar either, but I still had to wear my glasses.

"Wow, who is this handsome young man?" Dorian asked as she came into the bathroom.

"Just call me Edward, my alias."

"Okay, Eddie, ready to go?"

Before I could answer, the punk rock teleporter touched my arm. One purple flash later and we were in the courtyard of the Chicago Institute of Art.

"That was risky," I said as soon as I'd had the chance to look around and see that no one had spotted us.

"They closed at six, so I figured no one would be here."

"Shall we?" I took her hand like a gentleman, and led her into a long hallway connected to an even longer hallway connected to a hallway not unlike an airport hangar, with a high ceiling that had red banners hanging from it. For some reason, the juxtaposition of the white and red reminded me of the Rising Sun flag. I didn't know if this was the motif the Art Institute was going for, but that was the first thing I noticed.

And that's all I'm going to say about our visit to the Art Institute.

I'm also not going to brag about the fact that we saw a ton of famous paintings, including the sad guitar playing man picture that Picasso painted before he got his cubism on; some amazing works by Van Gogh; a little bit of Monet; a touch of Pollack; and Grant Wood's *American Gothic.*

The whole point of our little trip had been to inspire Dorian, and by the time we left, I could see that she had been moved by some of the pieces. She'd also picked up a little more about the history of art, be it in Africa or the Americas.

And while there had been hors d'oeuvres and wine at the museum, we hadn't had a proper meal. So Dorian and I did what anyone visiting Chicago would do in our situation: we got a deep-dish pizza.

Since we planned to go out that night, we ended up west of the Magnificent Mile, at a place called Giordano's. The pie was good, and we probably shouldn't have ordered a medium.

"It's so big," Dorian said as the thick pizza came to the table. "Michelle's going to be so jealous."

"Yeah, but I'm sure Grace has got them something."

"Without a teleporter?"

"Grace has ordered pizza over the phone before, and if that doesn't work, she'd just have a neighbor do it. I hope Veronique doesn't drain the pizza delivery guy, though."

"Yeah, that wouldn't be good at all."

Because of the thickness of the pizza, we had to use our knives and forks to dig into it, and as Dorian sawed into hers, she complimented me on my newest idea. "I think it will take them off guard, going after two facilities at once."

"That's the plan," I told her, swallowing my bite of pizza. "We have to finish destroying the Sacramento facility; we didn't, clearly, and they're not going to be expecting that. Plus, we have to get to the next facility, which is on an island off the coast of California. So we split up. Hit them at the same time."

"The teams you picked seemed to be well balanced too. Chloe, Veronique, and our weakest member, Michelle, are compensated for by the fact that you will be on our team."

"Thanks?"

"You're welcome," she said as she took a bite of pizza. Once she was finished, she continued. "Grace, Stella, Ingrid and Fiona can handle what's left of the Sacramento facility, and with your ability to communicate with Grace, we'll stay in contact."

"We haven't tested how far, yet, which could create an issue with our plan."

"But if you're both rocking the telepath schtick, I'm pretty sure it will work."

"It's not working right now."

To prove my point, I closed my eyes and tried to thinking a message to Grace. No response. I currently had both of Grace's powers and Jules' power negation ability. Even with the boost in telekinetic goodness, we were way too far apart to communicate.

"I think it will work when you are closer. I don't know, just a hunch. But it's a good idea, and I'm excited to do some more training." She smirked at me. "We have trained a lot harder than the times that we trained with you."

"I don't doubt it," I said as I cut into another slice. "Combat really isn't my area of expertise. I'm trying to get better, though, and I'll try to remember things that I have learned from some of the superhero books I've read."

"Like what?"

"I feel like we really haven't thought about the type of power users we are. I mean, we all know what we are – for example, I'm a mimic – but we haven't thought about using them better together. We are very much a ranged team, though, and our best fights are ones that we can win quickly from a distance. Close-up, we're much more vulnerable to attacks. Anyway, I'm still thinking about all of it."

"It is a new role for you, from sci-fi writer to superhero mastermind."

"You really think we're heroes?"

"Eye of the beholder?"

"Yeah, maybe."

Dorian shrugged, taking another bite from her pizza. The waiter came, and I ordered a couple beers, which was followed by another round, and another round after that.

A lot was on my mind when we finally left the pizza place, drunk and full. We headed down the street, towards the club scene around Chicago's Magnificent Mile. I had to stay focused on keeping my appearance up, because standing and moving around required real effort, and after throwing a few beers back, it also required effort to stand.

And to walk, for that matter.

The street was uneven, and I hit my toe on a raised bit of concrete, stumbling forward. I caught myself, but definitely scraped my forearm a bit on the pavement.

"Are you okay?" Dorian asked, stepping in front of me as my face quivered, the form I had taken nearly going away. With a deep breath in, I was able to modify my face again, and looked down at my arm, which looked pretty raw.

"I've got Father's blood," I told her, which sounded weird to the person passing by us. Luckily, it was a big city, and there were crazies everywhere, like the homeless man across the street, his legs splayed out and an empty 7-Eleven cup near his body just in case someone wanted to donate to his misery.

"Let's go to the alley, you can heal up."

"Sure."

I wasn't really scared about stepping into a dark alley in Chicago. I had Dorian with me plus Jules' superpower to boot, and besides, we were in the tourist area, not the South Side, so there were no thugs with guns or anything of the sort.

Hell, the alley was empty, and it was surprisingly clean.

I took the vial of Father's blood from my pocket, pressed my thumb over the end, and turned it upside down, just getting a little. I mentally pushed Grace's psychic ability out.

I sensed the two energy directions, one being Father's healing ability, the other being his ability to manipulate the future. I had heeded his warning thus far, never dabbling with his other power.

As my arm healed up, I began to think about this, and because I'd been drinking, I thought aloud: "You know, Father actually has two powers."

"He does? What's his other power?" Dorian asked.

"Aside from his ability to heal, Father has the ability to manipulate the future."

"Manipulate the future?" Dorian crouched next to me and helped me up.

"Thanks. That was quite a fall I took back there, but, as you can see, my arm's all healed up. Anyway, yes, his power to manipulate the future is something that I haven't messed with. He told me not to, and I don't know how I could utilize it anyway, nor do I know what it would be like."

Dorian's thin eyebrows rose. "Are you telling me that you have the ability to modify the future and you haven't tried it out? That is not like you at all, Gideon."

"What do you mean?"

"You are the type that charges in and does something without thinking about it. I mean, no offense, you act like you've thought about it, but the truth is, you haven't really thought much about it aside from surface level thoughts, if that. Then you charge in and you just do it, and notice what I said in that last sentence before you give me a dirty look."

"I'm not giving you a dirty look."

"My point is, *you do it.* However crazy it may seem, from what I've seen of you, you pull it off. So that's why it's surprising that you haven't tested Father's power. You should totally test it out. What's he going to do? We can't even find him."

"Dorian, you're right." I pointed at her to emphasize my statement. "You are so fucking right."

"Of course I'm right, and I'm also right when I say that you should get another tattoo."

"More tattoos?"

"Yes, but we don't have to do that tonight. Instead..." Dorian nodded to a club across the street. It was called the Havana Bar, and there was a crowd gathered inside, moving to salsa music. "Want to dance?"

"I never really could get into salsa, mostly because the 'one, two, three, one, two, three' felt unbalanced without the four."

"Come on," she said as she hooked her arm through mine. "It's *our* night out, let's have some serious fun."

"Can you salsa?"

She giggled. "Does it matter?"

So that was how I found myself in a salsa dance bar drinking a minty mojito and trying to avoid the sweaty crowd.

It seemed like the bar had brought everyone out, from the pair in the corner enjoying a couple steaks, to Chicago's preppiest douchehats from Hyde Park in their tucked in polos. There were a ton of beautiful women too in low-cut dresses with glitter across their chests, going for the glass skin look on their faces, most of them ignoring me.

That didn't really matter to me, though; Dorian was next to me, and she put most of these women to shame. She could dance too, maybe not salsa, but she had her own thing going on as her hips swayed to the music, immediately finding the groove, making me look like a real chump in the dance department.

It was nice to let my hair down, and I didn't feel my phone buzz as we kicked up some dust on the dance floor. Even if I had, I wouldn't have looked at it.

No, I was too busy enjoying myself, enjoying the moment.

"This is so fun!" Dorian said, sipping from her mojito. I had to kiss her in that moment, my focus less on my kiss now and more on keeping up my facial features.

Melty face was a no-no.

Eventually, as it always does, nature called, so I headed downstairs to the basement bathroom. As I aimed my little writer at the urinal, I got the urge to check my phone. It was a stupid place to check one's phone, but that never stopped a man from holding his cock with one hand and scrolling through GoogleFace with the other.

I had received two emails, and the second email caused me to lose my grip on my member, immediately covering the wall with a stream of piss.

"No... fucking... way."

I jammed my phone back in my pocket, returned my little writer to his writing nook, washed my hands like a gentleman, got haggled by the bathroom attendant who tried to dry my hands for a fee, and headed upstairs.

I saw Dorian dancing with a group of cute girls, and as soon as she locked eyes with me, she invited me over, on the verge of introducing me to the people she'd just met.

It only took her a moment to see that my borrowed face had gone from drunken pink to white. She excused herself and grabbed my hand, the two of us heading back downstairs.

"What is it?" she said as soon as we could communicate clearly, our voices no longer drowned out by the music. Dorian glanced around, moving into the opening of another alley partially covered in shadow.

"It's an email..."

"Okay?"

"Can you take us back to our hotel room?"

Before I got the sentence out, we were standing in a hotel room at the Allerton, the room cold and nicely kept, the sheets on the bed a little bit ruffled from the baby-making we'd done earlier. It was entirely alien to me; even after teleporting dozens upon dozens of times, to go from a loud, hot and sticky club to a cold hotel room bathed in silence was utterly bizarre.

"What is it?" she asked, moving closer to me. My features returned to normal; I was everyday Gideon, glasses, shaved head, scar across my cheek.

As my ears adjusted to the quiet, I turned the phone to Dorian to show her that it was a message from Dr. Ken Kim. All the message contained was a video file.

With Dorian next to me, I pressed the triangular 'play' button.

*"Gideon, if you're getting this, it means I have died. I've recorded several messages to be delivered to you over the following months. I know this is a little cryptic, but believe me when I tell you that these AEFL experiments run deep, and AEFL isn't the only group that has successfully performed these experiments."*

Dr. Kim swallowed hard, a clear look of terror on his face. I couldn't tell by the background what time of day he had recorded the message, but I did recognize his bedroom. It wasn't so long ago that Dorian and I had been in his place, seconds before a homemade bomb tore it to shreds.

*"I honestly have no way of knowing if you've made it this far. I hope for Sabine's sake you have. God, I really hope you've done it..."* He trailed off for a moment, anguish furrowing his brow. *"Fine, fine, I'll get down to business. I have a code for you that should unlock a power or stat boost in any AEFL super you encounter. Jim programmed several of these codes to be used in his modifier, but he lost track of them all. I had a program go through and run millions of inquiries. So here's one you should try."*

A code appeared on the video; ph4ul3CR0NK. The code stayed in the bottom corner of the clip as Dr. Kim continued. *"I have more codes to share with you in the future, but that's it for now. I'm going to assume you've taken out the facilities."*

I glanced at Dorian and shrugged. "Working on that," I said under my breath to Kim as he continued:

*"Well, there's more, a lot more, Gideon. Asia should be your next target. You need to get in touch with Jim Mathis, who holds more of the information about the Asia equation. The situation in Asia is different than it is here. The facilities are not as readily defined, the supers are already active and there are a few faraway places that are seriously feeling the squeeze from these powered individuals."*

"But how do I get in touch with Father?" I whispered.

*"It's a little harder to reach Jim than it should be. Send an email to the address on this screen, and hope that he gets back to you. That's all you can really do,"* said Dr. Kim, as if he had heard my question. Father's email address appeared on the screen above the code: songsmith51@googleface.com.

*"So that's it, Gideon. This email won't self-destruct or anything silly like that. You can watch the video again. After all, I'm dead, which..."* He took a deep breath. *"Jim will make his own decision as to if he should meet you or not, but he's who you'll want to talk to next. Good luck, and another email will go out in the future, so look for it."*

The video ended, and the icon appeared asking me if I wanted to play it again.

"We've got to get back," I told Dorian, lowering my phone.

"I know we do, but…"

"But what?"

Dorian came to me, her hand falling into mine. "Just a little longer, Gideon," she said, as she led me to the bed. "You promised."

**The end.**

## *Back of the Book Content*

**Reader,**

Another chapter of Cherry Blossom Girls comes to a close.

**Please take a moment to review the book and tell other readers what you liked about it.** After all, your reviews are what drive all my series and encourage me to really let loose and explore. This is a love or hate it series, it seems, so if you love it, please let other readers know.

I have big plans for this series, and see it continuing for quite a while as Gideon and the CBGs encounter new enemies (next book!) and shift more toward superheroes, well, flawed heroes, but heroes nonetheless.

So thanks for reading along, and stay tuned for more CBG goodness. I will be looking over the next year to venture into comic book territory with this, as I am a longtime comic book reader and feel like this story would translate in such a cool way. So we'll see.

A boy can dream, and he already did, and you're holding evidence of his dream in your hands.

--Harmon Cooper

Hate your job. Win the lottery. Get a superpower. House of

Dolls.

A fantasy harem adventure inspired by *Pokemon Go!*, *Scott Pilgrim vs. The World*, and the *Persona* family of video games. Check out this Amazon best seller!

Tokyo, Japan meets online fantasy gaming and South Park-styled humor. Yakuza, goblins, action, intrigue - add this book to your inventory list!

What if Ready Player One was a multi-part epic? Gritty LitRPG action, gamer humor, fantastic fantasy worlds, and a killer MC. Read now!